MW00476134

A Pie
to
Die For

Also available by Gretchen Rue

The Witches' Brew Mysteries

Death by a Thousand Sips
Steeped to Death

A Pie
to
Die For

A LUCKY PIE
MYSTERY

Gretchen Rue

CROOKED
LANE

NEW YORK

Published in the United States by Crooked Lane Books, an imprint of The Quick Brown Fox & Company LLC.

Crooked Lane Books and its logo are trademarks of The Quick Brown Fox & Company LLC.

Library of Congress Catalog-in-Publication data available upon request.

ISBN (hardcover): 978-1-63910-625-7
ISBN (ebook): 978-1-63910-626-4

Cover design by Tim Barnes

Printed in the United States.

www.crookedlanebooks.com

Crooked Lane Books
34 West 27th St., 10th Floor
New York, NY 10001

First Edition: February 2024

10 9 8 7 6 5 4 3 2 1

To Kristyn,
who deserves a book that's all hers.
I'm lucky to have you as a friend.

Chapter One

The saying goes that there are only two certainties in life: death and taxes.

I'd like to offer a third: that on the first of November every year, the island of Split Pine, Michigan, will shutter its doors for the season and bid farewell to any tourists until the following spring.

It happens like clockwork, which might be the only thing that happens like clockwork in Split Pine, since the locals have their own Northern Michigan take on "island time," which means punctuality is more frequently a pleasant surprise than the expected norm.

In a town where business hours could be considered a gentle suggestion rather than expectation, I still liked to keep them. Perhaps that was just a March family thing, since my Grampy Chuck's days, but the Lucky Pie Diner *always* opened at seven o'clock sharp.

As a teenager, I'd thought seven in the morning was an absolute nightmare, especially when picking up shifts over the summer when I wasn't in school, but as an adult I'd found that the early-bird thing had unfortunately grown on me, and now I woke up at five every day whether I liked it or not.

I walked down the middle of the street and smiled at the quiet town around me. Front yards were still decorated from the festivities of the previous evening. It was still dark outside, and the mornings were growing increasingly darker every day as we crept toward winter. As I walked alone, enjoying the quiet, it felt like I was the only person awake while the rest of Split Pine slept off their Halloween candy hangovers.

Split Pine takes Halloween more seriously than any other holiday in the year, because not only is it All Hallow's Eve, it's also Close of Tourist Season Eve. The island's two hotels host massive parties, local kids get to stay up well past bedtime and gorge themselves on sugary delights, and all the local businesses have late hours to account for the last-minute crush of tourists wanting to stock up on goodies from the island before leaving the next day.

There would still be new arrivals today. The last inbound ferry from the mainland would arrive at nine o'clock and leave at five, taking with it anyone who did not have a permanent address on the island.

We weren't exactly shut off after that. Boats and small planes would still come periodically with mail, packages, and essentials for the grocery store, but there wouldn't be any more outsiders spending their time with us until next spring. It was simply too cold, and the island too shut off from amenities, to have tourists here over winter. Locals understood that they could lose power or go weeks without their favorite foods.

A small gray cat walked past me, tail held high, and mostly ignored my presence. "Good morning to you too, Cinder," I said, tipping an imaginary hat. Pets on the island were afforded a lot more outdoor freedom than those on the mainland. Since there were no cars on Split Pine—horses and golf carts only—people were much less concerned about their animals running afoul of a vehicle, so many cats wandered freely about town at all hours. And since I took the same route to work every morning, I got used to the usual suspects. Cinder lived three doors down from me, and while gray cats were exceptionally common on the island, she was the only one with a sparkly studded collar.

Darkened pumpkins were on every doorstop and set of stairs I passed, their empty mouths seeming to laugh at me. Inflatable lawn ornaments that had seemed larger than life the night before now lay flattened and dormant on the ground. It was a little sad, honestly. When I'd walked home from the diner the previous night, everything had been aglow and the air filled with that chilly magic present only around Halloween. Now everything just felt a little emptier.

I pulled my fluffy plaid jacket more tightly around me and picked up my pace, eager to get inside the diner and start the ovens for the day. We'd had two brand-new—and crushingly expensive—ovens installed over the summer, thanks to the ones Grampy had installed in the fifties biting the dust. The added cost had set us way back in our expected earnings, so I was holding my breath that a last-day rush would nose us into the black.

The Lucky Pie Diner had been around for over seventy years on the island and had seen many other local institutions brought down by the volatile seasonal nature of trade. We had to make almost our full year's worth of income from May to October, something that a lot of businesses simply weren't able to accomplish.

The diner was open year-round, serving locals daily through the offseason, but we certainly couldn't pay for all our expenses on what a handful of locals ate in the winter months. We were exceedingly lucky—no pun intended—to own the building outright, with the mortgage having long been paid off, but a mortgage wasn't the only thing required to keep the lights on and stove running.

I reached Main Street, where a few other shop lights were glowing. Bruno Espinoza was obviously already at the General Store, as all the lights inside were on, and Melody Sharpe must have gotten to the post office early as well, since they didn't open until nine, but she often liked to get a head start on sorting the mail deliveries for the day.

Lucky Pie Diner was at the very end of Main Street, right at the crossroads of Main and Harbor, and so close to the harbor that we had added a big outdoor patio a few years ago that extended out over the water. We'd left a few picnic tables out there for the last day, knowing some brave souls would ignore the chill in the air and eat their food alfresco.

When it wasn't pitch black outside, the view from the diner was second to none. Split Pine was isolated, yes, but it was also close enough to the surrounding mainland that you could see the changing leaves on three sides of the island, while the fourth was a fairly oceanic vista looking out over Lake Huron. The diner had the best of both worlds, and people-watchers could see the ferries and boats as they arrived into Split Pine Harbor.

It also meant we were the first restaurant people saw when they got off the boat, which often meant they looked no farther for their first island meal, and it also inspired them to stop on their way out of town to take a pie or box of treats back to the mainland.

Based on years of previous experience, I knew today was likely to be the busiest day of the year, and I had spent an enormous chunk of my Halloween night not partying but making pies. Dozens and dozens of pies.

While, in an ideal world, they'd all be going home fresh, the biggest seller for the final day of the year was our frozen pies, which visitors would load into their coolers and take home to keep on ice until they were ready for whatever big event merited a Lucky Pie Diner pie.

I walked up to the one-story building that was our family diner. A white picket fence surrounded the front yard, and potted mums lined the sidewalk up to the front porch. Along either side of the door were café tables, whose white paint had faded over a busy summer and would need to be touched up again over the offseason. The porch itself was decked out in its best Halloween finery. A plastic skeleton sitting on hay bales held a grinning jack-o'-lantern, and more gourds and pumpkins decorated the bales surrounding him. I'd stuffed cinnamon brooms into the potted mums on the patio to give off the inviting scent of warm cinnamon as people entered the diner. It put them in the mood to order something sweet.

I'd changed the chalkboard on the wall next to the door before leaving the night before. Where it had previously said *Have a Ghoulicious Halloween—Candy Corn Pie Is Today's Special*, it now read *We'll Miss You—Take a Piece of the Pie-land With You—Frozen Pies $20*.

I love a good—or terrible—pun better than just about anything, and it shows on my signs. I'd leave the Halloween decor up for the day, and when things settled into their normal offseason pace, I could box everything up and put it into storage for the winter. Most of the current display would be good through Thanksgiving, I'd just need to swap out my skeletons for turkeys.

Unlocking the front door, I stepped into the familiar warmth of the diner and brushed my fingertips over the horseshoe mounted just above the light switch. Its rough metal coating had become buffed and shiny over decades of hands touching it, making it look like an important historical relic and not just a shoe Grampy had taken off an ornery stallion in his farrier days.

Signs of his time working with horses were everywhere in the diner. There were lushly painted artworks of horses on almost every wall, along with black-and-white vintage photos of Grampy and of the island when it was first settled in the 1930s—before his time, even—and historical maps of the town in its early days.

The diner was like opening a horse girl's scrapbook, and I loved every inch of its overcluttered walls.

The tables were all made of reclaimed barnboard that had been filled and sealed to make them safe for customers, and the walls were painted an ocher orange that you could barely see with all the photos on the wall but gave the diner a year-round autumnal vibe even in the height of summer.

As I made my way into the kitchen, the entire aesthetic changed. Here, rather than my grandparents' design choices, my fingerprints had been left everywhere. I'd come back from the mainland ten years earlier to take over the diner when my mother passed away, and since then I'd turned the overly dark kitchen and prep area into a soft, warm, dare I say feminine space that made me look forward to spending hours in front of the oven every day.

Whereas the restaurant was moody, in here I'd painted things a creamy off-white that reminded me of meringue or fresh custard. The cabinets had been repainted a lovely sage green, and the overall effect made it feel like I was baking inside a cloud nestled over a fragrant green forest. At least that's how it felt for me, and since I was the one running the place, that was all that mattered. I think Grampy was a little affronted I'd changed things—he didn't love change—but at the end of the day, it was my decision to make.

I'd kept my grandmother's old mixing bowls on display, though I no longer used them for fear of damaging them. What did get used still was my mother's stand mixer. While most of the baked goods were prepped in larger industrial mixers, there were small-batch items offered daily that I made either by hand or by using the old mixer. Those particular dishes were given a little extra love and attention.

Those were the pies people lined up for, but I was very specific about who got them. You could certainly ask for the daily special, but asking was no guarantee you'd get one. I usually had a pretty good idea of who needed them most.

I hung my coat up in the back office and briefly headed back into the main dining area to assess if I'd left anything unfinished the day before. Each table was decorated with a red-and-white gingham table runner and a little bouquet of fresh flowers in seasonal colors. Turning my attention to the glass counter that ran the entire length of one wall and separated the dining area from the kitchen, I checked all my labels as a reminder of what I still had to do for the day.

The Lucky Pie Diner was obviously best known for its pies, but that wasn't all we served. The menu offered pies whole and by the slice along with an assortment of hand pies, tarts, and Danishes. We had two daily soups on rotation and kept our meal offerings basic—classic sandwiches, the best fries in town, and an ever-changing list of specials that depended on the season and whatever fresh produce I could get my hands on.

Today would be my last major order of produce from the mainland. For the rest of winter, I'd depend on what I could get from the General Store, because demand was going to go way down. Through the tourist months I made so many pies I needed to order my ingredients in bulk. The expense was astronomical but usually made worth it by the sales.

I headed back into the kitchen and plugged my phone into the sound system, queuing up a playlist I'd named Bake it Off, and the peppy opening chords of "Pour Some Sugar on Me" started to play. It was an eclectic mix I was constantly trying to perfect. Before we opened for the day, I'd switch it over to either a classic fifties playlist or some ambient jazz. I found that if I kept the pop going too long, it was distracting, and I wanted to keep the diner experience limited to the food and the view and not have people focusing on what song was playing.

But that rule didn't apply when I was here all by myself.

I slipped my battered sage-green apron over my head and out of sheer habit ran my finger over the stitches that spelled out my name, Este. Esther if, and only if, my parents were annoyed with me; Essie if it was my cousin's baby daughter, who couldn't say the *t* sound; but Este to everyone else.

I had four matching aprons, because they got dirtier much faster than I could keep them washed, which reminded me that I needed to switch the laundry I'd thrown last night over to the drier. Once I'd done that dismal domestic chore, it was time to get cracking.

In the walk-in freezer, there were quite literally hundreds of pies stacked up and ready to be taken to their new homes. Each one was neatly labeled with one of our six signature fall flavors: Maple Pumpkin, Butterscotch Pecan, White Chocolate Raspberry, Caramel Apple, Classic Lemon Meringue, and Buzzy Blueberry Billions. The boozy secret ingredient in the last one burned off in the prep process, but people still liked to pretend they were being a little naughty sometimes, and who was I to stop them?

With the big six already taken care of—I had ten of each pie set aside in our standard cooler for by-the-slice serving today—the only thing I needed to worry about would be the daily specials. The soups and diner fare would be championed by my cook, Seamus, when he arrived in about forty minutes. Seamus had come to Split Pine in his teens, and while he'd left briefly to get formal training and spent several years working in some of the best kitchens in the world, he'd never outgrown his love for a greasy burger and some fresh-cut fries. When he came back to the island to visit his old stomping ground, he'd seen the *Help Wanted* sign in our window and simply never gone home again. That had been twelve years ago, when my grandparents were in their last years of running the place.

Seamus had been a gift from the heavens, Grampy used to say, but the truth of the matter was that when the diner needed something, it didn't take long to find it.

Our family was just sort of lucky that way.

Chapter Two

I heard the door open not long after I started to collect the ingredients to make my daily specials. Seamus walked past me wordlessly and deposited his coat in the office, then made a beeline for the coffeemaker parked behind the service counter.

Split Pine had three incredible coffee shops, which is an impressive per capita amount when you consider that our offseason population hovers around five hundred people. Two of the three—Daily Grind and Island Café—would shutter for the season after today, as their owners lived on the mainland and, truthfully, there wasn't enough business to keep them going all year. Elevated Grounds, however, stayed open year-round and served some of the finest coffee I'd ever tasted in my life. Because of that, Lucky Pie didn't really try to compete on the coffee front. We didn't sell lattes or fancy beverages, but you could get a coffee with cream and sugar, and if we were feeling adventurous, we might brew some decaf.

I'd had a cup at home before coming, so I didn't need another fix just yet; however, it seemed Seamus wasn't in a mood for chatter until he had a little hit of the good stuff.

Soon the smell of fresh-brewed coffee mixed with the sugar I was pouring into a bowl, the typical sign that the day was really getting started.

Seamus came into the kitchen, taking a big sip from his mug, and rested a hip against the counter. He didn't *look* like a cook; he looked like he'd just stumbled off a fishing boat from the twenties. His reddish-brown hair was perpetually covered by a dark-green beanie, and while he was clean-shaven during the summer, the moment September hit, he began to grow what he lovingly called his "face sweater." He shaved it a little less each month, going from barefaced to mountain man one iconic facial hairstyle at a time. At present that represented a ginger handlebar mustache. It would be a full beard by the end of the month.

He was in his late thirties but looked considerably younger, and I knew more than one local lady who went a little bit batty for the tattoos on his arms and the fact that he sometimes sat out on his porch at night, strumming an old acoustic guitar.

It didn't hurt that he was an incredible chef.

"What'll it be today?" he grumbled into his coffee.

One thing Seamus was *not* was a morning person.

"We have a ton of potatoes in the walk-in, so I'm thinking you might do that potato and corn chowder? I know we froze a bunch of the corn when it was fresh in August. Plus, that one always sells out so quickly."

"People love to eat chowder by the water." He shrugged. "I think it makes them feel nautical."

He wasn't wrong. Even this time of year, people would take their steaming bowls of soup outside and watch the boats.

"I'm open to suggestions on soup number two. What did you have in mind?"

He brightened a little. I knew Seamus always had a million and a half ideas for specials in his head, but occasionally they could get a little too "big city" for the types of folks our diner drew in. That said, I was willing to let him make just about anything, since it was the last day. We could go back to tomato-basil basics tomorrow.

"It's not that bold, but I'd really love to do this fall soup my mom used to make us every year. It's a butternut squash and bacon soup, but adding apple for some extra sweetness."

"Apple." I raised one eyebrow at him, not doubting his choices per se but having a slightly hard time imagining the flavor. That said, I was down for anything with butternut squash and bacon in it, so before he could even defend the fruity ingredient, I said, "Sure, go for it."

I just had to hope that Bruno would have the squash at the General Store, because I certainly didn't have enough to make a diner-sized serving of soup with. As if reading my mind, Seamus pulled out a notepad and started jotting down the ingredients he would need.

We kept the diner fridge and freezer especially well stocked in the high season, but that didn't mean we were a greengrocer. Sometimes we came up with ideas that meant we needed to seek out those special ingredients.

Together, Seamus and I hammered out the rest of the daily menu. The diner served five basic sandwiches and two daily specials, one anyone could eat and another that we tried to keep vegetarian or vegan friendly, or at least capable of being easily adjusted. The big five were the turkey club, Seamus's special grilled cheese, a Michigan Cuban (which was just a standard Cuban sandwich, but it didn't feel right to call it authentic so far from Florida), our veggie delight, and a chicken and Brie sandwich served with an ever-changing variety of fruit jam spreads.

One of the two sandwiches of the day would be a caprese sandwich on fresh ciabatta buns, which was suitable for vegetarians but would lose a lot of oomph for the vegan crowd.

"Maybe see if Bruno still has any vegan cheeses?" I suggested. The grocery store tended to stock a lot more in the way of food for special diets over the summer than it did later in the year. In the winter, I was lucky to be able to find oat milk creamer, but Bruno seemed to have realized how cranky I got when it wasn't on the shelf and had become diligent about keeping some around all year.

Seamus made a face at the idea of buying vegan cheese—I don't think he fully understood how someone could eat *no* dairy—but he was at least willing to make concessions. Even now, I felt a bit bad at how few of our dishes were suitable for vegans, but I hadn't been able to find alternatives to butter and lard that made the pies and tarts taste as good as they did with my grandmother's original recipes. Sure, I'd made my own tweaks over the years, but I still hadn't found that sweet spot. I made sure there were at least one or two vegan options in the front window, but unfortunately, not all the pies had gotten there just yet.

The non-veggie sandwich of the day was going to be one of my favorites that Seamus made: his spin on an Italian hoagie. He mixed iceberg lettuce, banana peppers, red onion, and a creamy, slightly spicy dressing together and put it on long hoagie buns that had been toasted to melt sliced provolone cheese and warm deli-shaved turkey. Then he would load the incredibly messy lettuce mixture on top.

It was not a sandwich to eat while walking around town; it was an elbows-on-the-table and napkin-bib kind of sandwich that was a sloppy disaster to consume but sheer bliss the second you took your first bite.

Seamus did a quick check of the fridges and freezer and made a list of everything extra we would need to get us through the day. I had a produce order coming that would supplement a lot of the greenery, but most of what I'd ordered was fruit. So much fruit. I was planning to do a lot of canning and freezing once it arrived so that I'd have plenty to get me through at least the first few months of winter.

I could get more from Bruno later on, but even his fruit supply wouldn't be as nice in February. He had groceries brought in by boat, but neither of us got visits from the produce-specific driver after this. Whatever else he'd get this year would come from a standard grocery wholesaler.

I snatched the list out of Seamus's hand before he could go for the door.

"Boss," he protested. "I really don't mind."

"Nah, don't worry. I know you're a miserable grouch before you get to the bottom of that cup, and I don't want to subject Bruno or anyone at the store to that this early in the morning." I gave him a wink to let him know I was only teasing, but we both knew I was right. Seamus was a bear before eight, and I was doing everyone a favor by going in his place.

Main Street was still dark outside, and I was glad it was only a short walk from Lucky Pie up to the General Store. The chill I'd felt in the air on my earlier walk hadn't dissipated, and if anything, it only felt colder now that I was leaving the warmth from my preheated ovens.

I jogged up the slight slope of Main Street, my calves burning even though I made this same walk at least once a day, every day. A few more shops had interior lights on now, but not many. Elevated Grounds was open, but I'd resist a morning coffee until later on. If I overdid it on the caffeine too early in the morning, I was setting myself up for a crash later on, and I couldn't afford to be a zombie on the busiest day of the year.

A bell jangled overhead when I stepped into the General Store, and I gave an aimless wave over the top of the shelves. I wasn't sure where Bruno was, but he'd have seen me come in. Or at least heard the bell.

He was kind of like a grocery store ghost: you didn't always see him until he popped up out of nowhere to give you a scare when you least expected it. I knew that wasn't his intention, but he was just so darned *quiet* it was a little spooky.

Today, I could hear his familiar Brazilian accent on the other side of the store as he softly spoke to someone else, though I couldn't see either of them over the store shelves.

I went down the aisles with purpose. Left to my own devices, I could happily wander through a grocery store for hours, putting things in my cart with the good intention of planning a future meal or making something special, only to entirely forget why I'd bought a certain spice or what the reason was for getting a dragon fruit in the first place.

I didn't have time for dreamy wandering today; we needed to get the soup on, quite literally, and get the diner ready to open in less than an hour, and I still hadn't started the special pies of the day.

I put a few bits of produce I had forgotten to include in my own order in my basket, like a big bag of basil for the caprese sandwiches and a few extra balls of mozzarella, in case what I had in the fridge wouldn't cut it. We had so many tomatoes that I had no fear whatsoever of coming up short and was hoping I'd have a ton left the next day, because one of my favorite things to make with them was a rustic feta and tomato tart. Any basil we had left over would complement that nicely as a special for the locals.

Distraction took over briefly as I added some red onions to my basket, thinking about making some delicious pickled onions that would create a pop of flavor on the tart.

"No, *bad* Este," I scolded myself. "That's *tomorrow's* special." I still took the onions, but I redirected my focus to Seamus's list and filled up my basket with the remaining items we'd need for today's meals.

"This is *madness*." Bruno's voice cut in over the mellow store music. "This is not at all what we agreed. You are a cheat."

"Hey now," came another masculine voice I didn't recognize. "A deal's a deal. You want it or not?"

"This is *no* deal," Bruno spat out.

I picked up my pace and headed around the corner to where the voices were coming from. Normally I'd try to keep my nose out of other people's business, but two things were preventing that. One: in a town of five hundred people, it is simply not possible to stay out of anyone else's business.

And two: I could count on one hand the number of times I'd heard Bruno sound this angry, and I'd known him for over twenty years. Of those times, almost every single one of them had been related to someone saying something insulting about football—European football, not American football, and no one dared to call it *soccer* in front of him.

The moment I got around the corner, I could see this was no mere football-related anger. Bruno, who was in his early forties but looked like the dashing hero of a Latin telenovela, was so red in the face I thought he might actually swear. Bruno *never* swore. He would sometimes say things in Portuguese that didn't sound altogether friendly, but usually only to summer shoplifters or people who were rude to his cashiers.

Right now, he looked like his head was going to explode if he didn't let it out.

"Hey, Bruno, everything okay?"

Almost immediately, the ticking bomb was diffused. When he realized he wasn't alone, he let out a deep breath and took a moment to smooth his already perfectly smooth apron, checking the array of pens in his pocket and straightening his name tag. This was a little ritual I had watched him do a million times.

When he was finished, he looked calmer already.

"I am very sorry, Miss March. My voice was too big for my words, I think." He offered me a small smile, but it was pinched.

I looked at the man he had been speaking to. He didn't *look* old but had the vibe of a person who had lived a little too hard and was worn beyond their years. While this stranger was probably only my age, in his midthirties, he had a sharply receding hairline and skin that looked as if it had never been introduced to sunscreen before. Something in his eyes gave me the shivers; they were flat and sharklike, and while he presented me with a toothy smile, there was no warmth in those eyes at all.

I instinctively recoiled from him by taking a step back, but I tried to match his fake smile with one of my own.

"Is anything the matter?" I pushed. Bruno had to have good reason for getting so angry, and I was just nosy enough to want to know who this guy was and why he was pushing our beloved grocer to the point of explosion.

"I'm sorry, I don't think I recall you being a part of this conversation," the new man said. While his voice remained friendly, like he was telling us a joke, the words were obviously not intended kindly.

"I don't believe we've met. My name is Este March. I run the diner down the street." I did not offer to shake his hand, even though I knew my Grampy would have been appalled at my lack of manners. Some people just didn't deserve a handshake, and I had a feeling this guy fit that bill.

"Oh, March, yes. I'm actually coming to see you next. If you'll just let me get back to my business here, that is."

"I'm sorry, who are you?" I tried to keep my tone light and not accusatory, but I felt like he was ignoring my obvious invitation to an introduction, and that was much ruder than skipping a handshake.

Seeing that he would not escape me so easily, he let out a little sigh and said, "Name's Jeff Kelly. I'm from Evergreen Produce, here making the rounds."

I squinted at him, trying to understand what he was saying, but even though the words were simple enough, they weren't making any sense. Evergreen Produce had been our sole distributor on the island for decades, and we had only ever dealt with the family who owned it. Not seeing our usual guy was unheard of.

"Denny has been doing our deliveries for years. He didn't mention he was going to be replaced." We'd seen Denny McAvoy about a month earlier, and at the time he'd warmly told me he'd see me for the end of the season and confirmed my order personally.

He'd never mentioned Jeff Kelly, or that he might send someone else to do his sales. In any other circumstance this wouldn't have felt so dramatic—it was just a produce delivery, after all—but on the island things so rarely changed that when something unexpectedly did, it tended to ruffle feathers.

"Yeah, sorry. Denny couldn't make it." Jeff turned his shoulder away from me, clearly trying to cut me out of the conversation so he could get back to business with Bruno, but I wasn't ready to let it go.

"Couldn't make it why? Denny's been out here for every delivery all year. I didn't know he worked with anyone else. Is he okay? Did something happen?" After ten years of even casual contact with someone, you get a feeling of who they are, and Denny had never struck me as someone who would let anything derail his plans unless it was serious.

"Mrs. March, I'm sure Denny is just fine, but I'm the one out here doing the delivery, so if you don't mind, I'd like to get back to my discussion, unless you want all those nice berries I brought you to go bad."

Well, now I knew he was a liar. There was no such thing as "nice" berries in November. I'd ordered plenty of them, but only because life without strawberry tarts is a dark and terrible place to live, and if I was going to be paying eight bucks a container for them all winter from Bruno, I was *going* to stock up while I had the chance.

But out-of-season fruit, no matter where it's imported from, is just never as good as what's grown at the peak of summer.

There was a farm on the island a good few miles from the town proper, and while they kept mostly to themselves through the year, they also operated a massive organic garden, and in the summer they grew more produce then they could consume or preserve for themselves, so at the weekly farmers' market I could glut myself—and the diner—on fresh strawberries, cherries, and other produce grown within walking distance of my front door.

I was sure Jeff's strawberries were fine, but I knew they didn't taste like Michigan soil and sunshine, and he knew it too. Denny never would have pretended otherwise.

"They'll do whatcha wannum to" was what Denny would always say when he unloaded out-of-season fruit for me. Peaches in October? Yeah, he could get them, but don't count on that sweet honey flavor you get in June. And tomatoes? You could get those all year long, but nothing was as good as a fresh heirloom still warm from the August sun.

Since I hadn't said anything else and was much too late to correct Jeff for calling me *Mrs.*, I relented and let him return to his conversation with Bruno, though I thought Bruno would have liked a reprieve.

As I walked toward the cash desk, I heard Bruno say sharply, "You are a scoundrel, and I won't stand for this. You won't get away with this."

The rest of the conversation was lost to me, but those words and the unexpected anger in Bruno's voice would linger in my memory for the rest of the day.

Chapter Three

Out on the street I was balancing my paper grocery bags when someone called out, "Anyone ever tell you that you that two arms can only hold so much?"

I recognized the cheery voice immediately and looked over my shoulder to see Kitty Cunningham bounding down the hill, a steaming cup from Elevated Grounds in one hand and an enormous smile on her face.

Her blonde hair was tied into a high ponytail that swayed back and forth as she walked, and in spite of the crisp, chilly morning she was wearing only a down vest over a mustard-yellow sweater rather than a jacket. Her cheeks were rosy from the cold, but it just made her look vibrant rather than uncomfortable.

"God only gave me two arms, Kitty. He never told me they had limits." I adjusted one of the bags again to keep it from tipping sideways, but gravity had other ideas. Before it could topple, Kitty relieved me of the burden and walked with me in the direction of the diner.

"You're up awfully early," I noted.

Kitty was the manager and part owner of Tom's, the only *dedicated* pub in all of Split Pine. While the two hotels had bars and the local B and B was licensed, Tom's was the only place you could go if you wanted to sit in a barely lit room with a beer in hand and chow down on stale peanuts while Willy Nelson played on the jukebox. Some kind of sports would always be streaming on the TVs overhead, and miraculously, with all of that magic blended together, there was almost never any kind of fighting.

I knew a lot about luck, and I still didn't know how Kitty managed that feat.

She also must have been running on fumes, considering how late Halloween festivities would have gone on.

"I'm just planning on pouring this into an IV bag later," she said, lifting her cup of coffee in my direction. "We're going to open up at eleven today, just in case the last crowd is feeling adventurous. Plus, I have about forty-five pounds of frozen mozza sticks in the deep freeze that expire next month, and I'd really like to get rid of them before they do. You know how Tom gets about food waste." She rolled her eyes, but I knew she was just as careful about not spoiling things as her big brother was.

"That doesn't explain why you're out here with me before seven."

"And miss who gets *the* pies this year? Are you kidding me?" She shook her head firmly. "You better do it before I have to leave for the bar, you wicked sneak."

"I have no idea what you're talking about," I said, but my smirk was a dead giveaway.

The thing about the Lucky Pie Diner was that our pies weren't just good, they were special. *Very* special. And over fifty-odd years of selling them, we'd started to develop a little bit of a reputation, to the point where people from all over Michigan, and now into the lower states as well, would email me and tell me they didn't care how much shipping cost, they needed to have a Lucky Pie pie for their big event.

If someone was getting married, or having a baby shower, or just any event that felt like it warranted a little touch of something extra, people would come to us.

But that was the key. They *had* to come to us.

Because not every pie we sold was going to bring luck to those who bought it. That was never a guarantee. I had never explained to anyone how the unique magic of our pies worked; once you explained magic to someone, it stopped being *magic*. And the more honest reason was that I didn't really know how it worked myself.

It was just something I'd known in my bones the first time I stood in the kitchen with my mother and she pulled out the well-worn wooden box of recipe cards we kept at the diner. As she kneaded the pie dough by hand that day, she playfully dusted my face with flour and told me, "Este, anyone can make a pie. A lot of people can even make a good pie. But in our family, we make *lucky* pies." And she never gave me anything more than that in terms of an explanation.

But as I grew and started to make the pies myself, I understood what she meant. It wasn't that I whispered some magic words over the pie filling, or that the recipe box was filled with a special luck-enhancing dust; it was an altogether different kind of magic, and while others could sense it, only those in my family could wield it.

While I might not understand *why* I was able to bake magical luck-inducing pies, I at least got to pick which pies I baked *were* lucky. It took a surprising amount of energy to imbue a baked good with luck, so it would have been impossible to make them all lucky. And we made sure people understood that, even when we were cagey about the *how*.

I baked two lucky pies a day, never the same kind on back-to-back days.

The luck itself was unique to the person eating the pie. Each slice would bring some kind of good fortune to the person eating it, but how lucky a person got really seemed to vary.

For some people, it could mean landing a great job or meeting the person of their dreams. For others, it could mean finding the perfect parking spot every day for a month or getting a good grade on a hard test.

One person told me they'd won the lottery after eating a slice of our Blueberry Billions pie, and while it had been a relatively small jackpot, it was impressive nevertheless.

Since I never told anyone how many pies were lucky, or which pies, people had started to create their own theories, and the general consensus seemed to be that there was a chosen pie every day. One pie to rule them all, so to speak. And so the legend became that one pie per day was *the* pie, and naturally that was the one everyone wanted, but since we'd never tell, they took chances on everything.

I wasn't sure how that rumor had started, and in my mother's day, when she'd run the diner, she had been no help at all in trying to squash it. She might have started it herself, for all I knew. But whenever someone would ask her, "Is this the pie?" she would just wink and smile and say, "It might be, honey. It might be."

Because the mystery of it had meant so much to her, I'd never had the heart to dissuade people from believing whatever it was they wanted to believe about the pies. I knew two things to be absolutely true: our pies were delicious, and sometimes the people who ate them had wonderful things happen to them that might not have happened otherwise.

Who was to say how the magic worked, right?

Kitty held the door of the diner open for me, and we headed in together, greeted by the warmth from the ovens and the old woodstove on the back wall that Seamus had gotten going while I'd been away.

"Honey, I'm home," I called out.

Seamus came out of the kitchen grumbling at me, but he took the bags graciously, putting his nose in to take a big whiff of the fresh herbs and smiling at them like they'd given him a compliment. "I'll get started on the soup," he said, and headed back to the kitchen, where I soon heard pots clanging and the fridge door opening and closing.

The whole place was going to smell heavenly in no time. It might have seemed too early to start on soup with it not even being breakfast time, but a good cook knows that the best soups need to simmer to really get that good flavor, and Seamus was a very good cook.

Kitty followed me into the kitchen, pulling up a barstool and setting it next to my workstation so she could watch me bake while she enjoyed her coffee. I didn't normally let others into my kitchen—only the diner staff were allowed—but Kitty wasn't just anyone; she had become an extended part of the family. No one complained about her presence, and even Dad and Grampy greeted her like a second daughter or granddaughter whenever they came by.

Single children were a thing in our family, but my dad had hoped for a bigger family. Whether Grampy had longed for more children, I wasn't sure; he had loved my mother immensely and always told me that he and my grandmother had gotten it so right on the first try that they'd simply never thought about tempting the fates to do it a second time. But Dad had always looked a little sad when I'd asked him about whether he and Mom had wanted more kids.

"I saw Bruno at the grocery store," I told Kitty as I unloaded the items I'd bought for my tomato tart, which I'd bake the following day, and put them in the standing fridge near my station. The walk-in was so full right now, it would be hopeless to look for room there. I pulled out some chilled doughs I had prepared the night before and set them on the counter so they'd be ready when I wanted to roll them out.

Kitty sipped her coffee and tried to act disinterested. "Of course you did; he's always there. Good old reliable Bruno." She smiled, and her cheeks reddened slightly. There were several unspoken questions that I knew she was begging to ask, like *How did he look?* or *Was he wearing that nice green sweater I like?*, but what she settled on was, "How was he?"

"Actually, not great. He was arguing with the new produce guy."

A metal clang drew my attention to the other side of the kitchen, where Seamus was looking at me agog. "*New* produce guy? Did he bring our existing order, though? Denny knew what we wanted. What happened to Denny?"

I raised a hand to calm him, "Whoa, bud. He said he was planning to deliver our order next, so he obviously knows we had things to be delivered. I'm not worried, so you shouldn't be worried." I *was* worried, but there was no sense in putting my anxiety on Seamus; he had enough of his own. I turned back to Kitty. "I've never seen Bruno that mad."

"Worse than the time we couldn't get the World Cup feed to broadcast and someone told him Brazil lost before he could go home and watch it?"

I nodded solemnly.

Kitty let out a low whistle. "That *is* mad. This guy must have really been grinding his gears. But what on earth is that vital about some fruit and vegetables?"

26

"*Some fruit and vegetables?*" Seamus interrupted, clearly fired up. "Kitty. Katherine. Why do you hurt me like this? Is it intentional? Is it a game to you?"

Kitty shushed him. "Go back to your potatoes, soup boy."

Seamus huffed. The two of them had, briefly and disastrously, been married for about a year. While the marriage itself had been a terrible mistake—their bad habits were far too similar and they were both a bit too quick to anger—they remained genuinely good friends after the fact, which meant I hadn't had to fire him, thank goodness. They still bickered like old marrieds, but now it came out of a place of love.

I wasn't sure if Seamus knew how Kitty felt about Bruno, but she played it pretty cool about the crush with everyone but me. Perhaps a little *too* cool, because Bruno didn't seem to have even the vaguest suspicion Kitty was interested in him. If he didn't get a little nudge, I worried she'd never get his attention.

It was a very Jane Bennett/Mr. Bingley from *Pride and Prejudice* scenario, but I hadn't managed to convince Kitty she needed to actually *do* something about it. I didn't want to push her too much, because I thought her hesitation might be more about a fear of being burned again than a result of general shyness.

Shy was not a word I would typically apply to Kitty Cunningham, but people get shut down about weird things.

I lined up my prepared doughs, which were half lard based and half vegetable shortening based. I was going to do two specialty pies today for the end of the season, and I liked to pair my doughs to the fillings. Whenever I was making something fruity that would have nothing in it that would scare off our vegan guests, it would get the vegetable shortening crust.

When the filling was savory and would have meat, cheese, or cream in it, I went with a classic lard or butter crust, because I personally liked them better than the vegetable ones and figured if the filling wasn't vegan friendly, I might as well use my preferred crust.

That's not to say there was anything wrong with the vegetable shortening crusts; they were still delicious, and no one complained. But crusts made with butter or lard just had a different kind of richness in the mouth. They were the pies I'd grown up with, so perhaps it was just the familiarity, but whatever it was, they were the ones I loved best.

I liked to do one sweet and one savory pie every day as my specials. Today's savory pie was going to be one I'd been wanting to try for weeks—I'd just been waiting for Denny to bring me a ton of sweet onions. It was a caramelized onion and potato pie with bacon. Just thinking about it made my mouth water, even though I had never actually made it before.

Even after the onions had been caramelizing for hours, both they and the potatoes had a ton of moisture. I prepared the savory pie crust, rolling it carefully into a deep pie dish and crimping the edges with a practiced speed one could master only after spending most of their life making pies. I emptied a container of dried beans into the bottom of the pie dish to weigh the dough down and keep bubbles from forming, then put the crust in the oven to blind bake. This would help avoid the dreaded soggy bottom. Even though Jeff still hadn't come with our delivery, I wasn't behind schedule.

The sweet pie of the day was going to be an orange cranberry cider pie. Once I got my cranberries, I would cook them in fresh apple cider to capture all the potent flavors of the beverage, then add fresh orange zest at the end for an unexpected shot of brightness. The two pies together gave me

Thanksgiving vibes, and since we weren't open to tourists during actual Thanksgiving, I didn't see the harm in giving some early thanks for a great season.

As I was rolling out one of my savory doughs, there was a knock on the back door. Since Seamus was already busy cutting up potatoes for his soup, I headed to the door to let our early-morning visitor in.

I was unsurprised to see Jeff on the other side. He'd told me we were his next stop.

"Mrs. March," he greeted me, his fake warmth on full blast, but I was left feeling chilly. Something about him rubbed me the wrong way, but maybe I was projecting because I'd heard him fighting with Bruno, and I generally thought Bruno to be a pretty good judge of character.

"You can just call me Este," I corrected him. "Mrs. March was my mother."

This level of familiarity seemed to leave him unsteady, and it took him a moment to nod. "Okay, Este. That's an unusual name," he added, regaining his used-car salesman smarm. "Is it short for something?"

"Esther, but if you call me that, I'm definitely not paying my invoice." I smiled at him to show it was a joke, and he laughed, but it was like a robot practicing a laugh and not a proper human sound.

I cast a quick glance over my shoulder to Kitty, who made a face like she had just smelled something terrible. Kitty could never play poker.

"Well, I've got your delivery here for you." He nodded backward, and I could see several Styrofoam coolers stacked on a wheeled cart. It was a lot of produce, but not nearly as much as I'd been anticipating for my last delivery.

"Is that . . . everything?" I asked nervously.

Jeff glanced down at his clipboard, counted something he had written, then turned around and counted the boxes. "Yup."

I held my breath, waiting to argue with him until I actually knew the order was wrong, but my gut was telling me this wasn't what I'd ordered. I had requested a small fortune in strawberries, enough that they should have filled at least half the containers he'd brought me, and that barely touched everything Seamus had requested on the root vegetable front.

"Okay, bring them in and put them by the walk-in, please." I gestured toward the big cooler doors, realizing he would have no idea what the layout of our kitchen was. By the back entrance, we had cold storage bins for things like onions and potatoes that didn't necessarily need to be refrigerated but lasted longer if they were at least a bit chilled. Next to that was our pantry proper, which had huge open shelving to store all the flours, shortenings, and various shelf-stable items that any bakery needed. It also had all the seasonings and base ingredients Seamus needed for the diner items. Beside that was the freezer, and next to it was the big walk-in fridge.

The kitchen was huge. We were blessed that the size of the diner allowed for it, and we made use of every square inch of space. On the wall opposite the storage was my workspace, and then the big standard fridge, and then Seamus's workspace. In the middle, separating the two areas, was a huge island with a butcher-block countertop that served as secondary prep space for both of us.

As Jeff started to load boxes in by the cooler, the front door jangled open and our only other full-time employee, Rosie Lewicki, came in. Rosie was a Split Pine lifer, born and raised on the island. She'd once confessed to me she had only ever left once, for a trip to Chicago, and that had been enough for her to know she didn't need to leave again.

She was only twenty-two, but she seemed pretty set in her ways for being so young.

Our part-timer, Marcel, would come before the lunch rush and stay until we closed at five.

"Morning, boss," Rosie greeted me, breezing through the kitchen and to the office, seemingly unaware of Jeff's presence. After ditching her coat and bag in the office, she mechanically went to the pantry, where our big cooling racks were stored at night. She grabbed a big tray of pastries I'd baked when I first arrived that morning and drifted back into the main diner like an efficient ghost.

She wasn't big on small talk until after her coffee, but once customers started to come in for the day, her sunny personality always netted her major tips.

Her dark curls were piled on top of her head in a messy bun, and under her Lucky Pie apron she'd donned a Taylor Swift sweatshirt that was one of her wardrobe staples. I'd seen that top so much that I knew it was starting to fade thanks to too many repeat washes. Like her beloved pop heroine, Rosie tended to sport an iconic red lipstick every single day of the week, and against her pale skin and dark hair, it gave her a perpetual Snow White look.

If Snow White was a Gen Z waitress who played in a pop-rock cover band on weekends, that is.

Rosie set about doing the front-of-house work: filling the pastry cases, making sure the milkshake machine was up and running—yes, even in November—and writing the day's specials on the big whiteboard we had mounted to the front counter.

I, meanwhile, turned my attention back to the load of fruits and vegetables Jeff was unloading next to my cooler. I started to peek into each Styrofoam container he had brought, mentally checking off the items I knew I'd ordered for myself and Seamus.

There was one glaring omission by the time I got to the end.

"Jeff, where are my strawberries?" I tried to keep my tone light, but even I could hear the edge of panic in my words. "Is there another stack of boxes somewhere?" I glanced around him to my closed back door and hoped it might open on its own to reveal several cases of strawberries.

Neither the door nor Jeff moved.

Out front, I heard the door open and close again and Rosie cheerfully greet the first guests of the day. I tried to remain calm.

"Strawberries? I didn't bring any strawberries. It's *November.*"

My eyelid twitched involuntarily, and I glanced over at Kitty quickly, hoping that looking at her was going to mellow me. Looking at Seamus wouldn't help, because I had no doubt that if I left this in his hands, it would probably end in fisticuffs.

"I ordered three *cases* of strawberries," I corrected him. "With Denny. And you said you had nice berries for me." Had he meant the several clamshells of blueberries?

"Well, sorry to tell you that got lost in translation somewhere. No strawberries. I did deliver some to the General Store, though, so if you're in need, might want to check with them."

"If I'm in need." I stared at him like he was speaking another language. As angry as I was, I knew there was no point in getting mad *at* him. It wasn't going to change anything. The berries weren't here, and if I started to yell, it wasn't going to make them appear by magic. It wasn't like I'd paid for them in advance, thankfully. Produce could be fickle, so Denny's business always operated on an invoice-on-delivery system.

I took a deep breath. "Okay, thanks."

He jotted something down on the clipboard he was holding, then handed the whole thing over to me with a pen extended. "If you'll just sign here, I'll be on my way. Usual terms." Meaning I had thirty days to make a payment on my account.

I looked down at the invoice in front of me, and my eyes nearly fell out of my head. Whereas moments earlier I had thought yelling wouldn't solve anything, I couldn't help myself as the words tumbled angrily out of my mouth. "Are you *kidding* me?"

The total on the paper was at least twice the highest amount I had ever paid for produce in my history of owning the diner. It was an amount far exceeding what I had budgeted, and it meant I'd need to sell every single thing on the shelves today, possibly including the shelves themselves, if I had even the faintest hope of calling it a break-even season.

Tears welled at the back of my eyes as I started to think about Seamus's and Rosie's offseason pay and the looming reality that the roof of the diner probably had only one more winter left in it.

"Is there a problem?" Jeff's tone was defensive, which didn't help matters.

"This is *not* what I was paying Denny."

"Yeah, well, market prices change, and Denny wasn't very business minded. Costs money to get these things and get them out here still fresh, y'know?"

I stared at the total on the page and thought it was pretty obvious that these things cost money, because he was asking for all of mine.

"This is highway robbery. This isn't just inflation. You can't just raise prices like this after an order has been placed. That's unethical." I could hear more people making their way into the diner, and I knew I'd to have to get my pies started soon if I was going to keep up with demand. Rosie had already come back into the kitchen twice to get frozen pies from the walk-in, but if she sensed the tension back here, she didn't let it show.

Jeff gave me a leering smile that sent a shiver of alarm down my spine. He leaned in close and tapped his finger on the bottom of the invoice I was looking at. "Prices subject to change based on market costs. Right there in black and white. Now if you don't mind signing, I'd like to get back to my boat."

I signed the paper, because I had no real choice. The produce was here, and I did need it. Pies and soups wouldn't make themselves. I thrust the clipboard back at him and bit my tongue to stop myself from saying anything I might regret. I could threaten to find a new vendor, but I didn't know if there *was* another vendor, so I needed to avoid burning any bridges before I had an architect to build me a new one.

I opened the back door of the diner, which was really on the side of the building, and could see a few more people making their way up the front path toward the entrance. My restraint buckled as Jeff wheeled his cart out.

"You know, if this is how you do business, you're not going to make a lot of friends on this island," I told him.

He doffed a fake cap at me and grinned again, something I sincerely wished he would stop doing.

"Mrs. March, I'm a man of business, and my business ain't making friends."

Chapter Four

The day flew by in a haze of customers both local and from the mainland. Like Kitty, many of the locals popped in throughout the day to either see if they were lucky enough to get *the* pie themselves or watch someone else get it.

Because I'd prepared so many of the pies in advance, there were more than a dozen lucky pies that went out over the course of the day, which meant quite a few people were going to think they'd gotten the only one.

I knew which ones were lucky, of course. I could feel it when I picked up the box. There was just something different about them, the way my fingertips would tingle and a little thrill would run up my spine, almost like an electrical current. But that wasn't something anyone else could feel. For them, it was warning enough when I smiled and winked while handing them their receipt and coyly said, "I think you're really going to enjoy that."

Perhaps that was my tell, and the locals had just learned to look for it.

Sometimes, once in a blue moon, I broke my own protocol and would guide someone to a specific pie. If they were looking at an apple pie but something about them gave me a good vibe, or if it was someone I knew personally who might be going through a rough patch, I would quietly lean over the counter and say, "You know, I think you're in the mood for chocolate cream today."

I was probably more my mother's daughter than I realized.

Unfortunately, what should have been a joyous final day in the shop was marred by my morning interaction with Jeff. The invoice was pinned to the corkboard in my office, waiting to mock me mercilessly when I got back there to do the nightly cash-out. Every time I let my mind go back to that encounter, a pit formed in my stomach that was an unpleasant combination of anger and worry.

I was grateful for how busy we'd been. I hadn't been able to look at the totals for the day, but based on the empty pots of soup and the dwindling pile of frozen pies in the freezer, I had a good feeling we were going to break even.

Barely.

With only a few hours left in the day, I decided there was enough time and ingredients to do a handful more of the day's special pies. I was tired, but I wanted to use all the cranberries I had on hand. It would be a shame to see them go to waste. Plus, it would be nice to send out at least one more *special* pie before we closed for the season.

I set my saucepan on the stove over medium-high heat and poured in the apple cider. The wafting scents of fresh apple and cinnamon immediately filled the air. Was there anything better than apple cider on a fall day?

The sugar in the cider would add a syrupy sweetness to the pies that didn't demand much extra sugar in the recipe, but I liked a good, sweet base to work with. Once the cider had been reduced to a thick golden syrup that looked like liquid gold, I stirred the whole cranberries and let them pop on their own as they heated. I didn't want it to be like eating the cranberry sauce you had with Thanksgiving turkey; I wanted some of the berries to remain whole so they'd pop unexpectedly in someone's mouth for a tart surprise.

As I baked, goose bumps prickled my skin, and my mind—once full of frustrated thoughts about my useless new produce vendor—started to fill with visions of shiny lucky pennies, shooting stars, and then of people gasping with delighted surprise. I saw people catching buses they thought they had missed, or hearing their favorite songs playing just as they got to their cars. I pictured a sad girl at a school dance being invited onto the dance floor by her crush. I saw exams aced and promotions won.

All of that poured into the baking, and I knew that someone was going to get a really nice treat with their dessert today.

Once the berries had begun to soften, I poured in the apple cider and reduced the heat. Earlier in the day I had zested a pile of oranges, so the fresh zest was ready in a bowl—one less step I'd need to take in assembling the pie. As I pulled the plastic wrap off the top of the bowl, the citrus scent filled the room, and when it combined with the aromas of apple cider and cranberry, it felt as if someone had wrapped a blanket made of Christmas around my shoulders.

While the filling thickened, I took one of the room-temperature balls of dough I had set out earlier and floured my workspace counter, then used an old family rolling pin to get the dough perfectly flat. After years spent making pies, I was pretty efficient at getting the ball to the exact size and thickness I needed with relative ease.

I loved the feeling of flour on my fingertips as I dusted it over the countertop. While my magic didn't require potions or tinctures, there was something inherently magical in the act of sprinkling sugar and flour into the air. I smiled to myself as I worked.

I folded the shell in half and rested it in a waiting pie dish, where I then unfolded it and gently worked it into the shape of the dish. I would add a lattice once I put the filling in, so I went for a subtle wavy edge before using a fork to score the bottom of the shell. Then I put a circle of parchment paper in the bottom and added a layer of dried beans on top.

Some bakers opted for fancy specialized pie weights that came in a chain. I had a nice set at home I liked for making my own pies, but at the diner I kept a few jars of old beans on the counter, finding they served the purpose of adding weight to my pie shell to keep it from bubbling or cooking unevenly when I blind-baked. I repeated this process with two more shells, then put all three into the oven and set a timer, which I clipped to the strap of my apron.

Rosie came into the back, and while she didn't look obviously frazzled, I sensed an extra quickness to her steps. "Need any help out there, Rosie?"

Marcel had arrived for his usual shift a few hours earlier, but today was a day that needed all hands on deck.

"That would be great, if you're not too busy."

I shook my head and turned off the heat under the saucepan with my cranberry pie filling in it. It had thickened up beautifully, with the glossy red cranberries and golden syrup creating a stunning combination that looked like a pot of precious gemstones. I couldn't resist sampling a taste from the back of the spoon. The added orange zest packed a powerful brightening punch that offset the ooey-gooey sweetness of the cider syrup perfectly. I tossed the spoon in the sink and mentally patted myself on the back, reminding myself to jot the recipe down later. The pie shells would need to bake for about fifteen minutes, which was plenty of time to head out to the front and help Rosie with crowd control.

In the main area of the diner, I heard the whir of the milk-shake machine and nodded in Marcel's direction. All the tables were full, and there was a lineup from the front counter to the door, where I could see more people lingering outside, waiting to get in.

For a few minutes, I didn't feel the slightest bit of worry about how our bottom line for the season was going to look. This was a *very* good day. Rosie took a tray of sandwiches and headed into the restaurant, so I took over on cash. A woman with a silver bob and an expensive-looking quilted jacket was waiting.

"It certainly is busy in here," she commented, with an emphasis on *busy.*

"Yes, ma'am. Last day of the year is always a bit wild. We're happy you could make it in. What can I get you?" I found that if you were incredibly nice to people who seemed on the cusp of making a complaint, they usually decided not to, and I was hoping not to have to juggle any customer complaints today. People were usually very understanding, but you could never tell when someone's patience might run out.

Her smile was thin, but she didn't make any additional comments about the wait. She ordered two frozen pies, and I added a fresh peach and white chocolate blondie to her order to make up for her inconvenience, though I couldn't imagine I was keeping her from anything important, considering she was a tourist and there were no scheduled events on the island today.

I wanted everyone to leave my diner happy, though. I wanted people to feel like they were better for having coming here. It was the way people had reacted when my grandparents ran the place, and when my mother was the one in charge, and I wanted to continue the legacy of being a force for good in the lives of our customers. Even the ones who complained.

Especially them, maybe.

The line moved smoothly, with very few people waiting for an eat-in spot and most either taking slices of pie or tarts in to-go containers or picking up whole frozen pies for their trips home.

I noted one person coming up in the line whose presence was unexpected enough to be considered a surprise. Wearing the muted-brown uniform of the group who lived on the compound across the island called Sunrise Acres, a man stepped up to the counter and offered me a soft smile. While the group was often referred to as a commune—or less kindly as a *cult* by some old-timers—they called themselves a *collective farm*.

I felt a bit guilty for not knowing the man's name, and for barely recognizing him. If he hadn't been wearing an outfit that signaled he was part of the farm, I would have assumed he was a tourist. I was fairly certain I'd seen him once or twice at the farmers' market, though.

"Afternoon," I greeted him brightly. "What can I get you?"

"Beautiful day," he replied. "We'd like to order one of each of the seasonal pies, if you don't mind. Big supper tonight." The *we* felt strange, since he was all by himself, but if I was being honest, everything about him was just a little bit strange. There was a vagueness about him that reminded me of the way cats sometimes look at shadows on the wall that no human can see. He just seemed to be smiling at something that wasn't there.

I brought out his pies and rang him up, but just as I was expecting him to leave, he said, "I gather you had a bad experience with the new fruit man today."

I blinked at him a few times, both because of what he'd said and the way he'd said it. His tone up to this point had been light and almost dreamy, and now his voice was firm and focused. "I'm sorry?"

"The new produce man. Didn't catch his name, but he was down at the harbor earlier complaining to Carey that he doubted he'd be around here again if you had anything to say about it."

I tried to laugh it off, but deep down I was genuinely mortified. Was Jeff actually going around telling people—Carey Wise the harbor master, no less—that I was trying to run him off the island? Sure, we'd had an argument, and I had found his business acumen lacking, but it wasn't like I'd chased him off with a pitchfork.

If anything, his own pricing would be the thing to drive him off the island for good.

Offering the farm collective man a smile, I said, "I think he was exaggerating a little."

"Thanks for these." He lifted the bag of pies and smiled.

"Anytime."

As I watched him go, I had only one thing on my mind: Just how much of a scene had Jeff been making if the hippie farmers had noticed and thought to bring it up?

I could have killed him.

Chapter Five

Where Halloween proper was an all-night party affair, by the time the last of the tourists left for the mainland on November 1, almost every local on Split Pine was ready for a pair of cozy pajamas, a big glass of wine, and an early night in bed.

Or perhaps that was just me.

We closed up the diner at five, precisely when the last ferry was leaving the harbor. There were a handful of nonlocal pleasure boats still moored, but they could leave at their leisure, provided they were gone by six the next morning when Carey did his rounds; otherwise, they would be levied a hefty fine. Some people who boated over by themselves wanted to stay for dinner or take in the final hours that a few of the shops remained open, but they wouldn't be doing it at the diner.

When Kitty came over that evening, I was sitting on the front porch of the converted carriage house I called home. It was a cute little cottage behind Grampy's house. I'd moved in after I returned for a little privacy and never gotten around to moving out. He still lived in the main house alone, now than Gran was gone, and my father had moved back to the mainland to be closer to his family when I was away at school. With my mom's passing more than a decade ago, I understood his need to be around the community he'd grown up with, but I still wished I saw him more than once or twice a year.

Grampy owned another piece of land just a block off Main Street that he kept offering to give me so I could build my own place, but the diner, though it was doing well enough to stay open, wasn't making me the kind of money that would allow me to build a house.

Plus, if someone built anywhere in the proximity to Main Street, the house had to fit a certain aesthetic requirement: nothing but a Victorian or Cape Cod design would do.

Once, about forty years ago, a woman named Evelyn Maximoff had gone rogue and built a storybook house about a hundred yards back from the designated historical zone, avoiding the bylaw. The "Witch's Cottage," as it was now called, was one of the most popular places for tourists to visit and take photos for social media. The lush overgrown garden and the way light hit the house around midday made it something truly magical. I, however, just marveled at Evelyn's cheek for using the house's precise location on her lot as a loophole.

The bylaws had changed after that, so even though Evelyn's house was a marvel and a delight, no one else would get to build anything like it unless they were blocks away from the heavy tourist zones.

"You look a million miles away," Kitty commented, sitting beside me on the porch swing.

It was cold, probably much too cold to be sitting outside, but I knew that soon enough snow would cover the ground and the only time I'd spend outdoors would be during my daily walks to and from the diner. I was trying to soak in the last evenings where it was possible to do so, even if my cheeks were red and I couldn't feel my fingers.

I tossed my throw blanket over Kitty's lap and was immediately warmer with her here.

"I was just thinking about Evelyn's house." Even if the tourists called it the Witch's Cottage, locally it was still called Evelyn's, though she had died about twenty years ago. It was now owned by her daughter Louise, but Louise wasn't a local, and so the house was used only at the peak of summer these days. It made me sad that it went vacant so much of the time. Someone should live there.

"I wish Louise would sell that place," Kitty said, giving voice to my own thoughts. "I'd love to see someone actually in there all year round."

"Me too."

"Look, it's freezing out here, and I know you love being cold for some reason, but I am a delicate flower, and I want to be able to feel all my extremities."

"So you're saying you're a wuss and it's too cold for you."

"I said half of those things."

"Fine, fine." I gathered up my blanket and wineglass, and we headed into the carriage house, where Kitty made a beeline for the fridge and poured herself a glass of white wine, then plopped down near the fireplace in her favorite armchair.

I took the couch, pulling my feet up under me and dropping the blanket over my legs. Now that we were inside, where it was warm, I had to admit it was a lot cozier than being out in the near-winter air.

"Tell me something good," I declared, setting my wine down and picking up a bag of knitting I had next to the couch.

For the longest time Kitty had called me a "junior grandma" because of my penchant for baking pies and knitting people things—not to mention my all-season adoration of canning—but after seeing the adorable cardigan I had knit for her and

Seamus's daughter one Christmas, she had stopped teasing and finally asked me to teach her to knit.

There was a project tote next to her on the floor, but she didn't make an effort to grab it. Our knitting lessons had long ago become an excuse to hang out together, and we no longer really needed the pretense now that we were actually best friends.

The insistence to start each evening with one good piece of news or information had begun over a year earlier when we had discovered—to our mutual horror—that we spent half our time complaining about things in our lives or the activities of others on the island, and we'd decided we wanted to be more proactive in our positivity.

"Piper is now officially better at math than I am," Kitty said, with a dramatic sigh for effect at the end.

I laughed. Kitty and Seamus's daughter, Piper, was five years old now and spent her days at a local day care program run by a retired schoolteacher. I guessed that rather than letting the kids have screen time or focus only on playing, Mrs. Mayberry was up to her old tricks of sneakily introducing arithmetic to the impressionable minds of Split Pine's youth.

"At least she'll have a leg up when she starts school next year," I reminded Kitty.

"She's just going to keep getting smarter than me from here. It's terrifying. I don't know where she gets it."

"Hey now, both her parents are pretty clever people who I like a whole lot."

"You're sweet, Este, but I think we both know that neither Seamus or I were winning any valedictorian awards when we were in school." She held both hands up in a *stop* posture before I could argue. "But I'm not complaining. I'm thrilled our kid is going to be a genius."

45

It occurred to me I hadn't asked where Piper was that morning when I'd seen Kitty. I knew she spent the day with Mrs. Mayberry, but usually Kitty went to work a bit later in the morning.

As if reading my mind, Kitty said, "I suspect Tom is teaching her things when I'm not around. He was with her this morning and dropped her off at day care on his way to the station, and when I picked her up, not only was she doing her pluses and minuses to perfection, she was also telling me why Hank Greenberg was the most underrated Detroit Tiger of his era."

I snorted into my wine. "He's indoctrinating her."

Tom Cunningham, the eponymous *Tom* of Tom's Bar, was Kitty's older brother. He had been the first of the Cunningham siblings to move to Split Pine, but once he realized he wanted to put down roots and stay, Kitty had ended up moving to follow him. That had been almost ten years ago and coincided with my own return to the island, which was probably how Kitty and I had managed to fall so easily into each other's orbits.

Tom, on the other hand, was a harder nut to crack.

He was kind, but he was quiet. He liked to keep to himself, which was why, even though he owned a sports bar with his name on the neon sign, he left the day-to-day operations to Kitty. In his life before Split Pine, Tom had achieved the kind of fame that comes only with notoriety.

The year he was drafted, he had been the hottest prospect in baseball—and he went to his hometown team, the Tigers, making him an instant success story across Michigan. And the thing was, he had lived up to the hype, maybe even exceeded the ceiling of where many scouts and baseball minds thought he would go. Then, in the final year of his initial contract with the Tigers, when he was set to reach free agency and make untold millions with his next contract, the unthinkable happened.

Tom "The Bomb" Cunningham stepped up to the plate one late September evening, with the Tigers poised for the postseason and their place in the division counting on one more win.

The manager, under normal circumstances, would have pinch-hit. I'm sure Tom—and every other baseball fan in the world—wonders what would have happened if he made that decision instead.

Tom swung. He made contact. The ball sailed over the outfield wall, and the crowd lost their minds cheering the win, but soon it was obvious that this was no normal home run, because instead of rounding the bases in triumph to greet his team at home plate and celebrate as the victor, Tom had never *left* home plate.

He was lying in a heap in the batter's box, his bat discarded, and it slowly became clear why: the way Tom had swung his bat, and the impact of the pitch, had created an unbelievably rare reaction, and broken his arm in three places.

The Tigers won that game, but Tom didn't get his life-changing free-agent contract.

He never played baseball again.

Instead, he moved as far from the fanfare of Detroit as he could get while still staying in his home state, and he'd found himself in Split Pine. Of course, everyone here knew who he was—we had TV, we were Tigers fans—but while the locals of Split Pine loved to be in each other's business, we also understood the value of privacy when it mattered.

Tom was welcomed, and even though we all knew what had happened to him, we didn't make him relive his glory days unless he wanted to. It had taken him a good three years before he'd even mentioned his playing days to anyone, and two more after that before he'd decided to take some of his savings and open the bar.

"Gotta do *something* with all that memorabilia," he'd said at the time.

There were two types of locals in Split Pine: the ones who'd been born here, like me and Rosie the waitress, and those who came to us from the outside world.

On the island, we had a saying: *You come to Split Pine precisely when you are meant to.* Some of us, it seemed, were meant to be here our whole lives, while others found the place when they needed it most. When you decided to make the island your home, you became family—it was as simple as that.

I think Tom appreciated that immediate sense of belonging, which was why he'd convinced Kitty to move as well, keeping his real family close to him and part of our community. And now Piper was an island-born local.

"Piper is lucky to have people around to teach her things, even though I'd argue that Bill Freehan is actually the most underrated Tiger." I set my wineglass down. I was getting to an age now—the dark ages of my midthirties—where unfortunately I no longer had the robust constitution I'd had in my midtwenties, and even just a little bit of wine went right to my head.

"She's been talking nonstop about going to the diner this week, so we'll probably come by on the weekend for lunch."

We'd be shifting out hours now that the tourist crowd was fone. Iver the summer we ran the diner in split shifts, from seven to one and three to nine, but in the winter we were just opening seven to six daily. This would still let us capture the lunch and dinner crowds but not stretch our meager staff too thin. One night a week we stayed open until eight.

Kitty stifled a yawn, and I was forced to hide my own. "We're not very good at this whole girls' night thing," I admitted.

"Maybe so, but I need my nights out where I can get them, so you're stuck with me at least once a week."

"How terrible for me."

She threw a pillow at me. Kitty was about six years younger than me, but motherhood and managing a business had given her the added maturity that most twenty-nine-year-olds were still struggling to find. It's pretty hard to be flighty and irresponsible with so many people counting on you.

"We didn't even pretend to knit this time." She poked her knitting bag with her toe.

I picked up my entirely forgotten pair of socks. "At least I pretended."

She yawned again and then sighed, clearly acknowledging it was time to call it a night. I didn't want to give in so soon either, but in all honesty, it had been an exhausting day, and I was ready to settle into the more relaxed routine of a Split Pine offseason.

I could definitely do with several drama-free months as I prepared myself and the diner for the next tourist season to come.

Chapter Six

Since I wasn't in a rush to face the morning wave of tourists, I decided to be brave and grab a to-go latte from Elevated Grounds on my way to the diner. I'd be buzzing through the day, but with a split shift ahead, it meant that when the inevitable energy crash hit, I'd probably be getting ready to head home for the day.

I was also, if I was being honest, avoiding doing the accounting from yesterday. I had done a preliminary cash-out and put all our money in the safe, but I'd need to thoroughly crunch some numbers today to see where we'd ended our season and whether I'd need to consider cutting back our winter hours to keep us afloat until spring.

Plenty of Split Pine businesses either shuttered completely for the winter or went to more limited hours, but I'd always been proud of the fact that the Lucky Pie Diner was open seven days a week all year round. We were a constant in town, and I didn't want that to change.

As I approached the diner, even through the dark of the too-early morning, I could see that there was someone sitting on one of the little benches in front of the white fence. I squinted and could only make out a masculine figure. Anything else was too obscure in the dark.

Maybe it was Seamus and he'd forgotten his keys. Yet even as I considered that option, I knew the shape of this man was all wrong to be my lean, overly tall cook.

When I got to the fence, I could see quite clearly that the figure was none other than Tom Cunningham, but what gave me pause was that he wasn't in casual dress. He was wearing his sheriff uniform.

Tom had, several years ago, been elected to the sheriff's office in Split Pine, and while I think he initially shied away from the role, he had come to grow into it in the years that followed. Split Pine had little to no crime, especially in the offseason, and I think that made the job a pretty relaxed one for him. Still, he took it seriously, which was why I was surprised to see him here so early, in his full getup. Usually he saved the uniform for tourist season and just sported his badge during the offseason, since everyone in town already knew who he was.

"Tom." I greeted him with a nod.

"Morning, Este." If you were to imagine a poster boy for All-American apple pie and Fourth of July fireworks, it would be Tom Cunningham. He looked like Steve McQueen with a dash of aw-shucks Jimmy Stewart thrown in to make him the slightest bit more approachable. In a word, he looked like he'd tumbled out of the 1930s, with his square jaw and tousled blond hair. He was impossibly handsome in a wholesome, old-fashioned way that made me want to make him a milk shake and ask him to a sock hop, which made no sense whatsoever, but it was the sensation he inspired in me whenever I saw him.

"You're up awfully early, Sheriff." I jutted my chin out at his uniform. "Can I get you a cup of coffee? Is it too early to suggest some pie?"

He smiled softly and pushed himself up off the bench.

"I'm afraid I'm here in an official capacity, so no pie today."

My heart sank into my shoes. I was so accustomed to Tom's presence in town that it had never occurred to me that something might actually be wrong.

"Is it my dad?" I knew Grampy was okay; I'd seen his light on this morning as I passed the main house. "Is it Kitty? Piper? What's going on?"

He raised both hands to calm me. "It's not like that. I'm sorry—I should have started by saying everyone is okay." He paused. "Well, I suppose not everyone."

I gave him a perplexed look and held the collar of my jacket closed against a suddenly chilly breeze. "You want to come inside?" I suggested.

Again, my offer was declined with a shake of the head. "Este, did you speak with a man named Jeff Kelly yesterday?"

I took a sip from my latte to keep the cold at bay. "Sure, new produce guy, right? The replacement Denny. A *lesser* Denny, if you ask me." I snorted.

Tom didn't laugh. In fact, his already drawn expressed edged closer to grave. "You mind coming for a quick walk with me?"

Alarm bells started going off in my head, and I looked toward the diner. "Tom, I really have to get things started in the kitchen. I don't really have time—"

"You've got time," he finished for me. "Or you'll make time. But either way, you're coming with me."

Suddenly, even with the warmth of the latte radiating into my palms, I felt ice cold right down to my core. "Am I in some kind of trouble?"

"I sure hope not." With that cryptic line, he headed off in the direction of the harbor, where much to my surprise I spotted the sheriff's office Jeep parked at the foot of the harbor gate. There were only three traditional motorized vehicles on the entire island: a police car, an ambulance, and a fire truck.

Needless to say, seeing any of them out and about signaled reason for real concern. Cold sweat beaded my brow as I trailed behind Tom like an obedient puppy, still clinging to my drink, even though my stomach was now too much in knots for me to even consider taking a sip.

It was only when I got closer that I noticed the gates had been opened and the ambulance was also present, its lights off, parked at the very top of the main dock. While the island's fire service was largely volunteer based, there was one dedicated EMT on Split Pine, and if she ever needed assistance, she'd call on someone from the fire department.

Even in the darkness of the too-early morning, I recognized the imposing figure of our EMT, Caprice Washington. In her pre–Split Pine life, she'd actually spent several years as a professional wrestler whose stage name was Lady Fear. Like Tom, she'd had her career cut short by an injury, but you could still see her former life in her build. She was slim but had broad shoulders and well-defined muscles, and I'd once seen her pick up two men at the same time when someone challenged her to do it at the pub.

She didn't often need a helping hand when it came to her job.

Today, however, the equally familiar and slighter figure of Elgin Glick was hovering nearby, wearing an EMT uniform that looked a little too big on him, as most of Elgin's clothing did. He had lost about seventy pounds in the last year but hadn't yet committed to replacing his wardrobe. Caprice and Elgin made an odd pair—her tall and imposing, him shorter and more accustomed to shrinking into the background.

Caprice nodded at me, but she wasn't smiling, which definitely wasn't like her and made this entire thing all the more surreal and unsettling.

As we approached the ambulance, one of the local stray cats darted out between us, almost tripping me in its eagerness to get away from the docks. While I normally loved all the strays on the island, this one's insistence on almost giving me a heart attack thanks to my already jangled nerves wasn't endearing.

Close up, I noticed that the reason Elgin was hovering a good distance away was because he and Caprice weren't alone. There was a gurney—or whatever the ambulance version of a gurney was—standing in front of Caprice, and on it was a black bag roughly the size of . . .

Well, it was roughly the size of a human body.

Tom was looking back at me now, but I could barely take my eyes off the body bag. "Tom, what the heck is this? Why have you brought me here? What's going on?" I clutched my paper cup more tightly, because without it my hands would have been shaking.

Tom nodded to Caprice, who took a long pause to steel herself, then slowly unzipped the top of the bag.

"See, from what we can tell, Jeff Kelly only visited a small handful of people when he was on the island, and we're pretty sure he stopped at Lucky Pie last. So, along with a lot of other questions I've got for you, you're possibly the best shot we have of making a positive identification."

"A . . . wh-what?" I couldn't look at the bag now that it was open. My gaze tried to focus anywhere else and landed on Caprice, who also seemed to be avoiding looking directly downward.

"Este, when Carey Wise did his rounds this morning, he found one unauthorized vessel hadn't left the docks. And when he tried to get the attention of whoever was aboard, there was no answer, so he called me down out of caution, and when we went onto the boat, well . . . we found something. Someone." Tom nodded toward the gurney again. "Can you tell me if this is Jeff Kelly?"

I swallowed hard and finally forced myself to look down, not sure what kind of grisly scene I was expecting. Instead, it was just Jeff. A more grayish-pale version of Jeff, whose eyes were open and whose mouth was fixed in an expressive O of surprise, but nothing too grim. Still, he was dead, and I didn't feel like looking at him longer than I had to.

I turned away, and Caprice quickly zipped the bag up again. "Yes, that's him."

"Thank you. I have one more question, then."

"Sure." Anything that would let me get out of here and back to the comfort and security of my diner's kitchen.

"Can you tell me why we found him holding on to this when he died?" He held up a plastic evidence bag, and inside was a crumpled piece of paper. I recognized it immediately.

It was the carbon copy of the invoice for the Lucky Pie Diner. With my signature clear as day on the bottom line.

Chapter Seven

I had lived in Split Pine my entire life—with the exception of my four years at university and living briefly in Detroit afterward—and I had been inside most of the businesses on the island. But in my thirty-five years, I had never once been inside the sheriff's office.

I'd certainly never been in what they were presently using as an interrogation room but I suspected was probably the staff room on most days, based on the single-pod coffeemaker on the counter and a mug that said *World's Okayest Deputy*.

I still had my jacket pulled tightly around me but had disposed of my now-frigid latte, which meant I had no idea what to do with my hands. I didn't want to look standoffish, so it seemed too aggressive to cross my arms, but I also didn't want to look too nervous, because I might come across as guilty.

Was that what Tom thought? That I was guilty?

In the ten years he'd lived on the island, I'd spent significantly more time with his sister than with him, but surely he knew me well enough that he didn't think me capable of murder.

Because that had to be how he assumed Jeff had died, right? I was certainly no expert on death or foul play, but it seemed unlikely to me that a healthy-seeming guy like Jeff would just drop dead all of a sudden while clutching *my* invoice, of all things. Perhaps he had, though. I didn't know if Jeff had actually been healthy; we'd known each other for about five minutes. Maybe he'd smoked a pack of cigarettes a day and eaten only bacon.

Maybe, then, Tom didn't think I had killed him myself and only thought that a diner sandwich might have been the final bit of cholesterol to tip the scales.

I had no way of knowing what Tom was thinking, because he wasn't in the room with me. I was, admittedly, worried that Tom might believe I was involved in Jeff's death, but my anxiety was also in high gear because I was concerned about the diner. It was already after seven, which meant things were well behind schedule and there would be no fresh pies to sell until I got there.

Hard to have a good-luck pie when the baker is stuck in jail.

Tom couldn't have believed I was much of a criminal, though, because he'd left me with my phone and bag, which meant I'd at least been able to text Seamus and Rosie and let them know I had run into an unforeseen issue and they'd need to open up without me.

I considered texting Kitty to see if she might come rescue me from her brother, but if this was all just innocent questioning, I didn't want to force Tom to face the wrath of an angry Kitty Cunningham.

I settled on what to do with my hands and focused on wrapping and unwrapping a piece of my bright-red hair around it, hoping to distract myself.

Just as I was plotting out my next haircut, Tom entered the room and sat down in the chair across the table from me. He was still wearing the same intense and grim expression I'd seen on his face earlier in the morning, but now under the much harsher overhead lights, I could also see the sallowness in his complexion and the bags under his eyes.

He looked exhausted.

He placed a mug of coffee on the table—this one just had the Split Pine Sheriff Department logo on it—then glanced from it to me. "Can I get you a cup?" he asked.

"No. I'm so sorry, Tom, I really don't mean to sound pushy, but is this going to take long? It's not that I don't trust Seamus, but I really need to get to the diner."

Tom's face twisted momentarily when I mentioned Seamus's name. Even though Seamus and Kitty had a good relationship for a divorced couple and were very amicable about how they shared custody of Piper, I knew there wasn't a ton of love lost between Seamus and Tom. As Kitty told it, Tom had told her not to marry Seamus in the first place, and there had been a fair number of *I told you so* looks after they got divorced.

Seamus wasn't everyone's cup of tea, so I could certainly see why he and Tom had never gotten on, but I also felt protective of my friend and bit back a defensive comment.

"I'll try to keep things as quick as possible, and then you can be on your way," he said.

Well, at least I wasn't in so much trouble that I was under arrest, so that was a positive start.

Tom opened a notebook and asked, "Could you just go over your meeting with Mr. Kelly yesterday?"

"Calling it a meeting is probably too generous. He came by the diner to drop off my order."

"We have a witness who mentioned seeing you and Mr. Kelly argue."

I could bet dollars to doughnuts the witness was just Carey Wise, who spent most of the time he wasn't monitoring boats monitoring what was going on in town. Carey was also probably the only person currently awake in Split Pine who might have been around yesterday. Since the Lucky Pie Diner was right next door to the harbor, I wouldn't be surprised if he'd overheard my parting shots to Jeff the previous morning.

I wasn't particularly proud of myself for how I'd behaved, but that didn't make me guilty of murder.

"Yeah, I'm not going to pretend he made a great first impression. And not just with me—I heard him arguing with Bruno before he came to the diner."

Tom's eyebrows went up, and suddenly I realized just how easy it was to start spreading gossip. "He argued with Bruno?" This he jotted down on his notepad, and I felt guilty for having potentially thrown Bruno under the bus.

"In fairness to both me and Bruno, Jeff was gouging us with insane price hikes, and he shorted me on my order considerably. It might have been the same for Bruno too. I can't say I was too impressed with him." My hand flew to my mouth even as the words came out. "Geez, I'm sorry. That's a terrible thing to say about someone who died."

Tom wrote something down before saying, "He didn't make a great impression with Carey either, so I think it's safe to say you aren't alone in that sentiment."

Was that the faintest hint of a smile?

It was gone faster than I'd even processed seeing it, so it was hard to say, but what was unmistakable was the slight flutter in my chest. Impressive that even in *this* scenario I could find myself a little twitterpated by Tom Cunningham.

I returned to what Tom had said about Carey. For the harbor master to have noted someone being *especially* rude would have taken considerable work. Carey Wise dealt with the daily arrivals and departures of the island, and while he didn't have anything to do with the operation of the ferries—other than making sure they left his docks precisely when they were meant to—he did spend almost every waking hour of his day dealing with people.

So. Many. People.

And between the entitled yacht owners and the drunk tourists who didn't think signs applied to them, Carey had met more than his fair share of bad eggs in his many years working the docks.

"Wow, if Carey didn't like him, he must have been a real piece of work."

Tom glanced up from his notebook at me, and I thought perhaps I should apologize again, but this morning my mouth was operating entirely independent of my brain, and there was simply no stopping it now.

If I'd been thinking at all, I probably would have requested that a lawyer be present for this entire discussion, but I was still having a hard time imagining that Tom could actually think I might have something to do with any of this.

"What time would you say Jeff left Lucky Pie?" Tom asked, apparently deciding not to address my comment.

"We had just opened, so a little after seven."

"And you didn't see him again after that?"

"No, we were pretty busy, it being the last day and all. I was at the diner all day, then went home after that."

"Can anyone corroborate your whereabouts during the day? More specifically the evening? We believe he probably died after nightfall."

"I'm sorry, are you implying I need an alibi?" My skin went cold again as I realized the gravity of the situation I was in.

"Let's not be hasty, Ms. March. I'm just doing my due diligence."

Well, we'd gone from *Este* to *Ms. March*, so that couldn't be good.

"Up until I left the diner, I was with my staff. Seamus, Rosie, and Marcel, as well as a bunch of regular customers, can certainly attest that I was there all day. In the evening, Kitty stopped by around eight and stayed for a little over an hour. I went in to see my grandfather before that, maybe at seven, but only for a minute or so. After Kitty left, I went to bed."

"Alone?"

"With Agatha Christie, but I don't know that she'll be much help to you."

"What book?"

I stared at him, unable to fathom how any of this was helping him solve a crime and slightly indignant that he wasn't just taking me at my word. "*A Murder is Announced.*"

He gave me another quick look, like he couldn't decide if I was being cheeky or genuine. In this case, it just happened to be an overly on-the-nose truth.

"I like Miss Marple," I told him flatly.

"More of a Poirot guy myself," he replied, his gaze back on his notepad again.

"Tom, do you think I had something to do with this?" I asked. After this long, this many years of living so close together in such a small place, it hurt to think he could believe that of me.

He closed his notebook and locked his eyes on mine, those cool baby blues giving nothing away.

"I sure hope not."

Chapter Eight

If I thought my day couldn't get any worse, I was in for a rude awakening.

Not ten feet outside the sheriff's office, still bewildered and shaken from my interview—but notably not under arrest—I found a big bloodhound with a regal stature and a little extra gray around his muzzle standing in the middle of the sidewalk.

He wagged his tail when he saw me.

"Morning, Mayor," I greeted him, approaching the handsome old hunting dog and scratching him behind the ears as his tail thumped loudly on the sidewalk.

There was a long-standing and somewhat ridiculous Split Pine tradition, dating back at least eighty years, which dictated that the mayor of the island was always, without fail, a dog.

The reason for this has been lost to time and retellings, but the general consensus, as passed from the mouths of grand-parents, is that one year not long after the town was founded, there was a bitter rivalry between the Sullivan brothers over which one would run for mayor, and the rift it created divided town loyalties. As a result, the people of the town didn't vote for either Sullivan brother and elected a scrappy terrier mix named Trixie, owned by the then harbor master, to be the town's mayor.

Trixie remained mayor for the next six years until she passed, and ever since then, the town has unanimously selected a dog to be the next mayor when the previous one dies, and no one really questions how ludicrous this is.

All the major financial decisions and other important choices on behalf of the island are made by the town council, but the mayoral title is strictly canine.

Mayor, the bloodhound, wore a maroon bow tie on his collar, something his owner had added to lend a little extra polish.

His owner was, unfortunately, the reason I had mixed feelings about seeing Mayor out and about.

"Well, well, well, Este March." If a voice could be made of fish oil and metal shavings, that voice would belong to Mick Gorley. It made me feel greasy and uncomfortable in equal measure. "You skipping out on work today?" He clucked his tongue as if were a truant child who'd gotten busted running from classes.

"Good morning, Mick," I said, punctuating my greeting with an obvious sigh. I gave Mayor one more scratch behind the ears, wondering how such a very good boy could be owned by the worst person to ever have lived in Split Pine.

In my distraction of having been unceremoniously dragged into the sheriff's office—okay, so I was politely invited, but that was neither here nor there—I had totally forgotten that the quaint little building sat almost immediately kitty-corner to one of the two hotels on the island.

It was, unquestionably, the fancier and larger of the two, but its being owned by Mick Gorley meant I always recommended Sullivan's Lodge, the hotel located closer to the harbor. Better view, better host.

I glanced up at the Pine Hollow Hotel, which had the distinction of being the tallest building on the island at six floors and was so wide you could see it from everywhere on the north side thanks to its location on the highest point of land we had. It escaped being an eyesore by showcasing a very pretty colonial style that made it appear as if it had been constructed much earlier than the 1980s.

Mick liked to act as if the hotel were a rich part of Split Pine history, when in fact the Pine Hollow had replaced the original first hotel built on the island, the Grand Michigan, which had been built in the 1920s and sadly burned down in 1978. The newly rebuilt hotel borrowed from images of the original, but it wasn't quite the same, and there were certainly elements of it that in retrospect were very assertively eighties and had not aged well.

All that being said, it was an exceptionally popular tourist destination and was fully booked for the duration of the season every year. In the offseason, several of the floors were closed entirely, but Mick managed to keep business steady by hosting weekly Sunday brunches, discounted spa staycations, and events for the locals like the annual Christmas ball and the only New Year's Eve party in town aside from Tom's.

It also housed one of the few year-round restaurants in Split Pine, which suddenly made me wonder: What if the Lucky Pie *hadn't* been Jeff's last stop on the island? Mick had to get his produce from somewhere. Sure, the Lucky Pie Diner was right beside the harbor, so we made the most sense as a final delivery, but Jeff was new and might not know the layout of our town that well.

This, unfortunately, meant I actually had to *talk* to Mick if I was going to find out if he'd known Jeff or seen him the previous day.

Mayor dutifully trotted over to his owner, and I turned to face the man whose voice so repelled me. His appearance, at least, wasn't as disquieting, but knowing what kind of person he was dampened any favors his genetics had done for him.

I was willing to bet that when Mick was in his twenties and thirties, he had been considered a genuine catch. He had the strong jaw and arresting features that were considered classically handsome, though he had put on weight in his sixties and now had a general softness of figure that dulled the sharpness of his cheekbones and chin.

He had muddy brown eyes and black hair going salt-and-pepper at the temples, and in the past three years he must have started to rewatch *Magnum, P.I.*, because he'd grown a very bushy mustache and never gotten around to regretting it.

He still wore the clothes of a smaller man, so his suits were all a little too tight, but I think he liked being the only man in town who regularly *wore* a suit, so he wasn't willing to let it go and switch to jeans like the rest of us common folk.

"Did I just see you leaving the sheriff's office?" he asked. He wore cowboy boots every single day of his life, at least as far as I'd ever seen, and today they looked to be a pale . . . crocodile, perhaps? Whatever it was had deserved better than to end up on Mick's feet for the rest of eternity.

"You did, yes."

Mayor sat next to Mick, wagging his tail, but kept his gaze locked on me as if ready to bound over at a moment's notice if I called to him. There was a long-running theory that Mick had named the dog Mayor solely with the intention of getting the bloodhound elected, which had certainly worked, because how do you *not* vote for a dog named Mayor? But the general opinion around town was that Mick had thought he might somehow get to act as proxy mayor in the stead of his dog.

He'd been very disappointed to learn this was not the case and had spent the years since Mayor's election trying to take over the town council.

If there was one thing in this world that Mick wanted more than anything, it was for people to think he was important.

I had to wonder if Jeff's sneering, belittling attitude had been upsetting enough to Mick that he had felt compelled to do something about it.

I'd never *liked* Mick, but I'd also never believed him capable of murder. Annoying? Absolutely. Backstabbing? Most certainly. But murder was an entirely different kettle of fish.

"You in any kind of trouble?" he goaded, giving me a leering wink.

"I don't think they're going to lock me up and throw away the key," I answered. It felt too dishonest to just say no, because I didn't really know if I was in trouble or not.

"Well, good, you keep your nose clean. Now listen, I've got a bone to pick with your grandfather."

I should have been prepared for this, since Mick and Grampy were always at each other's throats about something, but I was off my game this morning and had been looking for a way to ask Mick about Jeff, so the comment took me by surprise.

"Oh?" I immediately regretted how open-ended that one vowel sound was. It invited Mick to continue, which was the last thing in the world I wanted him to do.

"I keep making him offers on that plot on Main. Keep telling him it'll be good for the island if he lets me put up another hotel there. Something real cute, boutique like, you understand?"

I did understand. And while I also fundamentally agreed that another hotel was a very good idea for the island, I also knew why Grampy wasn't ever going to budge on selling.

"I can appreciate your interest, Mick; it's a wonderful location. But that lot is where I'm going to build my house."

"Now, Esther." He clucked his tongue again, but before he could continue, I had to interject.

"I'm sorry, Mick, but only my mother and grandmother ever called me Esther, and since you are neither and I'd like to think we're . . . friendly . . . I'd appreciate it if you wouldn't mind calling me Este."

"Oh, naturally, naturally. You know how the old brains work after a certain age."

What I knew was that he wanted to exert a parental influence over me by using my given name, but my full name wasn't even used by my father or Grampy unless they were feeling especially paternalistic, and I liked to keep it as a memory of the women in my life.

"Este, what I mean to say is, your family has had that lot for several generations now. And while I know you all had a place there once, it's really just going to waste. You've been back more'n ten years now. I think if you were going to build something, it'd be built by now."

This ruffled my feathers. The original plan on my return *had* been to build my house the following summer, just a cute little Cape Cod bungalow. I'd had the plans made, approved by the council, ready to break ground.

And then the freezer at the diner had died.

And the next year there was a leak in the dining room roof.

The year after that there was a winter storm so bad it had literally blown the deck off the back of the diner.

Every year there was something new that chipped away at the bottom line and took another bite out of my savings—not that I'd ever tell Grampy or Dad that was how we had financed most of those repairs—but it meant the house dream kept moving further and further away.

I didn't need Mick Gorley to remind me of that.

"I wasn't aware there was a time limit on using a plot of land my family has owned since we first came to the island." I was a March thanks to my dad's name, but it was actually my grandmother's family who had lived on the island longest, and she used to joke that the women of our family lured unsuspecting men into loving us and they ended up never leaving the island.

Grampy was a Davies, but my Gran, Ruthie, had been a Rose, and there were still Roses on the island now, my second cousins or great-aunts or other relatives through marriage and blood alike. We were all deeply rooted in Split Pine history and could trace our line back to the original founders.

Mick couldn't do that.

"I'm sure you can appreciate that it would do more good for the island to be able to put something there." He shrugged like this should just be common sense and I would suddenly change my mind about his offer of sale after a decade.

Heaven only knew how long he'd been on Grampy's case about the property before that, since Grampy was the one who currently owned it, but Mick knew perfectly well what the intended purpose of the land was.

"Mick, I'm sorry, I'm late to get to the diner, and I really don't have time for this. I can appreciate your goals, and I'm sure there are other lots on the island that could make a suitable location for your next business. But it's not going to be the lot on Main."

Suddenly his face took on an ugly red hue and his false nice-guy act dropped away. "Now you listen here, Este, I've had drawings done up. I've made a business plan. I'm going to take it to the town council, and they'll agree with me: that lot should be developed."

I had to keep my mouth from falling open in surprise. I knew Mick could be a real jerk sometimes, but I was genuinely stunned that he was threatening to take this issue to the town council.

Not that it would matter. Ownership meant something here, and no one could force Grampy or me to sell, but I couldn't believe Mick wouldn't let this go.

"We're not going to sell the lot to you. I think we've spent ten years making that clear. I'm sorry you wasted your time, but that's not my fault."

He pointed a finger at me, his eyes laser focused and filled with anger. "You're not sorry at all. But mark my words, Este, you will be. And I *will* get what I want, no matter what."

Chapter Nine

My argument with Mick Gorley had been so unsettling it had made me forget why I'd been at that end of town in the first place. It wasn't until I got back to the diner and looked over to the harbor, where Jeff's boat was still tied to the dock, that I recalled the rest of what had taken place this morning.

Today really wasn't my day. Not only had it started off with a corpse, it wasn't even nine in the morning and I'd already been interrogated by the police and threatened by someone.

Mick's words left me on edge for plenty of reasons, but it was his quick shift from calm to vicious that had my skin crawling. Before our argument, I hadn't thought Mick capable of being more than an annoyance and a pest, but what I'd seen in him this morning was scary.

Was Mick capable of murder?

He'd proven today how quickly his anger could be triggered, and I was someone he'd known for years. What might have happened if a stranger had pushed him the wrong way? I'd certainly seen how uniquely capable Jeff was of making everyone he met angry, including me. But angry enough to kill?

And if Mick *had* killed Jeff, why put the Lucky Pie invoice in his hand? Had he already predicted I'd say no to selling him the land and thought of how he was going to get me out of the picture? I tried to imagine Mick being clever enough to frame me for murder in order to sway the town council into giving over our family property, but it didn't add up. The plot was too highbrow, too clever, and too prone to failure. I realized I was probably just looking for an extra reason to dislike him.

Still, if I removed the invoice from the equation, there was Mick's intense anger. I'd seen how Jeff brought out the worst in Bruno at the market, and he'd managed to bait me into yelling at him as well. Had he pushed Mick's buttons in the wrong way, and had one thing led to another?

I shook my head, trying to chase off the questions. They were just taking me around in circles, and I still didn't want to think Mick was capable of killing someone.

But if not Mick, who? I knew I hadn't done it, obviously, but depending on when Jeff had died, if it really was after the rest of the tourists had left Split Pine, then the only remaining option was that it had been a local who had killed him, and that was unsettling and scary no matter who I pointed the hypothetical finger at.

I knew everyone on the island and had for my whole life. If one of them had done this, it made me question everything I knew about every single one of them. Sure, there were people I liked, people I disliked, but I couldn't picture any of them sneaking onto Jeff's boat and . . . well. Tom hadn't been forthcoming about *how* Jeff had died, but based on what I'd seen at the harbor, I had to assume he'd been hit from behind, since his face had looked untouched and his expression had seemed so surprised.

I let myself into the diner through the side door, not wanting to fake niceties with the locals out front while my mind was so diverted. What I needed was to lose myself in making some pies and let the magic of the process make everything okay.

There was no day so bad, no situation so dark, that I couldn't bake myself back into a good mood. Unfortunately, I couldn't bake lucky pies if I was worried or cranky, which meant I needed to make some normal ones until the cloud over my head was gone.

As anxious as the morning had made me, I knew two things with certainty: I was innocent, and Tom was a smart guy. He would figure out who had done this.

I had nothing to worry about, or at least there was nothing I could do about any of it right now, so I might as well bake.

"Mornin', boss," Seamus greeted me after I'd hung my coat in the office. The kitchen smelled incredible, so I had to assume my intrepid cook had gone rogue and picked his own daily specials.

"What's cooking?" I asked. The nice thing about Seamus was, whereas others might have been curious as to why I was suddenly late when I was almost *never* late, he didn't care. Seamus just assumed that if you wanted him to know something, you'd tell him.

In the case of his and Kitty's marriage, this had proved a difficulty, because she wanted him to show interest in her and ask her things and predict her needs, but Seamus figured if she needed something from him, she would tell him. It was a mess.

I'd learned in my kitchen relationship with Seamus just to be direct, and it had worked for us for years, but I could only imagine how frustrating it might be to be in an actual romantic relationship with him.

"Figured we'd go hearty today. Beef barley and a creamy tomato bisque. We had a lot of fresh basil left in the fridge, so I went tomato-basil on the soup."

I gave an enthusiastic nod. "That sounds incredible. Great choices." Beef barley was one of my favorite soups. My mom used to make it for me all the time over winter, and it was such a thick, stew-y meal of a soup that it rarely needed to be paired with anything. I was already craving a bowl, and it wasn't anywhere near lunch.

Not that Seamus's soup would be an equal to my mom's, but it would be a pretty close second, I was sure.

"Sandwiches?" I inquired.

"It's our first slow day, so I'm going to go easy. Brie, cranberry, and chicken, to use up some of the extra cranberries from your pie yesterday, and I'm itching to try this hearts of palm lobster recipe for the veg option. You season hearts of palm and fry them up and they taste just like lobster, so I was thinking vegetarian lobster rolls."

"Dang, that sounds incredible, Seamus. You have my wholehearted blessing. Get Rosie to add the sandwiches to the specials board, and if you need anything extra, just head over to the General Store." I had a hard time imagining we had enough hearts of palm in the pantry to make it a special, but Seamus was in charge of monitoring his own supplies, so perhaps he'd been stockpiling them for just this situation.

I left him to his side of the kitchen and the luscious aromas of two simmering soups. A few scant breakfast orders were on the queue, so I hazarded a quick peek into the main dining room.

As predicted for the first day after the island closed, the crowd was thin. This was how it would look for the remainder of winter. In one of the booths were three older gentlemen seated together with a coffee each and only one Danish that I could see.

Anita O'Dell, a teacher from the elementary school, was having a coffee and the breakfast sandwich—easily our morning best seller by a mile—and dribbling a generous amount of hot sauce onto the sandwich with each bite. Anita, a confirmed bachelorette, had made Lucky Pie a part of her daily morning routine for the last five years or so, since she'd moved here to take over a vacant teaching position.

Split Pine wasn't exactly a much-sought-after destination for professionals like teachers or doctors. Because of the over-winter closure, you had to be open to becoming close to your new community, since you'd be stuck with them from November through March. Anita had started out quiet and mousy, making a lot of the parents place bets on whether or not she would make it through her first winter. But she had thrived, and now in addition to teaching at the school, she offered a weekly learn-to-sew class at the community center beside the church over winter.

I nodded in her direction, and she smiled.

The last full table was a few of Mick Gorley's hotel employees tucking into breakfast before heading off to work for the morning. It made me feel a little smug that they would rather eat here than at the restaurant at the hotel where they worked. I'd take the tiny victories where I could get them.

The group of employees had their heads bowed together, sharing whispers, and even though the dining room was busy, I caught a snippet, enough to hear the words *dead body*.

I froze. I shouldn't have been surprised that word was already getting around. The ambulance being out was bound to cause a stir. Still, I was impressed and horrified that people were already sharing gossip about Jeff's death. How long would it be until they learned it was a murder? And how long after that until they knew I'd been questioned?

The curse of living in a small town with nothing else to talk about was that inevitably, any news was fair game, and this was *big* news.

I tried not to worry about it for now and turned my attention back to work. Behind the counter, Rosie was busy preparing a new pot of coffee. The front display windows were polished so well it looked as if there weren't any glass in them, and she had already added the two soups Seamus was making to the lunch specials board.

I knew this place could run just fine without me, but it was still nice to see that they hadn't missed a beat with my late arrival. Maybe that meant that after ten years of running this place, I could actually consider taking a day or two off every week.

My staff had been pestering me about it for ages, but I had been so focused on keeping the diner operational that I had sort of forgotten to have my own life in the process. Visions of a short vacation or even just a trip to Marquette or Detroit danced in my head. I had left the island only once since I'd been home, to attend the wedding of a friend from university, and it was while I was gone that the roof had started leaking, convincing me that perhaps if I was away, the Lucky Pie magic started to wear off. Probably a silly thing to think, but it had made me wary of going away again ever since.

I gave Rosie a quick thumbs-up of approval and headed back into the kitchen to decide what the specials for today were on the baking end of things. Just because *I* hadn't had a very lucky start to the day didn't mean I couldn't bring some luck to someone else.

I wanted to do something simple for one of the pies and settled on a chocolate cream, but because of the changing season, I wanted to add a bit of a Christmas punch to it. A peppermint chocolate cream, I thought—not quite as overtly Christmasy as my candy cane cream pie, but it would give that element of excitement about the pending holiday all the same.

I knew Elevated Grounds waited until after Thanksgiving to bust out the Christmas drinks, but I personally couldn't wait to bring peppermint back in full force.

I put a saucepan on the stovetop to start making my chocolate cream filling, then went to collect Oreos from the pantry. While I used a traditional pie crust most of the time, I liked to use an Oreo crust for chocolate cream–themed recipes.

With the milk heating, I took the prepared Oreo shells out of the plastic container we kept them in. Once a month or so, I would sit down in the kitchen for about an hour and use an off-set spatula to separate cookies from their cream filling. I kept the cookies in an airtight container, and generally ate enough of the filling to make myself sick, which was why I did it only once a month.

Since I could bake this pie on autopilot, I crushed the cookie shell under my rolling pin and started to think about what I would do for my savory option. It was hard to concentrate on the idea of savory anything with chocolate powder wafting into my nose and making my mouth water, but such was the danger of such a delicious job.

I wanted to make something hearty that would help anyone stopping in feel strengthened to take on the dropping temperatures outside. It wasn't even cold yet, at least not by Michigan standards, but there was a bite in the air that reminded us of what was around the corner. We'd had a few light snowfalls already, but with the fluctuating temperatures, none of it had stuck around just yet.

I made a mental note to be sure to dig the diner's shovels out of the little storage shed outside so they would be ready to go in case we got something in the next week.

A beef stew pie was just the thing to warm a chilly day, I decided. It was, for all intents and purposes, the same general concept as a chicken pot pie, but given the different flavor profiles, I didn't like to use the "pot pie" description. I went to take out several premade pie doughs from the fridge to give them time to come to room temperature and was grateful to see that Seamus had already pulled out two of each, realizing I'd be behind schedule.

"My pie dough hero," I announced. "Thank you."

He waved away my compliment, but when I glanced over, I saw him smiling. Seamus, for whatever reason, didn't want anyone to *know* he was a genuinely good guy. I guess it ruined the mystique he was trying to establish by looking like a longshoreman. Well, too late and too bad for him—I was in on the secret.

What made the beef stew pie a good idea today especially was that it didn't require a bottom crust. This meant that deep down I felt a little like I was cheating to call it a pie, but I also knew it was delicious and we would sell out over lunch, so I wasn't going to be pedantic about its name.

I went to the walk-in and gathered a hefty amount of precut sirloin stewing beef, carrots, onions, and a bag of frozen peas. I tried to ration the peas, since they weren't store-bought but rather grown in my father's big garden; I shelled and blanched them myself before I put them in the freezer for days like today, when the warmth and brightness of summer felt very long gone.

I had similar bags of frozen corn, which I used to have to rely on Denny to bring me, until the farm collective had started growing a ton of it in recent years. It was a bit more expensive to buy it on-island, because they could only grow so much, given their limited space, but it definitely tasted better than the stuff that had to be shipped in.

I decided at the last minute to grab a bag of the frozen corn as well. It wouldn't exactly be a purist stew pie, but then again, who made the rules on these things? I'd tried different veggies in the past in an effort to find out which variation worked best and had learned that while I loved potatoes in real stew, they weren't a good fit for a stew pie. There was just something about their density and texture that didn't work nicely with the crispy crust, so the potatoes never made a return.

I set about making the stew first, since that took the most effort and the pies would need to bake several hours, putting them just on schedule to be served for lunch.

First, I braised the meat. It would mostly cook in the oven, but I'd learned long ago that braising it first gave it a nice initial caramelization that really helped make it tender and juicy rather than chewy as it cooked. When the meat was browned, I took it out of the Dutch oven and added the chopped onion and carrot. Once those had cooked slightly but not oversoftened, I added beef stock, red wine, a mix of herbs, and some extra umami kick to deepen the overall flavor profile. Alongside soy sauce and Worcestershire—two classics in the umami oeuvre—I had a secret weapon: mushroom powder.

I'd never been a fan of mushrooms, so they were almost entirely absent from the diner's menu, but it was impossible to deny that mushroom flavor could pack a lot of punch in certain dishes. I'd learned about mushroom powder a few years earlier and discovered that it didn't repel me the way actual mushrooms did, and it soon started finding its way into many of my savory dishes.

In this one especially, it was a natural fit, and made those who actually *liked* mushrooms not feel as if there was anything missing.

Once the general stew base was ready and seasoned to my liking—I tended to use more thyme than most people might—I added the frozen peas and corn. I wasn't going to overcook them on the stove, just give them enough heat that they broke apart into the meat mixture. They'd do most of their cooking in the oven, and this way the peas would actually maintain some of their firmness.

The oven beeped to let me know it was preheated, and I transferred the big Dutch oven in. The stew would cook for a little over an hour before I spooned it into pie plates and added the perfect flaky crust on top to finish it off.

With the filling in the oven, I got to work on the chocolate peppermint cream pie, but I was barely in the process of turning on the stand mixer when I heard a raised, high-pitched voice from the front of the shop.

While the words weren't entirely clear, the tone definitely was, and I knew the voice well enough to know this wasn't just your average, run-of-the-mill annoyed customer. I let out a long sigh, putting my forehead against the cupboard door in front of me.

"You want me to go?" Seamus asked, sounding almost delighted by the prospect.

"As fun as that might be to watch, no, I'll handle her."

"I don't know why you don't ban her. She just keeps doing this."

I wiped my hands on a dish towel and steeled myself to enter the main dining area, letting out one more long sigh before I did as a brief meditation to remind myself to be patient.

There was one thing my grandparents had taught me as a small child as I observed the way they ran the diner, and that was that the popular saying *The customer is always right* was generally nonsense. They'd told me that not everyone in the world had learned how to respect those who served them and some people just wanted more than they were owed.

As I reached the main counter, I quickly assessed the situation. A lineup of people were waiting to place their orders, and several customers at nearby tables had obviously turned to listen to what was going on. In front of our glass display case was a beautiful woman with sleek blonde hair pushed back from her face by a pair of designer sunglasses. She wore an expensive-looking blue silk blouse tucked into even more expensive-looking black pants, and a huge purse dangled from the crook of her elbow.

She was flushed red and glaring at Rosie as if the girl had just spit in her coffee. I put a supportive hand on Rosie's shoulder and reminded myself of the lesson I had learned from my grandparents, which was to kill with kindness, even if that kindness was not earned. The idea was that if someone wanted a fight with you, you were the only one capable of denying them that.

"Good morning, Jersey," I said calmly to the woman on the other side of the counter.

Jersey Gorley, only child of Mick Gorley, was precisely the kind of adult that a person becomes when they are denied nothing as a child and given gifts and money instead of love and attention. I was very sure Mick loved his daughter, but I also thought that as a single father, he hadn't had the first clue of how to raise a child on his own, and the result was that unfortunately Jersey had grown up to be a demanding, mean, short-tempered menace. She *was* beautiful, but the kind of beautiful where a person knows it and wields their beauty like a weapon, making her pretty face feel more like a threat than anything pleasant to look at.

Right now, that face was red cheeked and wore a furious expression. "Good, someone with some common sense is here." She said these words directly to Rosie, making a maternal rage boil in me. I had no idea what had transpired here before I'd arrived, but I knew Jersey, and I knew Rosie, and I was absolutely certain whose story I believed before one bit of it had been spoken.

"Rosie, why don't you go check on everyone's coffee? I've got this."

Rosie gave me a grateful smile and shuffled off to get the coffeepot, not even looking back at Jersey. I couldn't blame her; there was a kind of unhinged rage on Jersey's face that made me think she was eager to lash out, and I wanted to be a shield to deflect and minimize that fury rather than let it land where it was currently aimed.

"What seems to be troubling you?" I asked, my voice as sweet as the pie filling I should have been mixing right then.

"That *girl* won't tell me which pies are lucky today, and *I know she knows*." She said this last part loudly to Rosie's retreating back.

"Now, Jersey. This isn't your first time doing this. We've had this discussion before. The pies can't be requested. And no, Rosie doesn't know. Only I know. It really is just luck of the draw." So to speak.

What I didn't say out loud but emphasized heavily in my overly cheery smile was that Jersey Gorley would *never* get a lucky slice. Both I and the pies had a general standard of who deserved a little extra luck in their day, and while you didn't need to be a saint, by any means, it went a long way if you weren't a big jerk to everyone around you.

"Then *you* give me the good-luck pie. I need it."

"Why do you need it?" I asked politely, folding my hands on top of each other on the counter and acting as if I had all the time in the world to hear what she had to say.

Already the red fluster had faded from her cheeks, and she took a moment to smooth her already perfectly straight blonde hair before she spoke again. "As you know, Daddy is very keen to open a new property on the island."

I wanted to be bothered that she still called her father *Daddy*, but I was a grown woman in my midthirties who still called my grandfather *Grampy*, so I was hardly in a position to throw stones.

Her words also reminded me of the very recent argument I'd had with Mick, something I had hoped to keep out of my head for the better part of the day. No such luck for me either, it would seem.

"Yes, I'm aware of your father's plans."

She tossed her hair back over one shoulder. "Well, I intend to ask him if I can run it. And Daddy is a little protective of his properties, so I just wanted a bit of extra luck before I present my plans to him. That's all." She gave me a perfectly practiced pout, one that had likely gone a long way toward getting her extra slices of cake for dessert and many toys she didn't need when she was a child.

But it wasn't going to get her any lucky pie.

There weren't a lot of rules about the magic of the pie, but I'd learned a few things in my time making them. One, the luck didn't work on my family. It was a gift in the truest sense, because it could be offered only to others. But it was also built with some added protections, because the luck was never, ever granted to anyone who would use it against us. If a land developer was in town and wanted a harbor-front property, the luck they desired for that project didn't act in my family's favor. So, no matter how good a person they might be, no luck for them.

"I don't have the specials ready today, but perhaps I could interest you in a slice of caramel apple?" I gestured to the front counter. The pies we had in regular rotation I always premade before leaving for the evening, so Seamus had put them in the oven before I'd arrived, meaning we had plenty of fresh-baked goods and I just needed to focus on the specials.

"Is it lucky?" she asked.

I gave a noncommittal shrug. "I like to think all our pies are lucky."

She snorted at this.

I didn't like people knowing too much about how the luck was dispensed, so I tried to convince them that it was the pies that decided rather than me, but since I *did* control it, I wouldn't be handing over lucky pies to Jersey. Maybe that was unkind of me, but she wasn't the kind of person who tried to help others or make the world around her a better place, and I didn't think she'd use a sudden turn of good luck to benefit anyone but herself.

When I didn't immediately cave to her whims or show any signs of giving in, she put her hands on her hips like an irritated toddler and heaved the biggest sigh imaginable, like I was truly vexing her very existence, and finally declared, "*Fine*, I'll take the caramel apple."

I gave her the best fake smile a gal could muster and packaged up the slice in one of our custom-labeled to-go containers. She thrust a five-dollar bill at me and didn't bother waiting for her change. Still, I had enough time to notice the way she looked down at the golden-brown slice through the little window on top, and it was impossible to miss the hunger in her eyes. It was the kind of hunger that food couldn't satisfy.

For a moment I actually felt bad for her, which might have been a first for me. I could relate to Jersey in some capacity, because I knew what it felt like to grow up being part of the family business. There were expectations, both spoken and unspoken, about what part you were meant to play in the ongoing success of your family's legacy.

While my parents and grandparents had never insisted I take over the diner, I was an only child, and as I started making plans to leave Split Pine to go to college, I could read the uneasy looks they shared just as easily as I could read the look Jersey currently wore.

My family never told me I *had* to step up, and I knew they would have supported me if I decided not to, but I had to wonder if Jersey had ever had a choice in the matter. Mick had been grooming her to take over the business for most of her life, yet now that she was an adult and eager to prove herself, he seemed uninterested in giving her the chance.

I wasn't sure what went on behind the scenes of their relationship, but Jersey had seemed especially on edge lately, and if she was starting to demand magical pies to fix her problems, perhaps there was some Gorley drama that had managed to avoid being sniffed out by the town's gossip grapevine, because I hadn't heard anything.

She headed for the door, and I was on the cusp of giving her an overly sweet farewell when suddenly she turned around and said, "You know, it'll be a real shame when this place closes."

I could barely manage to get my wits about me enough to respond. "Wh-what on *earth* are you talking about?" A few people nearby who'd had their interest piqued from her initial outburst were *extra* attentive now.

"Well, first I was just looking forward to seeing your face when Daddy's plan goes into action. Though maybe I should wait for you to hear about that from your grandfather. But this is better. I can't see the doors staying open long after they arrest you for murder. Maybe we can get an even better lot when it's all said and done." She tossed her blonde hair over her shoulder as if she hadn't just said the most insane thing I'd ever heard. "Too bad, really. You do make an incredible pie."

And she flounced out without a backward glance, leading me to pick my jaw up off the floor.

Chapter Ten

I had to assure several diner regulars that I was not, in fact, a
murderess, after they overheard Jersey's comments. I'm not
sure if it was a good or bad thing that all it took to convince
them was some free pie, but thankfully, no one went running
for the hills, and Jersey's little declaration didn't hurt my sales
for the day. Business was slow enough in the offseason; the last
thing I needed was Jersey scaring off the locals.

But there was no way around it: whereas the buzz earlier
had been about finding a dead body at the harbor, the word
murder was in the mix now, and it was all anyone could talk
about.

I had no idea how Jersey had made the connection between
me and the slain fruit vendor, but if she was going around town
telling people I was suspected of being a killer, it wasn't going
to take very long before *everyone* knew Tom had questioned
me. I wanted to believe that most people around here who had
known me since I was a baby wouldn't think me capable of
anything like that, but there were two unfortunate truths I
needed to face.

The first was that some people just didn't like me, and those
people would be more than happy to believe any bad thing

they heard. There was a small subset of people on the island who had decided I'd gotten too big for my britches when I left Split Pine for school. Others had their own reasons for disliking me, and when someone makes up their mind that they don't like you, there's not a heck of a lot you can do to sway their opinion, no matter how silly it might be.

The second thing I needed to remember was that while I was busy worrying about how the town might react to this new wave of gossip, there was a bigger problem at hand. I knew *I* wasn't the killer, but the meager bits of information I'd gotten from Tom implied that the killer had to be one of the locals, which meant it was going to be someone I knew. Someone we all knew.

I leaned in the doorway between the kitchen and the dining room and surveyed the small crowd with more suspicion. Vin and Eddie, two local fishermen, were sitting in their usual booth. Vin had a coffee, a slice of cherry pie, and a very well-worn Tom Clancy novel in front of him. Eddie had a week-old *New York Times* folded open to the crossword, his own cup of coffee holding down the corner of the paper, and only crumbs remained of his slice of caramel apple.

The two were in their eighties now, but they'd been coming in almost every single day since the doors opened. More frequently in retirement, perhaps, but as steady as one could hope for in terms of customers. Vin's wife, Suze, had recently passed, while Eddie's wife, Moira, was alive and well—but there was something comforting about their friendship routine. The two never said more than a handful of sentences to each other or anyone else, but it seemed to me they would have been miserable if they came in alone.

Did I think Vin or Eddie capable of murder? Both of them would know the docks like the backs of their hands, and even in their advancing age, I suspected they would be able to find their way around at night without making much noise.

But no, try as I might, my imagination simply couldn't allow for it.

Then again, no matter which direction I stretched said imagination—and I liked to think I had a pretty good one, if my pie recipes were any indication—I just couldn't picture a single soul on the island who might be capable of killing someone.

Much like there were people who disliked me, there were certainly people around Split Pine I disliked, most specifically the Gorleys, but there were a handful of others who rubbed me the wrong way. That was just going to be a natural occurrence when you put five hundred people together on an island and told them they couldn't leave all winter.

But no matter who I liked or disliked, I couldn't conceive of anyone who could *kill* someone. That was just beyond belief. I hoped the island would feel the same way about me once the gossip mill got hold of Jersey's little declaration. Surely they couldn't think the worst of me so easily?

And what had she meant when she mentioned Mick having a plan?

What I did know for certain was that if the entire town of Split Pine was about to get a bug in their ear that I might harbor homicidal tendencies, I would need to do my own work figuring out who was actually responsible for this.

While Tom was smart and capable, he was currently aiming his abilities in the wrong direction. I was sure he would come to realize my innocence quickly, but he might miss out on something vital in the meantime.

A little help couldn't hurt, could it? It wasn't like we had a bustling homicide department on the island, so any observant eyes and ears could only be beneficial to the case. At least that's what I told myself as I started mentally reviewing everything I remembered from the previous day.

What I kept circling back to, no matter how badly I wanted to ignore it, was the blistering fight I had overheard between Bruno and Jeff yesterday morning. I'd never heard Bruno that mad before, at least not about something unrelated to football. And while I'd certainly been upset about the shorted order and the outrageous pricing, Bruno seemed to have taken personal offense to the whole thing.

That didn't make him a killer, but it did give me a good place to start poking around.

First, however, there was still a diner to run and pie dough to prepare for tomorrow. The thing I loved about specializing in pies was that I didn't need to be here at three in the morning like some other bakeries. I didn't have bread deliveries to make or extensive dough rising times to wait for. I was not a doughnut shop, where the pastries needed to be fried in batches before being decorated and set out before the morning rush.

While pie could be very involved—especially if I decided to do a custom lattice—normally it was the kind of baking that could be done at its own pace and was very forgiving if I ended up with a rustic final product. My pies were beautiful, but more importantly they were delicious, so no one really cared if the dough was stained purple from overenthusiastic blueberries that bubbled up during the baking process.

I put my big food processor on the counter and cleared away anything else that would get in the way of my work. Pie dough, while simple in its ingredients, was a bit persnickety in its execution, which was why so many novice bakers found it to be a cruel creature to defeat. After spending decades in a kitchen and baking thousands of pies, I knew one thing to be absolutely true about making pie dough: cold was key.

For a pie dough to be a success, you needed cold ingredients, most specifically cold butter and cold water. Some bakers swore by vodka, but if I was going to buy vodka, I would be putting it in a cocktail, not a pie. Besides which, I remembered the winter ten years earlier when the last liquor shipment of the year hadn't arrived in time and the island ran out of booze before spring. It wasn't pretty. I didn't need to rely on one other ingredient that could be hard to come by in a pinch, so water it was.

I filled a small bowl of cold water and added a handful of ice cubes so it would stay cold while I worked.

I kept most of my butter overstock in the freezer, and my lard and shortening were both shelf stable, meaning there was no need to keep too many ingredients in the fridge on a daily basis. I had a stick of butter and two blocks each of lard and shortening sitting in the fridge waiting for me. I grabbed some butter for my first batch and brought it back to the counter, where I cut it into cubes, then immediately returned it to the fridge. I could have cut it after mixing my dry ingredients, but this was an extra little step my mom had always done and I'd learned to make pies her way.

I mixed together my flour, salt, and sugar. Not all pie dough needed sugar, but for my sweeter pies I preferred the crust to be part of the treat. I would make both kinds. Once the dry ingredients were mixed, I got the butter back out of the fridge and scattered the cold cubes through the powdery base, then sprinkled in some of the ice-cold water.

A few pulses from the food processor gave me a nicely pebbled mixture, though I added a bit more cold water just to get the consistency my fingertips wanted. The whole thing looked like sand when I was finished, and I poured the mix out onto my clean countertop. There I worked it into a proper dough and formed the base into four equal patties, which I wrapped and put in the fridge immediately.

Cold is key.

The cold butter would melt during the baking process rather than during the mixing process, as it did with cookies and cakes. This delayed melt would create the rich, flaky pastry experience one expected from a pie. Putting the dough in the fridge was also important. Sure, you could bake with a fresh dough, but in my experience, dough that had been refrigerated for several hours, or preferably overnight, was easier to roll out, held its shape better, and actually tasted better because the dry ingredients had more time to saturate.

Dough could sit in the fridge premade for days, which was why pie was a delightfully easy dessert to make once you mastered the basics. Sure, there seemed to be a steeper learning curve on those basics than with some other dessert offerings, but once you could make pie dough, the world really was your oyster.

The variations available after you had that glorious golden puck in the fridge were only as limited as a baker's imagination. Take the sugar out of the dough and you could make yourself a quiche, a turkey pot pie, a Canadian tourtière meat pie.

If I left the sugar in and added a little more to almost any fruit I could conceive of, I'd have myself an ooey, gooey treat in no time. Pies were magic, even *without* the actual magic they sometimes came imbued with in our shop.

I repeated the dough-making process a half dozen more times until I had a decent stock of sweet and plain dough in the fridge. Worst-case scenario, I could always make more in the morning to use in the afternoon, but I also needed to remember to switch my planning brain from summer mode to winter mode. We'd still sell pies consistently through the day, but take-home traffic would be greatly reduced.

With that in mind, I felt like I could safely step out and leave the post-lunch crowd in Seamus's and Rosie's capable hands. I had a mission in mind, and I could use my blank-slate menu for the next day to get away with it.

"I'm going to pop over to the grocery store for a bit," I announced to Seamus. My voice was a little too loud, making it sound almost like I was lying. "Do you need anything?"

Seamus checked his spices and pantry staples and peeked in the fridge, then finally said, "Maybe a big thing of Greek yogurt. I've got this notion about doing a stroganoff-inspired soup tomorrow, and I think a big dollop of Greek yogurt whipped with chives would be a really nice topper."

Whipped yogurt with chives was perhaps a bit highbrow for the general Split Pine crowd, but it also sounded delicious, so I nodded and slipped my coat on before heading out the back door.

Outside, the November air was crisp, biting my exposed skin and making me regret leaving my gloves in the office. It was thankfully a short trek to the store, so I just shoved my hands in my pockets rather than going back into the diner.

A few fat snowflakes had begun to fall, and even though I was on a mission, I couldn't help but stop at the gate and look up in wonder. I'd been living here basically my whole life, which meant I was no stranger to the bitter mood shifts that came with a Michigan winter—the deep freezes and massive snow dumps were certainly interesting to deal with on an island—but no matter what, I always stopped to appreciate the first snow of the year.

It was late this time. Usually by now we would have had at least one pre-Halloween appearance, giving us just the tiniest taste of what was to come while children shook their tiny fists skyward because they didn't want to have to wear snowsuits under their costumes.

Luckily for the kids, we'd had an incredibly mild October and it had been downright nice on Halloween night. Things had almost immediately gotten colder when the calendar flipped to November, and now here we were, two days into the new month, and it was snowing.

This wouldn't be *the* snow. Anyone who lived in a place that got serious winter weather knew there was a big difference between snow and *the* snow. There were always early-season flurries that would briefly coat things white, as if the town had been dusted in icing sugar, but then a bright, sunny day or a milder turn of temperature would melt everything back to a clean slate.

The snow was the one that stayed. It would typically show up in late November, and you just knew, you could feel it in your bones. The ground would turn white, peppered with footprints, and snow would pile on tree branches and bushes and turn everything into winter overnight.

If you were smart, you saw it coming and had your shovel and winter boots ready by the door. If you weren't, you had to trudge out to your shed, your sneakers filling with the light, loose powder, and dig through your paraphernalia until you found your winter supplies buried in the back behind all the more optimistic gardening gear.

This early dusting was a reminder that I really needed to go through my shed and find my good winter shovels. Grampy had a pretty nice snowplow, but the thing kind of freaked me out. However, he was starting to get on in years, and while Seamus never seemed to mind coming by to help clear the sidewalks, it was something I should learn to do.

Last winter, shoveling the path at work had started to take a bit of a toll on my lower back, which served as a cruel reminder that I wasn't getting any younger myself. It might be time to bite the bullet and get a plow for the diner.

I sighed, adding yet another item to my mental inventory of things I needed but couldn't really afford.

Being your own boss was great until it meant you were actually responsible for everything; then it suddenly became a lot less fun.

I trudged up the hill, letting myself enjoy the feel of the snowflakes as they melted on my cheeks. I wasn't a winter person per se, but I did like the cold better than the overly steamy summer days. Humidity was not my friend.

A wave of warm air greeted me as I entered the General Store, and the bell overhead chimed to announce my entrance. It occurred to me then that if I was planning to observe the people of Split Pine, it was going to be very difficult to be sneaky about it.

"Morning, Este," called a voice from somewhere among the shelves. I couldn't see Bruno, but now I knew he was here.

"*Afternoon*, Bruno," I corrected him cheerfully.

"Ah, no. Already?" He grumbled something else I couldn't quite make out. Guess the morning had gotten away from him. I knew that feeling all too well.

I wanted to immediately start peppering him with questions about Jeff and the murder, but I also didn't want to make it too obvious what I was up to. I grabbed a basket and headed for the produce section, but of course seeing the produce made me think of the man who had brought it.

I hadn't known Jeff well before he died. In fact, I hadn't known him at all, and the very brief moments spent in his company had been markedly unpleasant, but I could say this: the man had brought some very nice produce. I was sure that was more a testament to the company than to the man himself, but Bruno's fruit and veggie selection looked incredible. It made me sad that I'd been shorted on my strawberries, because I was betting that even the offseason berries I would have received would at least have been in great condition.

While Seamus hadn't *asked* for chives, I couldn't recall if we actually had any in the fridge back at the diner, and it wasn't like they'd have an opportunity to go to waste. Maybe I'd make some bagels when I got back and we could have a special tomorrow morning. A breakfast bagel sandwich actually sounded incredible, but in my estimation there was nothing quite like a toasted everything bagel, mounded with cream cheese and topped with chives or green onions.

My stomach growled audibly, and I realized that in all my work this morning, I hadn't stopped to have lunch at any point, and I couldn't remember the last time I'd eaten anything.

Going grocery shopping on an empty stomach was never a good idea, and perhaps the same was true of amateur sleuthing. I filled my basket with a variety of items that just made me want to go back to the diner and make myself a meal. Caramelized-onion hummus. Mini cucumbers, the perfect size to make fridge pickles. A bundle of green onions. The most perfect-looking tomato I'd ever seen.

The tomato just made me think fondly of summertime, when the garden behind Grampy's house would be filled with heirloom tomatoes half the size of my head. I loved a lot of things about winter in Split Pine, but I missed the fresh produce immensely in the colder months.

As I walked through the shop, I passed two middle-aged women I knew but wasn't close with. They were huddled together in a fashion I was becoming all too familiar with today.

"I just can't believe it," one whispered. "On *our* island."

"I *know*. And on the last day of the season, no less. A murder here—can you imagine?"

Neither of them sounded particularly scared, though some of the discussions I'd been hearing today had an edge of anxiousness and fear to them. In this case, these women were mostly scandalized by the fact Jeff hadn't had the decency to take his own murder off-island.

Their conversation did remind me of my real mission in coming here today, and it unfortunately wasn't about tomatoes.

I found Bruno in the dairy section, stocking packages of cheese from a box at his feet. I grabbed a few containers of burrata, knowing it would be the last I'd get my hands on in quite some time. Rumor had it I could learn to make my own, but I was pretty sure my culinary skill began and ended with things I could bake.

I smiled and pointed to the packages of sliced cheddar in his hand. "Could I get three of those?"

Bruno chuckled, plucked one more out of the box, and handed them to me. "Anything else I can help you find?"

The difference between his behavior today and the way I'd seen him act with Jeff yesterday was hard to process. This was the Bruno I knew, charming and soft-spoken; the Bruno that I knew Kitty was carrying a torch for; the Bruno who would extend nearly unlimited credit to anyone on the island if he knew they were going through a rough patch and just needed to eat.

Surely *this* Bruno wasn't capable of murder.

But the Bruno I'd seen yesterday was a man I hadn't thought existed. I'd never seen him so angry in my life. He'd been brimming with rage, and if I hadn't intervened, it wasn't a stretch to imagine him grabbing Jeff by his collar and giving him a good shake, or even throwing a punch.

Yet I needed to remind myself that plenty of people on this island—and in the world, for that matter—had gotten angry at another person, even punched another person, and hadn't killed them.

I was making excuses for him because he was someone I thought I knew. A friend, and someone I liked. But Bruno and I weren't *really* that close, and the more I thought about it, the more I realized how little I knew of him and his history. He didn't talk much about his life in Brazil before coming here, brushing off most questions with a shrug and a "That's not my life anymore."

I'd always assumed he must have left behind a bad breakup, or perhaps some family drama that was too painful to talk about. Now my imagination was running wild, concocting stories in which Bruno had been a professional assassin in Brazil and had needed to come to Michigan to escape his sordid past.

"Este?" He raised a quizzical brow at me, and I realized too late I'd been staring at him.

"Gosh, sorry, I didn't get much sleep last night, and it's really catching up with me now."

He smiled. "I understand. Must have been something in the air last night. I also had trouble sleeping."

Because you were out murdering someone?

"Did you hear what happened?" I asked instead, curious if the gossip mill worked as quickly for murder as it did for PTA drama. I was pretty sure Tom wouldn't want me sharing details about the case around the island, but there was no way folks had missed seeing the ambulance out and about in the early hours, so they'd know something was up, whether it came from me or not. Tom had no chance of keeping news this big contained.

Bruno returned to stocking the cheese, giving his head a shake. "It's been quiet in here all morning. I'm afraid my connection to the grapevine is not flowering today." He didn't seem remotely curious either, which was typical of Bruno. If gossip were a chain and not a virus, any town rumor would hit Bruno and immediately stop there. He didn't care much for other people's dirty laundry and didn't seem to want anyone looking at his.

"You remember Jeff, the new produce guy from yesterday?"

Bruno's shoulders stiffened visibly. "Mmm," was all he said.

"Someone killed him."

All the packets of cheese he was still holding clattered to the floor. Cheddar and Swiss piled at his feet.

I suddenly had all of Bruno's attention, and I wasn't sure what to do with it.

Had I just made a terrible mistake?

Chapter Eleven

I had to resist the urge to take a step back from Bruno as his brown eyes locked on mine. Gone was the jovial, warm expression. There was something cold and unreadable on his face now, and it was making me incredibly nervous to be this close to him.

"What did you say?" he asked, his tone sharp.

"Someone killed Jeff last night."

Bruno, seeming to catch himself, crouched down to pick up the packets of cheese, putting them back in the box before dusting his hands on his apron. "Surely not, Este. A murder? You have been listening to gossipy old ladies too much."

I shook my head, wondering if he was trying to deflect or if he was being genuine in his disbelief. It was hard for me to tell at this point. How on earth did detectives do this?

"I talked to Tom this morning. The ambulance was down at the harbor." I didn't tell Bruno that I had talked to Tom in a makeshift interrogation room; that was an unnecessary bit of information that was better off not making the rounds.

Except Mick Gorley had seen me there and was probably keeping that fact like a loaded weapon just ready to fire when it suited him, though he'd obviously said something to Jersey,

99

because she hadn't hesitated for a moment to drop that bomb in my diner. She might not always be the sharpest crayon in the box, but when it came to getting to the root of gossip and spreading it around town like a really obnoxious plague, she was an absolute genius.

Bruno was staring at me as if waiting for me to say more, and I realized I'd been hoping my bit of news might be enough to spark a reaction in him. He just looked surprised.

"An ambulance doesn't necessarily mean a murder. Are you sure Tom said Jeff was killed?" Bruno was shaking his head. "No, that cannot be."

Bruno's compassionate, concerned tone sounded legit enough, but it didn't mesh well with my memory of his encounter with the produce man the previous day. I couldn't decide if I should bite my tongue or lean into this whole junior-detective thing. I didn't want Bruno to shut down, and I also hoped my questions wouldn't overstep a line in our friendship. This was a very, very small town, after all. I didn't want to poke around on this case to the point of alienating someone I needed to keep in my life. If Bruno realized I thought he might be guilty of murder—which I still couldn't believe—then not only would he zip his lip, but he very well might kick me out of the store permanently.

I personally didn't feel like trying to make it through the winter on canned beans and soup shipped in from Amazon, and the diner couldn't survive without regular access to groceries.

I had to be careful about how I proceeded.

"Bruno, do you mind if I ask you something?"

He had turned his attention back to stocking the cheese, but his posture stiffened when I spoke. "Certainly."

"When I was in the shop yesterday, I heard you and Jeff arguing."

"*Sim,*" he said with a nod, reverting for a moment back to his native Portuguese. He'd been living here at least twenty years, but sometimes little crumbs of his homeland snuck in to remind us of the entire history he'd had before coming here.

"I guess I just got the vibe that he might not have been the nicest or most honest man."

"Yes, well, I heard you had a very similar argument with him yourself, hmm?" There was something defensive in Bruno's tone, something that made me realize I was coming awfully close to crossing a line with my questions.

"Yeah, I guess Jeff wasn't really making himself many friends when he was here, was he?" I decided to try a less personal approach. "Had you ever met him before? I've gotta say I was kind of surprised to see a new guy on the delivery. What happened to Denny, do you think?"

Bruno's tension relaxed a little, and while he was done with the cheese, he didn't immediately turn his whole attention to me. Fair enough.

"I guess I never really thought much about Denny's business. I knew it was family owned, but in this economy, things change. Maybe he retired and Jeff took over. Maybe he was sick. Maybe he decided he did not like to come all the way out here for such little money when he could stick to larger towns." Bruno's shoulders lifted, but it was a halfhearted shrug. "I couldn't say."

"Jeff was kind of terrible, but I can't imagine someone killing him just because he was rude," I admitted. "There had to be something more to it. But I only talked to the guy for ten minutes. It was enough to make me dislike him, sure, but . . ." My voice drifted off and I couldn't think of what else to say. "I'll take a brick of the Edam."

Chapter Twelve

Well, so much for solving a murder before lunch.

I was back at the diner, and the kitchen was filled with the incredible smells of Seamus's cooking and the familiar sugary fragrance of my own baking station. With my fingers coated in butter and flour, I should have felt a soothing balm of peace, but instead my mind was too filled with my discussion with Bruno, and visions of the scene of the crime danced through my brain like demented sugarplums.

Bruno hadn't completely absolved himself during our conversation. In fact, he hadn't really said anything to dissuade me from thinking he was probably still suspect number one, but that was something I hated to think about, especially given how Kitty felt about him. My best friend didn't have a great track record with men, and the last thing I wanted was for her to fall head over heels for a guy who might just be capable of cold-blooded murder.

Now that it was the offseason, things in the diner were quieter, meaning I didn't need to churn out dozens of pies a day. One or two of each was usually more than enough, and even that usually ended with me selling off day-olds or stocking my own freezer with single slices that were left at the end of the day.

Still, I needed to keep my hands and mind busy. I needed a way to think without *over*thinking, because if I let myself focus too much on this murder, I was going to get obsessed. I didn't like to admit that to myself, but it was definitely an ugly little quirk in my character. I tended to lock on to something and get a very insidious single-minded focus on it. That typically manifested itself in my buying a dozen books on a topic, reading only one, and then moving on to the next thing. Or getting hyperfixated on a new hobby, buying hundreds of dollars' worth of supplies, and then abandoning it soon after. My current love of knitting had been sticking around a bit longer than its predecessors, oil painting and wine making, but I'd recently watched some YouTube videos about candle making, and the itch to buy myself an entire case of wax and turn my old mason jars into custom pie-scented candles for the shop was a very real desire.

All this to say that my diagnosed-in-adulthood ADHD was wanting me to focus on the murder like it was a puzzle.

Still, there was an inexplicable *need* deep in the bottom of my chest and an annoying voice in my brain telling me that all the answers were in front of me, if only I was smart enough to put the pieces together.

I needed a distraction; otherwise I was going to spiral.

And sometimes the universe gives you what you ask for in unusual ways.

As I was making a new batch of sweet pie dough, I heard a hideous yowling sound come from outside the kitchen window.

I froze, wondering if I had imagined it, and turned to Seamus, who had likewise set his kitchen knife down and was staring at the window.

"What the heck was that?" he asked, wiping his hands on his apron—which was already splattered with bits and pieces from his soups—and coming to stand next to me so he could peer out the window into the yard beside the diner.

The diner faced the harbor on the customer side and faced town by the front door, but our biggest kitchen window looked out onto a patch of empty lawn, where we put picnic tables in the summer, and that backed onto to a big, undeveloped wooded area.

Rosie had come to stand in the doorway from the dining room into the kitchen, a concerned look on her face. "Did you guys hear that?"

The yowling sounded again, a short, high-pitched sound of panic.

An animal.

A very scared animal.

I quickly wiped my hands on my apron and grabbed my coat from the door of the office.

"Este, where are you going?" Seamus asked. "We should just call Dr. McKnight."

Dr. McKnight, the veterinarian, owned the pet shop, and while technically semi-retired, she refused to actually stop practicing until the *perfect* replacement could be found. She had rejected at least ten completely suitable candidates in as many years. While she was a well-respected vet, she didn't really do much in terms of animal control on the island.

If we called her, it might be hours before she was able to come out and help whatever animal this was, and that was a big *if*—if she was able to come at all.

"I'm just going to go have a look. If it's a raccoon or something, I won't touch it."

What I didn't tell him was how much I needed this mental distraction. Anything to give me a five-minute reprieve from thinking about Jeff or the way Tom had looked at me this morning as if trying to figure out whether or not he really knew me.

The same way I'd looked at Bruno.

It was taking too much of my brain to worry about who could or couldn't be capable of murder, and I needed to think about literally anything else right now. Helping an injured animal—raccoon or otherwise—was a good solution.

I slipped my jacket on and headed outside.

It was overcast now, giving the midafternoon sky a gloomy, evening darkness, and the wet chill in the air told me that we should expect more snow—if not tonight, then very soon. The light powder from earlier hadn't lasted long, but we definitely had more coming. You learned to be able to predict these things without the help of a weatherman after a while. The scent and texture of the air could tell you all you needed to know about a coming storm.

But maybe we locals were born hyperaware of that because we lived on an island, and even though it was in a lake and not an ocean, that didn't mean the water wasn't always a risk to us in the right dangerous conditions.

We had to know when to worry.

I pulled my jacket more tightly around me and stood quietly in the empty field, trying to determine which direction the howling sound had come from. Behind me, the diner glowed cheerfully, an inviting beacon in the too-early darkness. We were already losing daylight so quickly in the evening that it seemed extra unfair for it to get so dark in the middle of the day, but the heavy gray clouds had blotted out any sun. This was the kind of day when people would want to stay inside with a mug of hot chocolate and build themselves a fire.

We would probably close the diner early if it started to snow heavily.

No one came out during the first big snow of the year. We needed to steel ourselves, prepare mentally for the long winter to come.

The high-pitched sound came again. I glanced back over my shoulder to where I could barely make out the faces of Rosie and Seamus in the kitchen window. Seamus looked concerned but made no move to follow me, and Rosie gave an enthusiastic thumbs-up of support.

I headed in the direction of the noise, which seemed to be coming from a copse of trees near the shoreline. Now that I was outside, the sound was clearer and had a distinctly feline ring to it, making me pretty sure it was a cat in some kind of trouble rather than a rabid raccoon out to take a bite of me. As I got closer, the sound grew louder, and I knew I was on the right track.

"Kitty?" I asked stupidly, like it was going to answer me. "Kitty, kitty?"

After a pause, the sound came again, so perhaps it actually *was* trying to respond, because now the yowl that had previously just been long and frightened became shorter and more panicked, as if the creature knew that either help or more danger was approaching.

I pushed my way through the branches, now just barely able to see the diner if I looked behind me, a warmly lit red smear through the trees. The ground here was soggy on account of rising and lowering water levels, and my kitchen tennis shoes were a poor choice to be traipsing through the muck in. The sound was so loud now that I had to be almost right on the poor animal, yet I couldn't see any signs of one as I scanned the leaf-scattered ground around me.

Thanks to tomcat Smokey, almost every cat in town was gray, which meant that this cat would likely blend pretty well into its surroundings. Still, I was sure I'd be able to spot it, just because it would be making so much noise.

Then, as I pushed my way through a bunch of low-lying bushes, I saw a large cooler wedged into some trees right by the shoreline, so close that there was water licking up against one edge of the large black box. As I glanced through the trees, I could see where Jeff's boat was tied up at the harbor. The wet ground sucked at my shoes, making a loud squelching sound as I got to the cooler.

This wasn't just some run-of-the-mill cooler you might bring drinks in if you were going to the beach. This was one of the big industrial totes I'd seen Jeff hauling into my kitchen the day before.

"What on earth?" I asked.

"*Meowwwwwww!*" replied the voice I had been following. I couldn't believe how loud the cries were. I'd heard them crystal clear from the diner, and now that I was closer, they were frenzied.

The voice came from inside the cooler.

"Oh. Oh no, you poor thing." Forgetting my wet shoes and soon-to-be-very-frozen feet, I worked my way through the wet underbrush, where my feet sank deeper into the noxious-smelling mud as I approached the cooler. Even while the ground sucked at me like movie quicksand, I was able to get to the cooler quickly.

There were lock clasps on the side, but they weren't engaged, meaning that it was probably more of an unhappy accident that had landed the cat inside rather than a malicious prank or intentional animal cruelty.

I lifted the lid, and the creature inside stopped midyowl.

We stared at each other, both equally surprised. The poor cat's green eyes had enormous pupils, and it was panting from fear. It took one long look at me before seeming to realize it was free, and then like a gray bolt of lightning, it shot past me and into the underbrush, disappearing back in the direction of town.

"You're welcome," I shouted after it.

I glanced back down at the open cooler, and another, different surprise awaited me. The cooler was filled with empty plastic clamshell containers, the kind that typically contained fresh fruit.

I picked one up, and a sinking sensation twisted in my stomach.

The containers bore the label of Jeff's produce company, and that label very clearly indicated *Fresh Strawberries*.

But Jeff had told me they had none, and he hadn't brought any with him.

I rifled through the empty containers, none of which bore a single pink or red stain, as if they had never actually had any strawberries in them.

So what the heck were they doing here, in the middle of the woods?

And why had he brought them at all?

Chapter Thirteen

I left the cooler where it was, replacing the empty strawberry container where I'd found it and closing the lid of the main box tightly so no other poor wandering souls accidentally found their way inside.

I would have liked to drag the whole thing back to the diner and show Seamus and Rosie the weirdness of what I'd stumbled across, but the much louder and occasionally smarter voice in the back of my mind insisted that this was very possibly evidence and I should call Tom before I did anything else.

Before returning to the diner, though, I snapped a quick photo of the cooler on my phone.

My mind was reeling. What was an entire case of empty strawberry containers doing out here? Why would Jeff bring produce without any produce in it and then lie to me about being short?

Had he brought the berries and sold them to someone else? He'd said he'd left a few containers with Bruno, but there had been dozens of empty boxes in that crate.

Had the berries been bad and he'd brought them out here to dump them?

Yet the containers looked too clean and new to have been filled with rotten berries, so what was the meaning of this bonkers discovery?

As I walked back across the field behind the diner, my shoes now sodden and muddy, I sent the photo to Tom in a text. *Found this behind the diner, I think it was Jeff's.*

I sent it before thinking about how it might look for me that I'd been the one to find the cooler; it was, ostensibly, on my property. Technically, the wooded area wasn't mine; it was public property. But if I was a suspect, then it probably looked pretty bad for me to be stumbling across evidence.

Or maybe the opposite was true. Maybe this would prove to Tom that I had nothing to do with it.

The other thing I had to consider was that maybe there was nothing nefarious about this discovery at all and the box had simply fallen off Jeff's boat at some point.

What if it fell overboard while he struggled with the real killer? I could imagine the scene playing out, with Jeff fending off an attack from someone cloaked in shadows whose face I couldn't see, bumping into objects on the boat deck, sending the container tumbling into the water, where it made its way to shore.

I sighed, knowing that an overactive imagination was not at all the same thing as actually solving a crime.

My phone buzzed with a text from Tom. *Where is this?*

I turned around halfway back to the diner and snapped another photo of the area so the edge of the harbor was visible, giving him some idea of the general location.

I sent off the photo.

I'll be there in five minutes.

In spite of myself and the sticky situation I found myself in, a little thrill went through me as I read that message. I had to remind myself that he wasn't coming to see me on a social call, and yet I still felt like a teenager at the notion of him coming by.

"Ugh, Este, stop that," I chided myself, coming back into the kitchen through the side door.

Seamus and Rosie were waiting side by side at the diner doorway, giving me big *Tell us a story* eyes.

I wasn't sure how much I could say without getting into the entire mess of the murder investigation, but I *trusted* these people, I spent all day with them every day, and if there was anyone around I believed I could easily scratch off my would-be murderer list, it was the two of them.

"It was a cat," I began. "One of the Smokey Juniors. Or Junior Juniors." The town had long ago stopped trying to name all the gray ferals running around. If people found them when they were young enough or someone managed to come across one who liked people, they would take the cats in as pets and get them fixed. But somehow Smokey's line always managed to find a way to continue, and the island never seemed to run out of little gray cats.

I quickly explained the rest of what I had discovered to Seamus and Rosie, and they looked just as confused as I felt.

"You're sure it was Jeff's?" Rosie asked, quickly darting a glance into the main dining room to see if anyone was in desperate need of a refill. Seeing that everyone was comfortably settled, she stayed in the kitchen.

"I can't imagine who else a big produce cooler might belong to. And the containers inside all had his company's name on them. That seems pretty hard to call a coincidence. Anyhow, Tom is on his way over, so maybe he'll actually figure something out."

"Poor cat," Rosie said with a sigh. "I'm glad you got it out."

"I'm glad it didn't take my eyes out when I opened up the lid," I replied.

Seamus, ever a man of many words, just grunted and went back to working at his station, not offering any additional commentary on either the cat or the possible discovery of evidence.

He really hadn't said much about the murder all morning, come to think of it.

Now I *knew* I had to focus my attention on something else, because I was starting to imagine that people I knew well, people I trusted, were acting weird. Seamus was always weird; that's who he was. He didn't care much about anything other than his daughter and his recipes. He wasn't a killer, he was just an odd kind of guy, and I had to remember that.

I gave my head a shake, kicking myself mentally for even letting my thoughts wander in that direction. Sure, whoever did this was going to be someone from the island, but that didn't mean I needed to start casting my net of suspicion at literally every person I knew. That was just going to make me nervous and paranoid, and I didn't particularly want to start jumping at my own shadow.

I went into my office and grabbed a spare pair of socks from my desk drawer and a pair of ugly but comfortable kitchen clogs. I was about to change out of my messy shoes when a knock sounded at the side door. Seamus grunted again and went to open it, letting Tom in. Man, he really hadn't wasted any time.

And I supposed there wasn't much point in taking off the shoes just yet.

"We meet again, Este."

I appreciated him coming to the side door rather than the front. The way the gossip hounds in this town worked overtime, the diners in the restaurant would announce his presence to everyone they knew before they were even out the door. And while Tom lived here and needed to eat, as soon as word of the murder really got circulating, I wouldn't be the only person in Split Pine looking at everyone they knew as a suspect.

If I could keep everyone's eyes off of me, that would be great.

"You want to show me what you found and walk me through the whole thing?"

I did exactly that, practically reenacting the entire scenario. Rosie very helpfully demonstrated the sound the cat was making, even though no one asked, and Tom winced. But it did manage to lend credence to the whole bizarre scenario to have my staff backing me up.

After I'd shown Tom the place in the woods I'd found the cooler—I'd half expected it to disappear before I returned—he pulled out some gloves, opened the lid, and looked inside.

His expression was utterly inscrutable, giving me no clues as to what he was thinking. All he said when he closed the lid again was "Hmm."

Hmm indeed.

"It's weird, right?" I asked.

"That's certainly a word for it. And you touched this?"

"I had to let the cat out."

"What about the contents?"

I'd been out here only a few minutes earlier, but already the whole experience felt foggy and I was having a hard time recalling whether or not I'd picked up the containers or just looked at them.

"Yeah, I picked up one of the containers," I said, feeling like I was admitting to something much more sinister.

"Mm-hmm." Tom pulled out his own phone and snapped a few photos of the interior of the cooler, then closed the lid and took some pictures of the surrounding area. When he was done, he felt around the sides of the large cooler and found a handle like one might find on a rolling suitcase. He extended it up and pulled the cooler out of the muck. "Let's head back."

"You're just . . . bringing it with you?" I stared dumbfounded as he dragged the cooler behind him, heading back in the direction of my diner.

"Yeah, you want me to leave it here instead?" he asked.

"Well, I guess . . ." I stared at the ground and realized I'd been picturing the whole area draped in crime scene tape with those little yellow evidence markers I saw on shows like *CSI*. "I guess I thought you would secure the scene or something, I don't know." I felt a little foolish now for questioning him.

"Este, I appreciate where your mind is at on this one, I do, but I don't have a crime scene unit that's going to come out here and scour the ground for clues, and I think we both know this isn't where Jeff died. I'll come back once I have this safely stored at the department to see if there's anything else around, but I think what I'm going to find is a bunch of your footprints and maybe some from a cat. It's not the most secure *crime scene* to begin with." While it sounded like he was scolding me, there was the faintest hint of a smirk on the corner of his lips, which he quickly hid, returning to his usual stoic self, so I wondered if perhaps I had imagined it just to make myself feel better.

If I could imagine he had smiled, then *maybe* he might not think I was a suspect. But that could also be some monumental wishful thinking.

"Do you think this could be important?" I asked.

"It's hard to say right now. I agree with you that it's a bit weird, and I'm not about to call anything coincidental at this point, but you don't need to worry about it. I appreciate you calling it in, but next time you think you've found something that could be related to a murder investigation, perhaps only touch it with your eyes, okay?"

"I sincerely hope this is the last thing I ever find that might be related to a murder investigation," I told him. Though this was not altogether accurate, because there was one more very important thing I wanted to find.

The killer.

Chapter Fourteen

The rest of the day went by with no excitement to speak of. I made considerably too much pie dough, which was all well and good to occupy me for one day, but it meant I'd have very little to distract me in the morning when I went in.

I decided to take one of the savory doughs from the diner fridge home with me and play with making a French Canadian–inspired tourtière, a tasty meat pie, special because of its unique spice blend. Trying new recipes was a good way to keep my mind focused on anything other than this murder investigation. But, at the same time, it would give me plenty of time to think about who the killer might be, if it wasn't Bruno.

I really wanted it to not be Bruno.

Evening was already settling in by the time I left the diner. Normally I'd have left earlier, letting my staff close up shop so I wasn't at the restaurant for a full twelve hours, but today I'd stayed right up until six, probably annoying the heck out of them. Even Seamus had left well before me, giving his head a shake as he saw me rolling out doughs after five o'clock.

I wasn't sure what it was, but I just wanted the distraction.

By the time I left, it seemed that word of the murder had fully made its way around town, based on the hot gossip I could hear out front while I worked. The responses to Jeff's death seemed to be split evenly between fear over a killer being on the island and intrigue over a real murder happening all the way out here.

People had shared their theories over dinner. As I cleared plates away from a booth, I'd overheard two older women weaving an elaborate story about what they thought had happened.

"Well, I heard someone say that he didn't actually come here alone, that there was someone else on the boat with him, and they haven't found that person yet."

"What, no. *No.* Like a stowaway?"

The older of the two, her hair stark white and just recently permed, shook her head. "No, I heard it was a business partner and something went south between them. Some kind of fight, so the partner killed him and then hopped on the last ferry out."

While it was probably wishful thinking to exonerate our friends and neighbors, it was an intriguing option I'd never considered.

What if the killer *had* been a mainlander?

Tom seemed sure Jeff had died later in the night, after everyone was gone, and the harbor master always insisted no new boats arrived or left after dark, but I could appreciate everyone's desire to point the finger as far away from our back door as possible.

While the diner was as busy as usual, I did notice that people's discussions about the murder became hushed, or else the topic changed, whenever I came out of the kitchen or made the rounds among the tables. No one was outright pointing fingers at me—unless you counted Jersey—but it was obvious the rumors had begun to spread. I'd worried that perhaps people might remember the fight I'd had with Jeff the day before, and it seemed enough people did know about that for word to have gotten around. If the town was buzzing about suspects, I was definitely one of them.

In Split Pine, there was a generally held belief that the women in my family were all a bit hotheaded, and at the moment that wasn't really working in my favor. I didn't *think* I had a quick temper, but my being a redhead was reason enough for some people to think I might snap one day.

Even though people were sharing their theories—including ones about me, it appeared—there were no obvious front runners in terms of islanders that the town gossips believed had done the killing. Everyone was far more wrapped up in concocting elaborate ways a mainlander might have stayed around. The spookiest one of these involved the real killer still being on the island somewhere, just waiting for a chance to steal a boat or find another way off so he could make his escape. There was plenty of undeveloped forest surrounding the town, so while it had never happened before, it wasn't completely impossible that someone might have stayed on the island and found a place to hide themselves overnight. But how they could have gotten *off* the island later was a mystery that no one could come up with a good solution for.

I liked this idea even less than the notion that one of my neighbors might be a killer, because I hadn't considered it myself. What if the killer *was* a stranger, and they were still here? It made me start to worry that someone could be lurking around any shadow, willing to do whatever it took to get off the island and make a clean getaway.

I couldn't stop thinking about Jeff's body being taken off the boat. It was chilling to realize that something like this could happen in our little town. But something about it was nagging at me as well, and not just because it was obvious that word was getting around that I might somehow be involved. Maybe it would be better if people *did* think someone was creeping around in the woods.

Gossip in this town spread faster than fire in a matchbook factory, and based on the way people on the street lowered their heads as I passed or whisper among themselves, I knew that whether Mick, Jersey, or the paramedics were to blame, people knew I was involved.

Funny how *involved* just meant the dead man had been holding a copy of my invoice, and yet some people were going to take that all the way to murder in a heartbeat.

I supposed I wasn't much better, because I was doing the same thing; I just hadn't narrowed down my targets quite yet. As I left the diner, I decided that if people in town were going to put me on their big imaginary bulletin board marked *Potential Suspects* and even now were busy cutting up red string and deciding I was guilty, I needed to help move things along for Tom.

He had to be in the same boat as me, frustrated and baffled that a killer could be in our midst, but I had a few things going for me that he didn't. For one, I had one less suspect to consider, since I knew I could scratch my own name off the list immediately. And second, I'd been able to watch Jeff interact with a few people, meaning I might be able to narrow things down to those he had pissed off: everyone he had spoken to, probably.

Rather than heading home right away—though I would have loved to ask Grampy if he had any clue about Jersey's mysterious veiled comments from earlier—I took off in the direction of the harbor. The best way to figure out what had happened to Jeff would be to look at where things had started— and ended—for him.

The air was crisp, and I smiled. The smell of fall in Split Pine was unique. There was the ever-present pine aroma, of course, but there was also the scent of the water. While it was lake water and not salty, it still had its own distinctly nautical fragrance. There was the earthy bog scent of the shore as well as a cold-water smell that I couldn't explain but made me feel like I'd come home.

Glancing up from the harbor, I appreciated the view with the sun setting below the trees. Split Pine had a slight hilly aspect, so the center of town rose higher than the shoreline. It gave Mick's hotel an impressive view over the lakes, but from down here it meant I got to see the leaves changing color and tumbling down over the streets. We should have made puzzles out of that view.

The island was roughly divided into four quarters. The main town was to the northwest, facing out onto the lake, with views toward the mainland. The town was then split down the middle, with the population and shops pretty evenly divided between the west side, or mainland side, and the east side, which faced more and more open water the farther away from town you got.

The southeast quadrant of the island had a small number of remote properties, occupied by people who wanted to live on the island but not in town. It also housed a driving range and a small airstrip as well as the boatyard. The final quadrant to the southwest was mostly wooded land, but that was also where the farm collective made its home.

The breeze off the lake tousled my hair, and I scanned the docks to see if anyone was still around. The harbor was relatively empty, which wasn't surprising, given that it was din-nertime. Since all the tourist vessels were long gone, there were only a handful of locals I recognized who were getting their own boats ready to go into winter storage. Stuart Kelso spotted me from his boat and gave a wave, but his wife Nonny quickly swatted down his hand and whispered something in his ear. He paled visibly, and the two of them watched me pass by wordlessly.

Well, this was fun. I couldn't say I was a big fan of being considered a murderer. I'd grown up here and known these people my whole life, but all it took was one rumor and suddenly I was a pariah. How long would it be before this started taking a hit on the diner? I couldn't let that happen. We were in a precarious enough position financially as it was, and while summer earnings should have been enough to keep us solvent, I also depended on our regular offseason income as well. So did Seamus, Rosie, and Marcel, because it meant they got to stay employed.

Things were okay now, but a lot of that was probably due to people who were devoted to the memory of my parents and grandparents. I just had to hope I could help Tom figure out who the real killer was before everyone on the island decided it was me, and it was too late to save my reputation or my diner.

The way Stuart and Nonny were looking at me now, I was starting to realize I might have made a huge mistake coming back to the scene of the crime. I wanted to have a look at Jeff's boat, but there was no way I was going to be able to do that with people on the dock watching me.

I bent down, putting the box of leftover pie I was taking to Grampy later on the thick wooden boards of the dock, and pretended to tie my shoe. I had to give myself time to think. While I faked the tying, I glanced up and over at Jeff's boat. While the harbor itself had been reopened, there was still distinctive yellow crime scene tape across the plank, keeping anyone from getting access. So much for that idea. I noticed a handful of peeling bumper stickers attached to the windows of the boat's bridge. One said *Farmers Like It Organic*, and the other said *Keep Michigan Green*. I was pretty sure there was a *Co-Exist* sticker on there as well, but it was too curled and sun bleached for me to be certain.

The irony of a *Keep Michigan Green* sticker on a gas-guzzling boat was pretty interesting, but more interesting were these ecologically minded stickers on a boat that belonged to Jeff. I supposed he *was* in the produce business, so it wasn't totally farfetched, but these sentiments didn't fit the idea I had of him in my head.

I stood up and managed to walk directly into Carey Wise, the harbor master. We both let out loud, almost cartoonish *oof* noises in unison. I dropped my cake box, and he dropped the clipboard manifest he was carrying. I scrambled to pick up his board, which had landed at my feet, but before handing it back, I scanned the top of the page. Jeff's name stood out immediately, with his signature and time of landing. But something else stood out as well.

Whenever someone comes to the island on business, they need to have a local point of contact—someone on the island who can vouch for them and verify their reason for coming. In Jeff's case, he could have listed Bruno or me. But he hadn't.

He'd listed Mick Gorley.

Chapter Fifteen

I stared at Mick's name for a long beat before Carey gently removed the clipboard from my hands and replaced it with the white takeout container I had dropped.

"Sure hope that was a bar or some cookies," he said solemnly. "Something sturdy."

"I'm sure it'll still taste okay." This was true, but the pie itself was certainly a crumble by now. Perhaps Grampy could put it on top of some ice cream as a little flavorful bonus. It was certainly going to bring up some questions. Or perhaps I would fib and say there hadn't been anything left, because as much as I knew he wouldn't care, I felt bad about giving Grampy a busted piece of pie.

"Look, Este, it ain't for me to say, and you know I think you're a good girl. Known your family a real long time." Carey heaved a sigh. There weren't many people I would let get away with calling me a *good girl* like I was nine years old, but Carey had known me my whole life; I wasn't going to bother making a point of it. But he obviously had something he wanted to say. "Y'know, with everything that happened here earlier, I just don't think it's so smart, you coming down to the harbor."

He wasn't exactly banning me from the docks, and he was right—I already knew that from the way Stuart and Nonny had given me the stink eye. But it still hurt to hear him say the words out loud.

He must have seen my expression change before I could hide my reaction. "I'm sorry, Este. I'm just thinking of you and Chuck, y'know."

I had thought about what this might do to my business, but I hadn't really considered that rumors about me might impact Grampy as well. "No, no, you're right. I guess my curiosity got the best of me. I should have been smarter." I patted the pie box. "I have places I need to be anyway. Thanks, Carey."

His warning should have been what I needed to hear to convince me to go home and stop snooping, but instead, the bitter sting of embarrassment coupled with the mention of Grampy had me boiling with irritation. Someone was responsible for Jeff's murder, and while I'd thought my imagination was giving me an easy target when I'd considered Mick earlier, I couldn't ignore his name in bold print on Jeff's line of the ledger.

Denny had done business with the hotel, so it wasn't like Jeff hadn't had a reason to use Mick's name. I had to admit to myself that I had no clue what name Denny had used when he filled in the form. Maybe it had been common practice for Evergreen Produce to list the hotel, but for some reason, I didn't think it was. I was sure most delivery vendors used the grocery store, as it was visible right from the harbor and an obvious choice.

Perhaps that was just me being biased against Mick, but I wouldn't have used him to vouch for me if I was paid to do so.

So there had to be a reason Jeff had picked Mick over anyone else he delivered to. I moved up the hill in the direction of the hotel. This route was steeper than my usual trek home and proved to be a sobering reminder of how out of shape I was, because by the time I walked into the hotel lobby, my forehead was damp with sweat and I was breathing hard.

I took a moment to make myself look presentable before heading up to the front desk. While the tourist season was over, the hotel still operated, just at a reduced capacity. Only one floor of rooms was left open in case any locals wanted to staycation, and the restaurant and spa reduced their hours without shuttering entirely. This meant there was only one person at the front desk, and she looked bored out of her mind.

She perked up when I got to her, and it was nice to see that someone on the island didn't immediately react to me like I was coated in poison. "Well hey, Este," she said. She was a little younger than me, but I recognized her, having gone to high school with her sister.

"Hey, Lulu. How's Carly?" Carly had moved to the mainland a few years earlier after getting married, and it had been a while since I'd last seen her.

"Oh, she's great," Lulu said, beaming. "She's going to have a baby in March."

"That's exciting," I said, genuinely thrilled. "Carly was always such a group mom as a kid. She's going to be a natural."

Lulu nodded in agreement, then got straight to business, something the Gorleys probably insisted on. "So what can I do for you tonight? Spa is closed, but maybe you want to book a massage for the weekend? You work too hard."

This made me bark out an unexpected laugh. I didn't disagree with her; I just admired the natural hustle. "No, but I might put that on my to-do list."

"A reservation at the restaurant, maybe?" Her tone said she already knew this wasn't likely.

"I actually just stopped in on my way back hoping you could maybe settle a bit of an argument we had at work this morning."

Lulu looked intrigued but also moderately concerned. "I'm not sure how I can help, but fire away."

"Well, I was talking to Rosie, and she insisted that when she was out last night, she saw Mayor wandering down by the harbor, but I told her that was probably impossible, because Mick is usually home that late. Except if he's working—then you know how old Mayor likes to go on his walkabouts."

Lulu laughed. "That old dog. He gets into so much mischief, he's lucky people love him so much. Last night, though . . ." She paused, thoughtfully considering. "I think Mick left here around nine o'clock. He actually made a pretty big deal of saying he was going. So I guess it depends when Rosie thought she saw the dog, but if it was later than nine, probably not. Maybe Mrs. Mercer's Lab? They might look alike if you saw them from a distance."

"Oh, that sounds like a possibility. Thanks, Lulu."

"Hey, glad I could help with *something*." She gestured around the empty lobby, which was precisely when Jersey decided to walk through the front door.

We locked eyes, and I could tell she was resisting every urge in her body to say something incredibly rude to me. I'd learned a long time ago that Jersey was desperate to win her father's approval, and acting like a high school mean girl within earshot of an employee wasn't the quickest way to take over Daddy's heart and empire.

What she'd said to me earlier was still gnawing at me, but I couldn't exactly ask her about it with Lulu right here. She and I were at a stalemate: she wanted to make me miserable, I wanted her to spill her guts. Neither of us was going to get what we wanted.

"Thanks again, Lulu. Give my best to Carly."

"I sure will. Nice to see you, Este."

As I walked out of the lobby, Jersey and I kept an eye on each other the entire time. She was hiding something, but so was her father. If Mick had left here last night at nine, that meant he'd had plenty of time to kill Jeff. There were much stronger suspects than me that Tom should be looking into.

I was so distracted by Jersey that I almost didn't see Mick walking into the lobby as I exited. We narrowly avoided a collision, and I managed to avoid dropping my pie yet again. Flustered, I immediately worried Mick would know I was onto him.

"E-evening, Mick," I stammered, hating myself for how obviously shaken I sounded.

"Leaving so soon?" he asked. He couldn't have come across as more of a villain if he'd been twirling that stupid mustache of his. "Thought you might be coming by to reconsider that discussion we had earlier."

I stared at him stupidly, not putting two and two together. After a moment, I remembered what our conversation had been about. "Oh. No. I just had a question for Lulu, and now I'm on my way home." I was being too nice now. Mick knew me well enough to realize I was always polite with a hint of tartness when it came to him. *Nice* wasn't a word that would ever apply to how I behaved toward him or Jersey.

He stared at me uncertainly for a moment, and a chill crept down my spine. I wondered if those sharklike eyes had been the last thing Jeff had seen before he died.

"You all have a nice night," I said, backing out the door.

"See you real soon, Este," he replied.

Chapter Sixteen

I kept checking over my shoulder as I walked back to my cottage, and before I locked myself in for the night, I headed into the main house to look in on Grampy.

His door, naturally, was unlocked, as most doors in town were, and I found him in his favorite armchair with the fireplace going. Grampy's house was a two-floor Cape Cod, painted a weathered gray with bright-white trim. All the warmth could be found inside, where the walls were pale yellow and the furniture practically screamed *grandparents*. The overstuffed couch was draped in one of Gran's quilts, and there were old oil paintings all over the wall that Grampy had done during his artistic phase. Now he preferred his spare time spent with a good book in front of the fire. He'd started losing the dexterity in his fingers a few years back, and holding a paintbrush was simply not an option for him anymore. It made me sad, but he seemed at peace with that chapter of his life being closed so he could move on to new hobbies.

He'd never been a big reader in his younger days, as he'd spent too much time running the diner, but now he practically read a book every day. He favored nonfiction, as he enjoyed reading about real people's lives, and the subject matter he chose was diverse, from long-dead political figures and royalty to modern social movements, the study of which allowed him to, as he put it, "keep a finger on the pulse."

I set my tote of pie-making supplies down inside the front vestibule and called out as I made my way into the living room, still carrying the tragically dented box of leftover pie.

As expected, he had the fireplace stoked, and a few lamps lit the room with a warm glow. His wall-mounted television was on, but he had tuned it to a ten-hour YouTube video that depicted a similarly cozy room where a mug of tea was permanently steaming and a small tabby cat dozed. He was obsessed with these animated room scenes, and I had discovered that there were a seemingly endless number of them, so he could change them through the season to suit his mood.

He sat in a recliner by the big front window, his legs propped up, slippers on. A plate on the side table next to him held a crumpled-up napkin, and a half-finished glass of Pepsi sat on a coaster. We fundamentally disagreed on our choices of pop, but Grampy could never be swayed from his love of Pepsi. There was even an old vintage Pepsi sign hanging on one of the diner walls, and he'd told me that if I even thought about removing it, he would disown me.

I was *pretty* sure he was kidding, but the sign stayed where it was, just to be safe.

"Hey there, angel. How was the old pile of bricks today?" He barely glanced up from the thick book in his hands—a bulky fantasy novel, which was one of the few types of fiction he treated himself to—and offered me a smile.

I wanted to point out that there were no bricks to be had at the diner, but since he'd insist on asking me this question every day until one of us died, I just went with it.

"Nothing out of the usual," I replied automatically, before realizing that wasn't actually the truth. I was too rattled by my interaction at the hotel to ask him about Jersey right now.

He raised one thick white eyebrow at me, and that was all I needed to see to know that *someone* had already gotten to him. Since he hadn't stopped by the diner, I didn't think it was any of the old guys in town, and he hated Mick as much as I did, so I also didn't think it was a case of enemies sharing information.

"Who told you?" I asked, narrowing my eyes at him.

He slid a bookmark into his current read and set it down next to his empty dinner plate.

"Marjorie stopped by earlier this afternoon. My most recent order had come in and she decided to bring it by, along with a bite of pot roast." He inclined his head toward the plate.

Marjorie Sheldon owned the little bookstore in town, and I was a bit surprised to learn she had started making home deliveries. With food. Over the past few years, I'd started to suspect Grampy might be about ready to get back out there. Even with me just outside the back door in the guest cottage, he got pretty lonely by himself.

Gran had been gone a long time, and I certainly didn't begrudge Grampy the opportunity to spend his golden years with someone who would treat him right. He was almost eighty, and he didn't get out as much as he used to, so perhaps a new romance would be the thing that would inspire him to stop being such a recluse.

"How did *Marjorie* find out?"

"Saw the ambulance this morning, I suppose. She's a bit of an early riser."

I made a small *mmm* sound, but he evidently wasn't finished talking.

"Ambulance wasn't all she saw."

"Oh?" I wasn't about to volunteer any information if he was just fishing. I wanted to see how much he actually knew.

"Says she saw you out there before light was up, talking to Tom Cunningham."

"Marjorie sees a lot, I guess."

"Gonna tell your old grandpa why exactly you were at a crime scene before dawn talking to a police officer?"

"He's the sheriff," I corrected him.

"Crime. Scene," Grampy retorted.

"Yes, well . . . as it turns out, I was one of the last people to see this murder victim alive." I gave a small shrug, as if this wasn't the big deal Marjorie was thinking it was. Actually, now that I knew Grampy and Marjorie were in regular communication, I was a bit hesitant to talk to him about the case, not knowing what he might share with her and by extension the rest of the town.

"Well, you're not in jail right now, so I suppose that's a positive sign."

"I appreciate that you didn't ask me if I was guilty."

"Are you guilty?" he replied with a sly smirk.

"Be right back; going to go bake you a poisoned pie. Hope you didn't fill up on Marjorie's pot roast."

He clucked his tongue at me. "You'd miss me too much, angel."

"Rest easy, I didn't kill anyone."

"Good, good."

"I have a question for you, though. I know Mom and Dad were running things before I took over, but I know you were always around still . . . *helping*." This was not how my father characterized Grampy's constant offers of advice, but I knew my mom liked having her dad there with her. "Do you remember Denny McAvoy, the produce guy?"

"Sure, he's been doing our deliveries for a good fifteen years. Took that business over from his dad."

I mulled this over, chewing the inside of my cheek. "So it *was* a family business."

"You betcha. Fourth generation, I think."

"And do you remember anyone other than Denny making deliveries to us after he took over the company?"

Grampy considered this, really furrowing his brow as if replaying fifteen years' worth of memories. "Can't say I ever recall anyone else, no. Never had anyone with him either."

"Yeah, that's how I remember it too."

"Why do you ask?"

"Well, the dead guy, Jeff, he was telling everyone he was taking over the route. But I thought that sounded a bit strange, since Denny never mentioned a partner or colleague, and then all of a sudden here's this new guy and he's jacked up the prices and doesn't seem too keen on making friends with any of us."

"Could be another member of the family, I suppose. I mean, we didn't really *know* Denny, aside from a few chats here and there. I think he had a son, he told me. Maybe that's this Jeff fella."

That explanation didn't sit right with me. Jeff seemed too old, for one thing. But there were other ways to be part of a family—brother, cousin, uncle—and while Jeff hadn't indicated he was related to Denny and had actually gone out of his way to avoid discussing him, I found it hard to believe there was no connection at all. You don't just come into a four-generations-old family business without some kind of link to the family.

I should know.

Rather than continuing to grill my poor grandfather about this when it was clear he didn't know much more than I did, I returned to the hall to collect my bag. From inside I withdrew the small carboard takeout container that I'd practically rolled all the way here, setting it next to the empty dinner plate at his side.

"It might be a little worse for wear tonight, sorry. I managed to drop it."

He peered inside, and all he said was, "Caramel apple. My favorite."

He said that about any kind of pie I brought him. According to him, everything I made, everything my mother had made, and everything my grandmother had made were all equally his favorites.

Except cherry. Grampy hated cherry pie.

I pressed a kiss to his forehead. "Don't let me keep you from your book. I'll be out back if you need anything."

It wasn't like he was helpless. Even in his eighties, he was still an avid gardener in the summer, and when he could be persuaded out of his reading chair, he loved to go on long walks around the island. He was fit and healthy, and I didn't begrudge him his new favorite hobby of doing as little as possible. He liked to joke that he had a lifetime of reading to catch up on, and that was bound to keep a man busy.

I just didn't want him to atrophy.

Slinging my bag over my shoulder, I made sure the front door was locked and then headed out the back door and toward my small cottage nestled in the garden. The porch light was on, because I left when it was dark and got home when it was dark, but there was something there I wasn't expecting.

At first, I thought someone had left something at my door. It appeared to be a small bag of garbage. It wasn't until I was closer that I could register what I was actually looking at.

A little gray cat.

Since the island was overrun with them, it wasn't a total surprise to see one out and about, but they were all largely feral, so it was unusual to have one just sitting at my back door staring up at me.

"Smokey?" I asked.

Honestly, it was a logical impossibility that the original Smokey was still alive, and yet everyone on the island would swear up and down they still saw him regularly. But this cat wasn't Smokey. The granddaddy feline had a white patch on his forehead that made him distinctive, and while it was possible one of his offspring's offspring might bear the same mark, convincing us all that Smokey lived on, this particular gray cat had no white mark. It also appeared to still be little more than a kitten.

"Hello," I said, approaching cautiously. I expected the cat to run away when I got too close for comfort, but instead it stood, placed both front paws out on the ground, and executed a long, luxurious stretch that made my aching limbs tingle with jealousy. Then it sat back and continued to blink at me with its large, green eyes.

Perhaps my imagination was in overdrive, but the longer I looked at this cat, the more certain I was that it was the same one I'd let out of the cooler earlier in the day.

But surely that was impossible, right? That cat had disappeared in a furry streak of panic, and it definitely hadn't stopped to ask for my address so it could come by and thank me later. Had it followed me home? Had it come here because of my scent?

I looked around, as if trying to see if there was someone else in my grandfather's fenced-in backyard who might own this cat, but a general dusting of woodland debris on the little guy told me this cat only belonged to him—or her—self.

"I appreciate the visit, but off you go." I pointed back toward the house.

The cat merely blinked, long and slow, and then yawned.

"You're not coming inside."

The cat just stared.

I reached for the door handle and tried to bypass the cat, hoping it would go away as soon as I went inside. It wasn't that I disliked cats, but this was, for all intents and purposes, a wild animal. I had no idea if it was healthy, or if its current friendliness might be a worrying sign of something like rabies.

The cat did not care a lick for my health and safety concerns.

The moment my door was open a crack, in it went. The space had been too small for me to imagine it getting inside, but cats have the ability to turn into air particles when it suits them, I swear.

"*No*," I howled, chasing it inside. "No, no, no. I am not a kitty Airbnb. This is not your place."

I knew enough about cats to know that my entire diatribe was falling on deaf ears. You could tell a cat what to do about as effectively as you could tell a river which way to run.

A tiny smudge of gray moved around my living room and into my kitchen. I had expected the thing to go into panic mode as soon as it was inside, knocking things over and generally creating a disaster once it realized the space was enclosed. The kitten defied my expectations, however.

It wandered from room to room at a leisurely place, as if it were a prospective buyer trying to get a vibe for whether or not the cottage might make a suitable investment.

My initial plan had been to chase it out, but now I was a little bemused by how calmly it was taking in the scenery. I left the front door open a smidge so that when it decided it had had enough, it could leave on its own.

I set my bag from the diner on the counter, keeping the cat in my peripherals so that it didn't decide to make a DIY litter box out of any of my plants, and unloaded the ingredients for tonight's dinner onto my kitchen island.

The dough had warmed to room temperature, making it perfect for rolling, so I grabbed my big French rolling pin. While some people favored the look and feel of a more classic rolling pin design—a long, evenly shaped cylinder with handles on each end—I vastly preferred the ease of use of the French design, which was longer and tapered at each end. No handles. I found that over the course of a full day of making pies, it was a lot easier on my hands and wrists, and I just liked the way it looked and felt.

I had a small jar of flour permanently on the island because of how many pies I made, so I removed the glass lid and liberally dusted my wooden countertop to prepare it for the dough. I also grabbed my favorite pie dish, a classic-looking red-and-white ceramic number, and set it to the side of the island. This wasn't a pie I felt the need to prebake the crust for, so I didn't bother grabbing my pie weights, even though I admittedly still delighted in using the little white porcelain spheres all these years later.

I divided the dough into two roughly equal portions and rolled the savory crust into an approximation of a circle. I didn't need to be too precious about it; this was just for me, and I'd be cutting the excess off the edges anyway. But since I'd spent most of my life in a kitchen making pies, the circle was about as close to perfect as one could get without a cutter.

I lightly wrapped the dough circle around my rolling pin, then brought my pie dish under it, unrolling the dough and letting it naturally sink into the dish. Every so gently I adjusted the pastry until it perfectly lined the dish and evenly overhung the edges so I could easily crimp on the top layer. I prerolled another circle and left it waiting on the island while I prepared the filling.

There wasn't too much to a tourtière, certainly nothing like what went into the beef stew pie I'd made the previous day at the diner. It was a mix of ground beef and pork with onion and garlic. The seasonings were scant: salt, pepper, thyme, sage, and the tiniest bit of clove that gave it a little something special. I had, over the years of making it, also started to add a minuscule splash of balsamic vinegar to my filling, which I was sure was sacrilege in French Canadian circles, but for the present moment I was not feeding my pie to any French Canadians, so I was going to cook it the way I liked it.

I fried the meats with a homemade seasoning mix that filled the air with an aroma of cracked peppercorns and thyme before adding the entire mixture to my waiting pie dish. I rolled the top dough on much as I had the first, then did a lazy baker's trick to finish my pie. Using kitchen shears, I cut around the entire circumference of the pie dish, removing any excess dough and giving my pie a nice, clean edge. I then crimped the top and bottom pieces together and cut vents in the top dough to allow air to escape while the pie baked.

There wasn't too much dough left from the edges and I hated to waste it, so I rerolled what was left and shaped the remainder into a few leaves, then made a simple dough braid to use it all up. The dough braid I used around the edge of the dish, and the leaves I placed between each vent. It was unnecessarily fancy for a pie that no one else would see, but my grandmother had always told me that sometimes the person you should most want to impress is yourself.

I smiled at the finished pie and popped it into the waiting oven, and when I glanced back up to the counter, I gasped to see the little cat now primly seated at one of the stools on the opposite side of my island.

"Have you decided to stay for dinner, then?" I asked. I wasn't sure why, but something about the way the cat sat, and how it regarded me, made me think it was female.

She didn't reply to my question, but she was polite enough not to climb onto my counter, so I decided that probably deserved a bit of a reward. There was some filling left that hadn't fit into the shell, and it had cooled on the stove to the point I didn't think it would be uncomfortable for the cat to eat.

I put some on a small side plate and set it in front of her. As far as I knew, the seasonings were all pet safe, and it was such a small amount that I didn't think I was putting her at risk. Besides, this was a feral cat who probably spent most nights eating literal garbage or whatever people left outside for them and also working to keep our island almost entirely rodent-free. This was a one-night fine-dining experience.

She sniffed the plate, and for a moment I feared she might reject the offering. Considering that about thirty minutes ago I hadn't wanted her inside my house, my worry that she wouldn't like her dinner was quite the about-face. But evidently my cooking was passable by cat standards, because after a sniff test, she quickly devoured what was on her plate.

"Oh my goodness, you were hungry," I announced. "I don't have any more, though, I'm sorry."

She didn't seem too offended and instead set about licking her paws and then using them to clean off her face and whiskers. Once she was satisfied with her post-dinner cleaning, she hopped off the stool and left through the front door, gray tail held high.

I waited a few moments to see if she might come back—surprising myself by secretly hoping she might—but when five minutes passed and she hadn't returned, I closed and locked the door.

I could try to pretend this was a one-off and that I was not suddenly a cat person, but I also knew perfectly well I was already planning a stop at Bruno's tomorrow that would let me pick up cat food.

Just in case.

Chapter Seventeen

I didn't sleep well that night.

I tossed and turned, restless and my head too full of thoughts to let me get comfortable. And then I got annoyed with myself for not sleeping, which meant that when my alarm went off at four thirty, I was still tired and also extra grouchy with myself.

Not the most ideal way to start my day.

I dragged myself out of bed, largely against my will. Part of me just wanted to stay under the covers for the rest of the day, but there was no reason to believe sleep would suddenly come to me if I played hooky from work for the day.

I turned on my coffeemaker and headed for the shower while the little pot filled. It only made enough for about two cups, which was all I ever really needed, so I had never bothered to get anything larger. Counter space was at a premium in the cottage, but I also couldn't see myself needing something different when—or if—I finally moved into a place of my own. Coffee was readily available at the diner, and it was pretty rare that I was ever actually home long enough to need a second pot in one day.

After a quick shower, I felt considerably more human, though no better rested, and I tied my damp red waves into a messy bun on the top of my head. I had neither the energy nor the desire to bother with styling my mop today, so it would just have to accept my poor excuse for grooming.

I didn't bother with makeup, but I was fairly religious about my skin care, slathering a mix of serums and moisturizer on my face and finishing off with my daily dose of sunscreen. Even though I barely saw the sun on any given day, my grandmother and mother had both imparted to me the importance of sunscreen, and the two of them had had unbelievably beautiful skin right up until they passed away, both looking years younger than their actual ages to the very end.

I did as I was told and never skipped my sunscreen.

Still, I had to admit the sunscreen step felt a little silly right now when it was still pitch black outside and would stay that way for my entire walk to work.

The prospect of walking alone in the dark had never bothered me before today. The island had always felt so safe that it was almost like living in the past, because where could you live in the world these days where no one bothered to lock up and literally everyone knew everyone else? It sometimes felt like living in a 1950s sitcom world.

Yet today I was uneasy about my short commute.

I drank my coffee slowly, prolonging the time until I had to leave, but soon enough my watch and the glowing digital light of my stove were telling me it was time to stop dillydallying and get my butt in gear—both phrases lovingly stolen from my Grampy.

I rinsed the coffee cup and slipped my warmest fall jacket on. I didn't want to jump right into winter clothes just yet, but there was a thin lining of frost on my windows—the dangers of living in a very, very old cottage—and my feet had protested touching the wooden floorboards this morning.

We might not have gotten a real, proper snow yet, just a couple of temporary dustings, but it was only a matter of time, and while we waited, the temperature was more than happy to give us a taste of what was to come.

I eschewed a beanie, because I was a Michigander and would allow myself only *one* pre-snow item of true warmth. For some reason we all insisted on proving how tough we were by continuing to dress like it was September until nearly December, and then a flip would switch and we would suddenly all start to wear appropriate winter attire.

I did slip on some gloves, though, just light ones, but I needed to be able to feel my fingers in order to do my work.

I locked the door on my way out and glanced over to Grampy's house. His kitchen light was on, which wasn't a surprise. The man had kept diner hours almost his entire life; he wasn't going to stop now just because he retired. It was a hard thing to train your brain out of. Even at college I'd gotten up obscenely early, but that had proven to be a lucky boon for me, because it provided me ample opportunity to study while others slept, meaning that when the evening parties and revelry interrupted everyone else, I was caught up on all my reading.

I couldn't see Grampy through his kitchen window, but I waved anyway, just in case he might happen to look out while I was passing.

The walk to work was short as always, but instead of feeling my usual confidence or drinking in the sweet charm of my hometown while it was at rest, I was too busy wondering what might be watching me from the shadows to delight in any new Thanksgiving decor.

Mrs. Duncan had gone straight from Halloween to Christmas, something that had repeatedly been brought up at town council meetings, but Mrs. Duncan didn't care if people thought it was tacky to put up Christmas decor before both Veterans Day and Thanksgiving. She insisted that it was her favorite holiday and she was going to take pleasure in it for as long as she could, so for her Christmas began promptly on November 1.

She must have tackled the inside of the house first this year, because the yard lights and wooden cutouts hadn't been up the previous two mornings, but now the yard was so brightly lit you could probably see it from the mainland.

While some people in town might have frowned at her enthusiasm, I wasn't one of them. Seeing Mrs. Duncan's yard set up to look like Santa's workshop—she had three distinct themes of decorations and rotated them yearly—grounded me to where I was and gave me a brief sense of familiarity and ease, something I'd been lacking for the last day.

Yes, something terrible had happened here, and it likely meant that *someone* terrible was here as well. But that didn't change Split Pine. It didn't suddenly mean this was a scary and dangerous place to live.

Well, a little more dangerous than we previously believed, maybe.

But I couldn't let Jeff's death make me afraid to be here. I couldn't spend my days jumping at every shadow I saw and assuming a murderer was lurking around every corner. In truth, the murderer was likely to be someone I would willingly let sit in my restaurant and wave at if we passed in the streets.

I couldn't just start to believe the worst in every single person I knew. That would be an unbearable way to live my daily life.

My resolve not to be so jumpy and paranoid took an immediate hit when I approached the diner and noticed that someone was sitting on one of the benches on the back deck that overlooked the harbor. Most of the outdoor furniture had been piled up under the porch and covered for the winter, and we'd fit in the shed whatever we could, but the benches were a permanent fixture.

With my pulse tripping and my keys gripped tightly in my hand as the only approximation of a weapon I could think of, I edged closer to the shop, trying to get a good look at whoever it was. The view from the bench centered pretty directly on Jeff's boat. Was this my killer, come back to revisit the scene of the crime?

Then I saw blond hair ruffle in the breeze and recognized the dark jacket.

I stuffed my keys back into my bag and gave one longing look at the diner door, where I knew it would be toasty warm inside, and instead went onto the back deck and took a seat on the bench.

"You know, you're going to give me a complex," I said.

"How do you figure that?" Tom asked without looking at me. He wasn't looking at Jeff's boat either. His focus seemed to be off in the distance, as if he'd sat down to think and simply forgotten to get up again.

"Well, either you're here because you want to keep an eye on me, which isn't great, or you're here hoping to spot the killer, and the proximity to my diner *also* doesn't make that feel great. So one way or the other, this isn't the best start to my day."

"Ouch." He placed a hand on his heart like I'd wounded him. "Maybe it's neither of those things. Maybe I was just here and waiting for you to open so I could get a cup of coffee."

I was going to be cheeky and remind him that Elevated Grounds was already open, but the little pulse of excitement in my chest told me not to. He was here for my coffee, which felt like a flimsy cover, but whether it was a cover to come observe me as a potential suspect or as a potential girlfriend, I couldn't quite tell. If the thing that finally made Tom Cunningham realize I was a nice eligible lady worthy of his attention was our little interrogation the other day, that was going to be an awfully weird conversation to have with our future children.

You see, kids, your father thought I might have murdered someone.

Except it seemed fairly likely he *didn't* think that, if he was sitting here waiting for me to let him into the diner. And I realized as well that it was a perfect opportunity to ease any community suspicion from me. If Tom was seen patronizing my workplace rather than just showing up to haul evidence out of my backyard, that was a good thing.

Too bad he was doing it at six in the morning.

"We're not open yet." I gestured to the darkened diner. "But I suppose I can make an exception."

"Hey now, no special treatment."

I made a *pssh* sound and got up, nodding my head for him to follow. We entered through the front, where my hand instinctively went to the horseshoe next to the door.

"So is that the secret?"

I started, having already almost forgotten someone had come in with me. I'd switched to autopilot mode the instant I crossed the threshold, my mind mentally going through the morning checklist.

"The secret?" I said, genuinely confused.

"Come on, Este. Ever since the day I first showed up on this island, people have not stopped talking about your pies."

"They're very good pies." I turned on all the lights in the front and lingered near the kitchen entrance.

"But everyone talks about them like they're magic or something."

This brought a smile to my face, if only because the idea of straitlaced, intense Tom Cunningham, former baseball superstar, asking me if my pies were magical in the most roundabout way, was incredibly charming to me.

"Are you asking me to share secret family recipes, Tom?"

"No. Just curious if the rumors have any merit."

"I suppose that comes down to one very important factor."

"Which is?"

"Do you believe that luck is magical, or do you think luck is just people giving too much credit to happenstance?"

The question took him by surprise. It was something I'd thrown at nonbelievers in the past, because the thing with our pies was that they weren't a magic potion and the luck they brought could come in many forms. People knew coming into it that not every pie was lucky, but they knew *some* were, and that was enough.

They came, year after year, for the chance.

The hope.

And what was magic if not hope?

"I guess I never thought about that," he admitted. "I don't think I really thought much about luck at all before you."

My heart skipped a beat, because while I *knew* he hadn't meant it as a line, it was still possibly the single most romantic thing a man had ever said to me. I drank it in, letting it feed my ego for a second. Then I set about turning on the coffee machine to get things ready for the early birds. Seamus would be here soon to start breakfast, but for now it was just me, Tom, and the coffeemaker.

He leaned casually on the front counter, thoughtfully watching me work.

"You're avoiding my question," he nudged.

"No, the horseshoe isn't what makes the pies lucky." It wasn't the framed four-leaf clovers either.

"Then what is it? Why do people insist your pies are so remarkable?"

I stopped where I stood and looked back at him open-mouthed, then began to go through every single interaction he and I had ever had. Granted, there weren't many.

"Tom Cunningham," I said slowly. "Are you telling me you have *never* had a piece of Lucky Pie Diner pie?" I let my words drip with offense, so he knew how he'd wounded me.

"I'm not a big dessert guy."

I made a face at this. I typically didn't trust anyone who said they weren't a dessert person, because dessert was literally the best part of any meal.

"We make more than just sweet pies," I replied instead. "I can't believe you've never had my pie before. Kitty is here basically every day; she's always taking leftovers home. You *never* had any? Tom. Tom. Tom." I was worked up now. "Are you trying to tell me that every single year you've lived here, and every single Thanksgiving potluck we've had in this town, not one single time have you had a piece of my pumpkin pie?"

He shook his head, and I mimed fainting.

"You know, I think the reason is a really stupid one too, if I'm being honest."

"More stupid than *I'm not a dessert guy*?"

He smirked. "When I first got here, it was right after the team released me. I was still so fresh out of baseball, I think a lot of people thought that me coming here was maybe a chance for me to regroup, get my head on right, and then come back. Even people here. *Especially* people here. Split Pine folks certainly love to share their advice freely, I've noticed."

"We are very fond of being right."

This got a chuckle out of him, and he continued. "Do you know how many people told me to come see you when I got here? Well, not you specifically. But your pies. So many people I spoke to when I was getting settled in said, *Hey, if you want to get back into baseball, go to Lucky Pie Diner.* They made it sound like one slice of pie was all it would take to get my career back. Like overnight it could solve all my problems."

"It's pie, but it's not a miracle," I said with a small smile.

"I think, if I'm being honest, it wasn't that I was worried it *wouldn't* work. At that point I was really used to disappointment. I was wallowing in it. I think what scared me was that it *might* work and I would have to go back to that life, only to find some other new way to let my team down. The injury was kind of . . . well, it was horrible, but it was also kind of a good thing. I never had to watch my career decline. I never needed to see fans turn against me, the way they often do when players get older. I guess what I'm saying is, I was so worried your pie might work that I never tried any then, and I just never have since."

I regarded him carefully for a long while. This was the longest social conversation Tom and I had ever had, the longest I'd ever heard him talk about himself at all, and he'd just spilled his guts about something incredibly personal. It felt like being given a gift, and I wasn't sure how best to thank him for trusting me with that level of truth.

"Are you glad you stayed?" I asked.

He nodded immediately. "The team did call me about a year after I blew out my arm. They were going to offer me a job as a hitting coach, which was an incredible opportunity, but . . . I don't know. This already felt like home. Baseball already felt like a version of myself I didn't know anymore, if that makes sense."

"Sure it does."

The coffee pot hissed, letting me know the brew was complete. I poured him a cup and set it down on the counter in front of him. "You take anything?"

"Cream, if you have it."

I raised an overdramatic eyebrow at him. "If I have it. Sheriff, what kind of diner would I be if I didn't have cream?" Little did he know this could actually be something of a contentious point, considering how expensive it could be to continue buying cream during the quiet season. Bruno got semiregular grocery deliveries, as did we, but everything was more expensive, and there was definitely a cutthroat element among the locals in being the first to get certain items, especially dairy-related ones. But for now, at least, we had cream.

I pulled a container out from the fridge beside the coffeemaker, poured a little in my empty cup, then set it in front of him. I made my own cup with a dash of sugar, and for a moment we just stood there, enjoying our coffee. There was an urge deep in my belly to say something, to fill the silence in any way possible. This was something I often struggled with, being able to just be quiet in a moment. Right now I was struggling against myself, wanting to blurt out something, anything, but specifically my brain really wanted me to let him know that I wasn't guilty of anything. I guess something inside me thought the only reason Tom could want to spend any time with me was because he wanted to see if I'd slip up and admit to something. That he was being so nice because there might be a deep, dark secret I was dying to share.

I'd gone years being in his periphery, being best friends with his sister, and yet this felt like the most attention Tom had ever paid me. It would be nice to think it was just good things happening for me at last, but the timing of it made me a bit suspicious.

I managed to avoid any unnecessary outbursts, and rather than letting myself continue to wonder if this was his sneaky way of getting information out of me, I decided it was okay to turn off the worry for a few minutes and live in the moment.

Just enjoy this, I told myself.

Tom was the one to finally break the silence, clearing his throat as he set down his empty cup. "I suppose I should get on with my morning," he announced. "But Este, you never did answer my question."

"Which question was that?"

"Are your pies actually lucky?"

I smiled as I collected his mug. "I guess you're just going to have to try one and find out."

Chapter Eighteen

The morning flew by in spite of there being a relatively regular-sized crowd. All the usual suspects were present, with Vin and Eddie sitting at their usual booth and bickering with each other instead of actually doing their crossword puzzles.

I did notice, though, that once again a vague hush would sweep the room whenever I emerged from the kitchen, giving me the uneasy sense of walking into a room where people had just finished talking about me. I tried to pretend it didn't bother me and that it was just a coincidence, but there was no doubt about it anymore: people were starting to think I was involved.

At least it didn't seem to be hurting business, which was a relief. Perhaps the local population's need for greasy diner food and tasty pies would outweigh their concerns over my potential guilt or innocence.

Though I wasn't sure what it said about my neighbors that they might be willing to overlook me murdering someone if it meant they could still have a burger and a slice of apple pie.

Still, I stuck mostly to the back, letting Rosie and Marcel handle the front-of-house traffic. At about three o'clock things had slowed down enough that I figured it was okay to head home and leave Marcel to hold down the grill for the final supper rush, which would hit right before we closed at six. The islanders had figured out our rhythm over the years, and last season I'd started an experiment of having one day a week where we would stay open late—if one could consider eight o'clock late—so anyone who was keen to eat dinner in rather than grab it to go could come on a Friday. Honestly, since the age of many town regulars did skew a bit toward the senior side of things, our hours had never seemed to bother anyone.

I double-checked that my prep was done for the next day, but thanks to keeping myself basically locked in the kitchen all day to avoid awkward silences in the dining room, I had once again gotten more work done than I actually needed to. With that in mind, I grabbed a bundle of sweet pie dough from the fridge to do some recipe testing with when I got home, then took a piece of our daily special—key lime—to drop off with Grampy on my way to the cottage.

As I got outside, the light was dim, thanks to the oncoming evening and the overhead clouds. Just as I'd thought, a few fat snowflakes had begun to fall, and while the weather forecast didn't predict any storms in the near future, it was an inevitability that the whole town would be covered in snow at some point in the next month.

There was a definite bite to the air that made me believe we were in for an early winter. Sometimes you just know, the way the chill prickles your skin and dives deep into your bones; it's just a sensation that says winter is on its way and it isn't messing around.

I enjoyed winter, which couldn't be said of everyone I knew. But if you were going to live in Split Pine, you needed to like the season, at least enough to grit your teeth and get through it. Our isolated status and how truly shut down we were in the coldest time of year meant that we Split Pine natives needed to be okay with being tucked away and cozy in our own little world, but it also forced us to create a sense of community that didn't exist in other places like the mainland.

Sure, sometimes it could be incredibly frustrating to have everyone in your business, but it was also a relief to know that almost anyone on the island would come to your aid if you needed help.

Except one of them is a killer, the voice at the back of my mind nagged.

A pretty major exception to the rule.

Kitty was planning to come by when she finished her shift at Tom's Bar, but I had a few hours to kill before I saw her and plenty on my mind to work through so I wouldn't be terrible company. I stopped by Grampy's place first, only to find that he wasn't home. I suspected he had made a stop at the local bookstore, in spite of a large pile of unread books sitting on the table next to his favorite chair.

I left the key lime pie in his fridge and headed back to the cottage. I had barely gotten the door unlocked when a smudge emerged from the shadowy side of my place, nearly making me jump out of my skin. My heart was pounding a mile a minute, and it took me a second to realize that it wasn't some nefarious attacker or monster come to get me but rather the little cat I'd rescued the previous day.

She let out a plaintive chirping sound, like she hadn't yet spent enough time around humans to figure out meowing for attention, then parked herself next to the door and looked at it expectantly.

"Oh, you think so, do you?" I asked, hiking my bag of recipe supplies up on my shoulder.

She blinked at me, her eyes a striking blue-green shade that was unusual to see in cats, in my experience.

I figured she was going to let herself in the minute I opened the door, so there was no sense in arguing about it. I turned the knob and let her in before entering myself, figuring that if any killers were present in my tiny home, she would get a scent of them first and hightail it back to the door, giving me enough time to do the same.

Much like the previous evening, she toured the space and deemed it worthy of her presence—and more important, killer-free—then jumped up on my love seat, where she vigorously kneaded the throw blanket I'd left there until all I could hear was the loud sound of purring. Once the blanket was thoroughly smushed to her approval, she curled into a little ball and closed her eyes.

I'd assumed she was here to be fed again, but it seemed that she was far more interested in making herself at home.

I wasn't sure what to make of that. I knew no one owned her; that was obvious enough from her dirt-stained fur and how skinny she was. A woman named Eva St. Pierre maintained a cat colony just outside the town proper, where she fed a great number of Smokey's progeny and did her best to catch the ones she could and get them fixed. But new kittens, like this one, popped up every year.

I'd never considered getting a cat, but I also had nothing against the idea in general. I lived by myself and certainly had the space and the means to take care of her, and I had to admit it was nice to have another living thing in my space with me. It made the cottage feel warmer and less lonely, something I hadn't even realized it had needed until right this moment.

I wasn't going to force the kitten to stay, but I was kicking myself for forgetting to grab cat food today. At the very least, if she came around again tomorrow, I'd keep her long enough to get her checked at the vet, have her fixed if she was old enough, and take care of her basic vaccinations.

But I knew myself well enough to know that once I went to all that trouble, there was no way the cat was going to have to fend for itself in the wild again.

"Guess that means I'm going to need to think of a name for you, doesn't it?"

She said nothing, because she was completely passed out and had no interest in making conversation with me. But seeing her splayed out on her back with her paws curled up against her chest, I couldn't resist snapping a quick photo on my phone.

I sent it to Kitty, adding, *Looks like I have a squatter.*

Kitty sent back twelve exclamation marks and a cat emoji.

I left the kitten to sleep and unpacked my bag of groceries from the diner. As I put things away, I dug through my cupboards to see if I had any human food that might be suitable to feed a freeloading fur baby for the night. After my discussion with Bruno earlier in the week, I wasn't in a huge hurry to go back to the General Store, because I didn't want him to think I was giving him the third degree yet again, and things had felt more than a little tense between us when I'd left. It wasn't that I thought I was banned from the grocery store, but I figured I might give him at least forty-eight hours without seeing me before I headed back in.

I still wasn't sure what to think about Bruno's involvement in this whole thing. I didn't *want* him to be the killer, but it was hard to ignore some of the signs. I just had to admit that I couldn't trust him completely until this was all sorted out, and that was going to make it very difficult to sit with Kitty later tonight and listen to her talk about him.

Luckily for me, Bruno, and the kitten, I found a can of tuna tucked in the pantry and set it down on the counter to await Her Highness's return to the world of the conscious.

I knew Kitty—my human friend, not the cat—would be hungry when she got off work, so I figured that rather than just recipe testing a new pie, I'd make a proper meal to go along with it. Nothing fancy—I had cooked all day, after all—but a little comfort food could go a long way, especially on a chilly night like this.

My favorite thing to eat on cold wintry nights was something warm and hearty. The perfect option would be a pie—but not a real pie. Shepherd's pie was one of my favorite quick-fix meals for keeping bellies full and smiles on everyone's face. I wasn't sure why it was called a pie to begin with, since there was no crust, though perhaps there once had been centuries earlier.

Technically, the version I made wasn't a true shepherd's pie, as that would have relied on ground lamb as the meat base. I had always had mine made with ground beef, which was a cottage pie, if we were getting pedantic about it, but I still just called it a shepherd's pie, and no one could tell me otherwise if they wanted to have a big serving of it.

I set a big pot of water on the stove to boil, salting it lightly for the potatoes that I would mash to adorn the top of the dish. Then, in a large skillet, I sautéed chopped onion, freshly minced garlic, and some salt and pepper. I liked to add a bay leaf just to give a little extra oomph to the final flavor.

I was grateful to my past self for leaving some ground beef in the fridge, knowing I'd want something like this. Perhaps it was a lot of ground beef for one week, after yesterday's tourtière, but to me these dishes were so infinitely different that it didn't matter.

I added the beef to the skillet to brown and got my secret weapons ready to go. A little tomato paste, a packet of onion soup mix, and a splash of balsamic vinegar added a good umami punch to the dish, and once the beef was completely browned, I removed the bay leaf.

Now for my two lazy tricks that made the pie all my own— or more specifically made it my family's, as I'd stolen these tricks from my mother, who had adapted it from her mother.

The first: frozen mixed vegetables. Sure, I could chop and mix and get fresh carrots and other goodies in there, but a frozen veggie mix worked just as well and everything was already cut to the perfect size. And then, last, a can of condensed vegetable beef soup, the kind for kids that had small alphabet noodles in it. I liked that it added a little extra tomato and also brought some potato into the casserole part of the pie.

With all these ingredients cooked, I poured the mixture into a waiting baking dish and turned my attention to the potatoes. On days where I had energy to spare, I would peel whole potatoes and cube them. Today, though, I was tired, and the word *peel* was, shall we say, una*peel*ing. I took a small bag of mixed baby potatoes and added them to the boiling water, skins still intact, and boiled them until they were soft enough for mashing. After pouring off the water, I added a healthy dose of butter, salt and pepper, and my other secret ingredient: Greek yogurt. Then I mashed the baby potatoes into a delicious and spreadable consistency.

If I made this in the summer, I would often cut in fresh chives and mix those with the potatoes as well, but I had no chives to spare tonight. I piled the potatoes on top of the beef mixture in mounds and then sprinkled the entire thing with some cheddar cheese before setting it aside. The shepherd's pie would bake in no time, so I could throw it in when Kitty texted that she was on her way. What would take a little longer was the *real* pie.

I wanted to do something creamy and simple to offset the heavier dinner, so I decided on a buttermilk pie. While the cream made it rich, the sharp tang of the buttermilk, topped with fresh berries, made for a surprisingly refreshing treat.

I hadn't made this pie in years and was trying to find a way to make it fancy enough for the diner since it often felt too simple to go into my regular rotation. When you're known for pies, and especially known for magical luck-creating pies, you sometimes feel like you always need to be outdoing yourself. At least that's how it often was for me. But I'd been looking for something a little simpler to add to the menu over the winter months, something that would tickle the fancy of people who just wanted a hint of sweetness, not a bomb of sugary delight.

In spite of how long it had been since I'd made a buttermilk pie, the recipe came together as if my fingers had been itching to bake it for eons. Soon enough the pie was in the oven, and when I turned around, there was a tiny gray cat perched on the island stool, her nose raised to the air, obviously smelling the shepherd's pie.

"No beef tonight, missy. I'm sure too much of that isn't very good for you."

She blinked slowly but didn't protest. She was a funny, quiet sort of thing, and the way she looked at me made me think she was judging me. Like this was her opportunity to determine if I was going to be worthy of taking care of her for the long haul.

I suddenly felt a desperate need to prove myself to this kitten.

"I'm not going to leave you high and dry, not to worry." I got out the can opener and found an old mini pie tin under the counter that would make a serviceable cat food dish until I got something more appropriate. She watched me carefully, nearly unblinking, as I emptied the can of tuna onto the plate and put it in front of her.

After a cursory sniff, she dug in, and an immediate wave of relief washed over me. I had appeased her.

I was beginning to understand why ancient Egyptians had worshipped cats like gods. The little fur beasts certainly had a way of making you feel about as small as an ant or as important as a queen with just one reaction. I didn't even technically own this cat, and she already had me wrapped around her little finger.

The pie baked, and I found myself with about an hour to kill and suddenly no distractions to keep me from thinking about the murder. Since I couldn't exactly wander down to check out the murder scene and I certainly had no interest in going to chat with Mick about whether or not he'd had an encounter with Jeff, that left me only one option: the internet.

Chapter Nineteen

I left the kitten at the kitchen island and moved myself into the living room, where my laptop was sitting on the coffee table, inviting me to do a little amateur investigating while I waited for Kitty to show up.

If anything, this was Tom's fault, because if he had reduced the bar's hours over the offseason, Kitty would have already been here and I wouldn't have had a chance to go poking around.

Yup, totally Tom's fault.

I couldn't exactly Google *who killed Jeff the fruit guy*, but there was something that had been nagging at me since last night after I talked to Grampy. It was bizarre how Jeff had just come out of nowhere, seemingly inserting himself into a multigenerational family business that none of us could recall him ever being part of.

What had happened to Denny? If he'd been planning to sell the business, he would have mentioned something when he'd been out to see us only about a month earlier. It was suspicious to me that Jeff had just popped up, acting like everything was business as usual when it was clearly anything but.

A good place to start would be the company's website, just to see if it mentioned Jeff at all or what his connection to Denny and his family might be.

I pulled up the website for Evergreen Produce, and it was a pretty lackluster offering, the kind probably made from a pre-existing template on a website-generating site. The company's logo was on top, unchanged, and brought me right back to those plastic strawberry containers I'd found in the woods.

That whole situation didn't sit right with me, but I also couldn't really see how it factored into Jeff's murder. More likely than not, the cooler had just gotten knocked overboard at some point during the murder and wasn't directly connected.

Still, seeing the logo made my stomach tighten in anxiety.

On the "About Us" page was a small blurb about the company being family owned for four generations along with an email form I could submit if I had questions. There was an address in Harbor Springs where the Evergreen orchard and fruit farm was located, and below that was a phone number.

I already had the number, but I jotted it down just the same.

The website didn't list any names or have any mention of who was in charge, just the brief write-up on the McAvoy family's fruit legacy.

I navigated through the pages looking at the scant few photos they'd included, most of which were of the orchard and strawberry fields and featured smiling families who'd come to enjoy the u-pick experience at the farm. Finally, there was a picture of several people wearing matching dark-green polo shirts in front of an A-frame storefront. The picture was small and it was hard to make out any faces, but I recognized Denny almost immediately, his round cheeks and distinctive dark beard making him stick out. Beside him I also recognized his father, Douglas, who had been our deliveryman when my parents had just started out, before Denny took things over.

One person I was absolutely certain I didn't see in the photo was Jeff.

That was weird, right? Someone who claimed to have taken over from Denny wasn't even on their website? Surely if he was part of the family, he would be in the photo. And if he wasn't and had just taken over operations, why leave up an old website?

The smell of baking pastry wafted through the house, applying a soothing balm to my growing uncertainty.

As I continued my search, the kitten appeared at my feet, apparently trying to decide if it was okay that I had stolen her love seat. I gently patted the pile of blankets next to me. "They're all yours if you want them. I promise I don't bite."

After another moment of indecision, she must have come to the conclusion that I was trustworthy enough, because she jumped up, resumed kneading the blankets until they were tenderized to her liking, and went right back to sleep.

Yeah, I was definitely going to need to start thinking of names.

With the Evergreen Produce website yielding nothing in the way of truly useful information, I decided to search for Denny McAvoy himself, wondering if there might be notice of a sale or other information that would help me make sense of things.

What I found instead took my breath away.

The first few hits were newspaper articles about the fruit farm, and one was a family reunion website, but the fourth listed result was an obituary. As I clicked, I kept a prayer in my heart that it would be someone else, someone with the same name, not the Denny I had seen for years on end with the jolly smile and unrelenting dad jokes.

The page loaded, and I was greeted with a photo of Denny's smile. He looked older here than in the photo from the farm's website, but this was the same face I had seen just over a month ago, looking hale and hearty as he loaded bins of produce into my walk-in.

I could barely process the words next to his picture as my eyes misted with tears. I couldn't believe it; surely there was some mistake. There was no way Denny was actually dead. He'd only been in his early fifties, not old enough by far to just drop dead.

Scanning the article with its usual niceties and remembrances, I stumbled on a line that stood out sharply against the rest.

Dennis "Denny" McAvoy died in a boating accident on Lake Michigan. Though his death is tragic, his family is grateful that he passed away doing what he loved most: spending time on the water.

So it wasn't a sudden heart attack or a battle with cancer that had taken him out; it was an accident.

An accident on a boat.

I thought of Jeff, dead on his boat, and while I was certain I was probably jumping to the craziest kind of conclusions, it was really hard to not draw a line between the two deaths. Denny had died suddenly and had clearly been an experienced boater, certainly not someone who would take undo risk or put himself knowingly in harm's way.

Just over a month later, the person who had supposedly taken over his business was dead as well.

Perhaps there was more to this than a fight over the price of strawberries.

And if that was the case, then this murder investigation had suddenly taken on a much more sinister angle, because there wasn't just one dead man; there were two.

I set the laptop down on the counter and turned toward the dozing kitten next to me.

"I think I need to tell Tom about this."

The kitten didn't answer, but my phone pinged a notification, a message from Kitty telling me she wasn't feeling great after her shift and she wanted to rain-check our get-together to tomorrow night.

I glanced quickly at the clock on my stove. It was just after eight o'clock, too late for anything to be open but not too late to be out. Just as I was considering my next steps, my timer buzzed to tell me the buttermilk pie was done.

And I knew one man in town who had never tried it.

Chapter Twenty

The light at the sheriff's office was off, making my first stop a bust and also shooting my *I was just passing by and noticed the light on* excuse to pieces. I mean, he was a smart guy; by the time I got to my second stop, he was never going to believe I'd just been walking by with a pie. It was going to be obvious I'd come looking for him.

I'd hoped to stage a casual run-in where I could drop the information I'd found into a conversation rather than making it too obvious I'd been digging into the case on my own. Still, this was information he should have, which meant I needed to find him even if it was apparent I'd gone out of my way to deliver it.

Thankfully, Tom's house wasn't far from his office, quite literally just down the block, and when I got to his front street, I didn't even get a chance to work up a good opening line, because he was sitting on his front porch swing.

The night air was cold, certainly not inviting enough to be sitting outside, but he had a bulky jacket on and a steaming mug of something in his hands. Still, I could see little puffs of his breath in the air, and I knew he had to be just as cold as I was.

"Now what was it you said to me this morning?" he mused, taking a sip from his mug like he was in no hurry to finish his sentence. "That me being on your doorstep either meant you were in trouble or you were in harm's way, but neither answer seemed like much fun to you?"

"That doesn't sound like me," I countered, knowing full well it was almost exactly what I'd said. My own tart tongue coming back to haunt me.

"So what does it mean for me if you're on *my* doorstep, Este?"

I held the baking dish up for him to see. "I come bearing pie."

His long legs were kicked out in front of him and he was rocking his ankles slightly to give the swing just a bit of movement. He didn't make any moves like he was going to get up, but he did scoot over sideways a few inches before taking another sip from his mug.

"My mother always told me to never look a gift pie in the mouth."

"I never met your mom, but I feel pretty certain she never said that."

"You've met my sister. I think if you stretch your imagination enough, you could *probably* think my mom said something along those lines."

I sat next to him on the porch swing, suddenly very aware of how small the swing was with his larger figure taking up half the space. Our thighs were pressed together, and even though there were many layers of bulky clothing buffering us, I flushed with a giddy head rush, as if I were a teenage girl who had just been asked to dance.

"So what's this you've brought me, then?" he asked, eyeing the foiled-wrapped pie plate that was still warm in my hands.

"Buttermilk pie with a strawberry compote."

"What in heaven's name is a *compote*?" he asked incredulously.

"Think of it like a jam that hasn't set."

"Mushy strawberries and sugar. Check."

That made me bark out a very unladylike laugh. I removed the foil from the plate to show him the pie. "It's a pretty basic pie. I figured I'd ease you into it rather than starting you out with a chocolate cream or something that isn't for beginners."

Tom raised a brow at me and sipped from his steamy mug again. From here I could smell it, and the fragrant bloom of cinnamon and apple told me he was enjoying a cider, which seemed like such an implausible thing for our former pro-baseball-playing sheriff to be drinking that I was both impressed and a little surprised.

"Este, I said I'd never had one of *your* pies, not that I'd never eaten *any* pie. I don't need a tutorial." He leaned in and sniffed. "Though if that means you're suddenly going to start showing up to my house regularly with increasingly fancier pies, then perhaps I shouldn't argue with a good thing."

"Hey now, first one is free; after that I expect you to pay like everyone else on the island."

"That's always how they get you." He gave his head a shake. "Y'know, if this were anywhere but Split Pine, I'd say this gesture was a little less *friendly neighbor* and a little more *bribe the authority figure*."

"Oh, are you an authority figure? I hadn't noticed."

He raised a hand to his heart. "Ouch."

"I promise, no bribes. Bribing would imply I had something I was guilty of, and I'm only guilty of making really tasty pies, I promise you." I waved the dish at him.

"All right, all right, come on with you, then." He got up from the swing, and the removal of his weight set the whole thing swaying until he took hold of the chain and held it in place for me so I could stand. He then held his front door open for me, and even though I knew how innocent this was, I still darted a quick glance around, trying to see if anyone was out and about who might turn this into some hot gossip for the next day.

Unless someone was watching from one of the nearby houses—always possible; people here were nosy like that—we were in the clear. And to be honest, I'd rather they were making up stories about my scandalous affair with the sheriff than telling each other I might have killed someone.

Tom's house was neat as a pin, and when I crossed the threshold, it occurred to me that this was the first time I'd ever seen it inside. I supposes that wasn't strange, considering he and I weren't close, but given my friendship with Kitty, it was somehow surprising I hadn't ended up here for a dinner or barbecue at some point before this.

It was a sweet little bungalow, probably only about eight or nine hundred square feet, and the interior was painted a pale-blue color while maintaining the original dark-wood trim that had likely been here since the place was built. At some point some upgrades had been made, because most era bungalows from the forties or fifties had distinctly small rooms, but this had been converted into a large open space where the living room, dining room, and kitchen all connected.

The open-concept room provided a great view through the big windows backing onto a deck through the kitchen side, and beyond I could see moonlight reflecting on water.

Tom didn't have a waterfront property, but his house was located on one of the higher hills in town, giving him a good view over other buildings and out to the lake. He'd probably paid a pretty penny extra when buying this house thanks to that view.

The living room was masculine without being overly *dude* in its presentation, with a large charcoal-gray sectional facing a fireplace and a truly enormous TV mounted to the wall above that. The kitchen was small, so it made me wonder if the renovation work had been Tom's—a bachelor opting for a large living room instead of a fancy kitchen.

On either side of the fireplace were built-in shelves, and I was surprised to see that he had displayed a lot of his baseball memorabilia out in the open. Tom didn't seem to like talking about his time as a player, generally changing the subject whenever it came up rather than using his glory days as an opportunity to hold court over a captive audience. Decorating the bar with all his sports stuff had been Kitty's idea, to appeal to tourists and Michiganders who knew his name. She'd told me he hadn't initially wanted to use his fame like that, which had made me think that perhaps he didn't like to reflect on that time of his life or that perhaps it made him uncomfortable to think about it, but in here it was evident that his pro career brought him a lot of pride.

Above each set of shelves was a framed jersey. On one side was one of his classic blue-and-white Tigers jerseys showing his name on the back, and on the other was a more stylized All-Star jersey with gold accents and an American League logo on the shoulder. The shelves contained framed photos of iconic career moments—like the home run that had secured the Tigers' trip to the World Series and earned Tom his nickname "The Bomb." Next to that photo was the home run ball itself in a clear plastic cube, signed by Pedro Cabrera, the pitcher who had thrown it.

Yeah, I lived in Michigan; I got excited about major moments for Michigan teams. Of course I knew what I was looking at.

Tom must have seen me staring, because he cleared his throat, bringing my attention back to him.

"It's a bit tacky, I know."

I looked away from the signed baseball, giving him a stern glare. "Tom. Tacky? Come on."

He shrugged in a way that made him briefly look like a teenager, and I thought I caught the faintest reddening across his cheeks.

"You should be really proud of what you did."

He made his way toward the small kitchen, and I followed after him. As he pulled plates down from an overhead cupboard, he said, "It's not that I'm not proud. I guess it's just been so long now since I played, and part of me is a different person now than I was then. I mean, I got drafted when I was seventeen. I didn't know who I was, what I wanted; I thought baseball was going to be my whole life. But baseball isn't an old man's game, not that I ever got the chance to try." He set the plates down on the counter and took the pie dish from my hands. "Maybe it's silly to hang on to things from what's basically a children's game played by millionaires—I don't know."

I caught him looking past me with a soft expression on his face, taking in the items on the shelves.

"How many people can say they've played major league baseball, Tom?"

"About twenty thousand," he answered almost too quickly.

"You just *know* that? My question was rhetorical."

He smiled and took a knife from the drawer, then cut the pie into slices. I bit my tongue to keep from offering suggestions on the best method and let him do it his way.

"Anyway, that's still a very small number, all things considered. Be proud. Getting to that point and doing the things you did is impressive as heck."

"Baking magical pies is impressive as heck," he retorted. "You might be more famous than I am, if online buzz is accurate."

"No one on this planet owns an Este March jersey, and I definitely still see Cunningham jerseys in the crowd at Tigers games every year."

"I notice you're not arguing about the magical pies."

"I notice you're actually going to try one." I smirked triumphantly. He had placed a piece of pie on each of our plates and added a fork to the side. The buttermilk pie was a lovely custard color and had a firm texture that reminded me a little of cheesecake. The strawberry compote on top would complement the tartness of the buttermilk, but the added sugar would keep things from skewing too sour.

I hoped.

It had been a while since I'd made this, and while I could do a caramel apple pie in my sleep, this might be a differently story.

"Well, here's to luck, then, I guess." He held his fork aloft, and I clinked mine against it like we were cheers-ing with glasses. "I could use as much luck as I could get, honestly."

I waited until he'd taken a bite before observing, "It's funny you should say that."

Chapter Twenty-One

I had to give Tom credit, because he managed to avoid giving me a lecture until the very end of me showing him what I'd learned about Denny and his mysterious accident.

When I wrapped up my miniature TED Talk on all things related to deaths on boats, Tom gave me a long look, a piece of pie still sitting on his fork, which he held halfway to his mouth, and after an exceptionally quiet silence, he let out the most overburdened sigh I think I'd ever heard.

"Este." At first that was all he said, just my name. I waited for there to be something more, but it seemed like he was hoping that might be all he *had* to say to make his point.

I looked at him expectantly, hoping he'd at least tell me he appreciated what I'd found, or that it had some kind of meaningful impact on his investigation. *Something* to make it not totally insane for me to have come over here tonight.

"Tom," I replied finally, hoping it might move things along.

He set his fork down, pie suddenly forgotten, and crossed his arms over his chest. I knew the movement was supposed to give off stern vibes, but I was momentarily distracted by how toned his forearms were and forgot to be properly chided.

Once he realized his silent efforts had failed against me, he said, "I can see you're trying to be helpful, and that's . . . nice. I won't say it's good, because you shouldn't be involving yourself in this case at all."

"*You* involved me in the case," I reminded him.

"Because we found *your* invoice in his hand. Have you forgotten that part? You're so dead set on doing your own investigating you seem to have completely brushed past the part that you're still a person of interest in this case."

It did not escape my notice that he said *person of interest* and not *suspect*.

"Tom, be real. We both know I didn't kill him."

"That's not the point. And that doesn't mean you should go around trying to solve the case on your own either; that's not how these things work. You don't get to point at a different potential killer and that means you're totally off the hook."

"I'm not the sheriff here, but I kind of think if I found the killer, that probably should clear me of suspicion, though." I offered what I hoped was a charming smile, but he wasn't impressed.

"Thank you for bringing me this. It was something I hadn't known, but I'm not sure if it means anything at all."

"How can it not mean anything?" I protested. "The old owner of the company dies suddenly in a boating accident, and Jeff also dies on a boat? That means something."

"Please promise me you're going to stay out of this," he said, ignoring my pleas for common sense.

"That's it?"

"I don't know what's going on in this case, but if you didn't do it—"

"Which I didn't."

"If you didn't do it, someone else on this island did, and if they think you're putting your nose in their business, that could be very bad for you. So please, Este, just leave this to me. I know you want to be helpful, but I can't be worried about you sleuthing your way into danger and also solve this case."

"I knew you didn't think I did it," I said triumphantly.

He shooed me to the door, clearly annoyed but also unable to keep that subtle twinkle of humor out of his eyes. I might be driving him nuts, but a part of him didn't seem to mind.

And as he closed the door behind me, it didn't seem he'd even realized that I'd never actually promised to stay out of things.

* * *

I got to the diner earlier than usual the next day, and even though I'd told myself after leaving Tom's house the previous night that I would keep my investigation strictly internet based, I stopped on the back deck of the restaurant to have a look out at the harbor.

Jeff's boat was still tied in its guest spot, with yellow crime scene taped fluttering in the wind attached to its railing. It wasn't a huge boat, maybe about fourteen feet, and while I was certainly no nautical expert, I recognized a basic cabin cruiser when I saw one. It wasn't as fancy or decked out as some of the models we had coming into the harbor over the summer, it showed signs of wear and tear, and based on its boxier design, I guessed it was probably from the eighties.

The stern of the boat was clearly visible from my deck, and I noted the port of call—Little Traverse Bay—and the boat's name, *Fishy Business*.

I couldn't have imagined a more fitting name for Jeff's boat, or the hot water it currently found itself in. Plenty of punny boat names had come through our harbor, but never one quite so clairvoyant.

I glanced around the harbor but couldn't see a sign of Carey Wise anywhere, and there was no one else out and about on the harbor front this early in the morning. Good—I didn't need to get glared at by my neighbors like I had the last time I went down there.

Plus, I didn't want to get *on* Jeff's boat, but I wouldn't mind taking a closer look at the deck to see if there were more crates like the one I had found. It would go a long way toward painting a picture of how that particular crate had managed to find itself going overboard. Boats in general were designed to keep things *on* the deck rather than in the drink.

Pulling my jacket tightly around me and my beanie down over my red hair—no need to make myself obvious—I skirted the edge of my property on my down toward the harbor entrance. Now that we were in the winter season and no one was coming and going daily, Carey often let himself sleep in or reduced his watch hours. After all, if there was nothing happening, there was no point.

Jeff's boat was moored on the slip closest to my diner, and when no one immediately yelled at me to stop what I was doing, I beelined in that direction.

There weren't many boats left at the harbor at this point. Local residents took theirs out of the water before the end of the season. A handful of smaller boats remained, and those would likely get pulled this coming weekend. The main dock was left clear for incoming deliveries from the mainland for as long as it was still safe to come by boat. When things got super frigid—though the Great Lakes never froze over entirely—the only safe and reliable way for us to get deliveries and mail was by plane. There was a small landing strip just outside of town, and after winter came, we would get things brought in every week or two, weather depending.

What the limited number of boats meant was that I didn't need to worry about anyone out here noticing me snooping. But it also meant I'd lost any kind of plausible deniability. I couldn't say I was looking for some other boat when the only one on this slip belonged to a murder victim.

I briefly considered turning around, as there was nothing I could really gain from this mission except sating my own curiosity. But right now that felt like reason enough, and I picked up my pace, partially against the sharpness of the wind coming in off the open water and partially to get this whole adventure finished with before someone spotted me.

In spite of how small the boat looked from my deck, it was surprisingly large up close. Certainly big enough for one man to comfortably rest and relax below deck in what I imagined were relatively small quarters. Denny was a bigger guy, so overnights on the boat had probably been more uncomfortable. Jeff had been more slight of build; he'd likely fit okay on the little boat bunk.

I moved to the stern of the boat, where the sides were lower and I could get a better look at the back. This would be the best place to climb aboard if I were inclined to do so, which I wasn't. As I craned my neck toward the storage space at the back and noticed a familiar-looking black case, something else caught my attention and caused my stomach to drop right to my shoes.

There was a light on inside the cabin.

I blinked, wondering if I was imaging things or if the light of the moon reflecting off the water was playing tricks on my eyes. But the moon had long since set, and the sky was turning a medium blue that signaled the sun would be on her way up soon.

No, I wasn't imagining it; there was definitely a light on in the boat's small cabin area. The light bobbed and moved erratically, making me realize it was actually a flashlight rather than a lamp or an interior fixture.

Someone was on the boat.

The realization that this wasn't just an accidental oversight by police or a light Jeff had left on made my adrenaline soar, and I knew that it didn't matter who was on the boat—whether it was Tom, the killer, or the ghost of Jeff himself. I needed to get out of here *now*.

I took two slow steps backward, keeping my eye on the light for a few moments longer. Now that I was farther back, I could see the faint glow from the flashlight through the closed curtains of the cabin. Someone was looking around, but for what? And why? Jeff was dead. Were they looking for something he'd left behind?

Or were they planting something to further point the finger of guilt away from themselves?

As I remembered the invoice that had been found clutched in Jeff's hand—something I'd seen with my own two eyes—I had to wonder if Jeff had actually been holding it when he died. Or had someone intentionally placed it there to direct attention my way?

While I wanted to continue to believe I couldn't imagine a single person on the island capable of doing something like that, there was one particular father-daughter team who were more than able to do what it took to make sure things went there way.

But how bad did the Gorleys want my property?

Bad enough to frame me for murder?

That was dark, even for Mick and Jersey.

I was so lost in my thoughts about who might be on the boat and what they might be up to that I almost forgot how troubling my current situation was. I was right out in the open and needed to get out of here before I came face-to-face with the stranger on the boat.

I couldn't just run full speed off the dock, though. Heavy boots on wooden planks would make too much noise and alert whoever it was to my presence immediately. I hadn't been trying to be subtle in my approach, but I'd evidently been quiet enough not to be noticed. Now I just needed to repeat the process in reverse.

I backed away slowly until I was about halfway down the dock. Once I felt I had enough distance to risk picking up my pace slightly, I started to take the widest, lightest steps I could imagine, basically doing walking lunges all the way back to the harbor entrance.

At least if anyone from shore saw me, they would have more questions about the stupid way I was walking than about why I was out on the docks before dawn.

The second I hit dry land, I ran. I ran until the docks were out of sight and only the little red building I called my daytime home was visible.

Even around the far side of the building, not facing the harbor, I was on high alert. What if they'd heard me? What if someone had followed?

My hands were shaking so hard that it took me three tries to unlock the side door and let myself in. Locking up behind me, I immediately made a beeline for the dining room and slid into one of the booths, trying to see if I could get a look at Jeff's boat.

The deck outside the window was too deep, though, blocking almost my entire view of the harbor, but also hopefully blocking the sight line of anyone down there doing their dirty business. I peered up over the edge of the window and could see a shadowy figure moving toward the harbor entrance, but it was dark, and they were wearing a heavy jacket and a cap of some kind. From this distance I could barely tell they were human, let alone who they were.

I pulled out my phone. The digital timer read *5:56*.

It felt too early to call Tom, and I wasn't sure how I could explain what I'd seen without implicating myself as well.

Still, even though I knew he'd get mad at me for sticking my nose in his investigation so soon after he had expressly told me not to, I also couldn't ignore that there was someone who had been trampling all over a crime scene only seconds ago.

I unlocked my phone and sent him as innocent-sounding a text as I could. *Hey, got to work and noticed that it looks like a light is on in Jeff's boat. Is that you?*

See, no guilt whatsoever, just an innocent bystander.

I had to admit to myself, though, that after this morning's close call, Tom might be onto something.

Maybe it was high time I leave the investigating to the professionals.

I returned to the kitchen to start the morning opening routine, and while my text to Tom was marked as read, he didn't reply, either to tell me off or to inform me of his next professional steps. He could at least have acknowledged whether he was going to take my report seriously.

As I huffed around the kitchen, turning on my ovens and getting pie dough out of the fridge so it could come to room temperature, a sharp noise at the door stopped me dead in my tracks.

Was that a scraping sound?

I listened carefully, but for a moment the only thing I could hear was my pulse hammering in my ears, blocking out any other kinds of noise.

Then there it was again, clear as day. *Scrape, scrape, scrape.*

I darted a quick glance at my phone, which I'd left on the counter. It could be Seamus without his keys or Tom coming to tell me what he'd found, I knew, but I also figured that either one of them would have knocked rather than scratching at the door like an unhinged psycho from some urban legend about a stupid diner owner who gets killed because she can't mind her own business.

Scrape, scrape, scrape.

I should have just ignored it. I should have waited until it went away. But in spite of my poorly honed survival skills screaming at me to keep the door closed, some other part of my brain was telling me how silly I was being. This was Split Pine, after all. There wasn't going to be a man outside my door with a hook for a hand.

That's probably what everyone in those legends thought too.

I sighed, trying to shake off this new nagging paranoia that had started to follow me around. I couldn't start to jump at every noise or convince myself that everything was a threat.

And while I *had* just seen something highly unusual at the docks, I'd also told Tom about it. By this point he must be either in the vicinity or on his way. If something happened to me, at least two dozen people were within earshot to hear me scream.

I told myself all of this just to amp my courage up enough for me to open a door.

When I finally did, cracking it open just a little, there was no one there.

"Oh, come on, what in the horror movie nonsense is this?" I declared to the now-pink morning sky.

A whine drew my attention down to where the large form of Mayor was splayed out at my doorstop. At first I worried maybe something had happened to him, as he was flopped over on his side, his large ears tossed above his head. But then he began to snore, and I knew he was fine; he'd just come to say hi.

I bent down and gave his belly a rub before closing the door again to let him nap in peace.

But as I turned the bolt, something else occurred to me.

If Mick Gorley's dog was at my back door . . . where was Mick Gorley?

Chapter Twenty-Two

My body felt like a live wire all day.

Tom didn't answer my text or come into the diner, and there was no sign of Mick or Jersey coming by to claim their dog throughout my shift either, though Mayor hung around for several hours, eventually moving to the front of the restaurant, where regulars would drop him french fries or little bits of their leftovers.

Everyone knew not to share the chocolate pie with him, thankfully.

Mayor's long stay should have made me feel better about his appearance being coincidental, but I just couldn't shake the feeling that it must have been Mick on the boat this morning.

I'd spent a lot of time focused on Bruno and his fight with Jeff, and it had kept me distracted from Mick, who was Jeff's *other* big client on the island and likely to be a lot less polite about his displeasure.

Mick was a piece of work, and everyone on the island knew it. He was pushy and rude and generally went out of his way to be obnoxious and confrontational. It was like he enjoyed the misery of others, so he did whatever he could to create it.

Not exactly the kind of guy you wanted to be best friends with.

Jersey wasn't much better, but how could she be when she'd been raised by a single father who was basically the worst person on the island?

Still, I *knew* Mick. I'd known him for decades. And while I wouldn't put things like lying, cheating, or manipulation past him, it was still a pretty big leap from trying to harass our family out of long-owned property to cold-blooded killing.

Though I guessed if I was going to believe it of anyone in town, I'd believe it of Mick.

By the time my shift ended, I was desperate to share my thoughts with someone. After what had happened last night with Tom, I didn't think he was going to welcome any further suggestions or insights from me, especially not if they gave him any further indication I was snooping around on the case by myself.

Plus, things this morning had taught me I needed to tread lightly if I was going to continue to snoop, because I'd felt a surge of genuine fear on the dock outside Jeff's boat. In that instant, I'd felt to my very core that I needed to be more careful about this.

So I wasn't going to go poking around and spying on Mick.

Not alone, anyway.

I made my way into Tom's Bar, the crowd fairly thin this time of the evening, as happy hour wasn't really a big draw for locals. The bar was open only until eight on weeknights, which was late by island standards, but on Friday and Saturday it stayed open until midnight, even through the winter.

People needed something to do and a place to socialize, and Tom's was that place, unless it was bingo night at the community hall and then *that* was definitely the place. No joke. Island bingo got cutthroat; I rarely missed it.

Since it was still a weeknight, there were only a couple of regulars at the bar and a middle-aged couple seated in one of the booths enjoying a pizza. Tom's menu didn't really overlap with ours, thankfully. You wanted a burger and fries or a good sandwich, you came to Lucky Pie. You wanted a pizza or mozza sticks, maybe a plate of nachos, or if you were feeling brave some fish and chips, then you came to Tom's.

You wanted to overpay for steak and cold mashed potatoes? You went to Mick's.

I hopped up on a stool at the bar. I didn't have a bag with me, as I rarely carried a purse. Most days I was just moving to and from the cottage to the diner and back again. I kept my wallet in my jacket pocket, and the only time I brought my purse along was if I knew I was going grocery shopping, because I stored several small grocery bags in it.

I toyed with the thick cardboard coaster on the bar in front of me and tapped my toe along to the Bruce Springsteen song on the jukebox. Tom's bar had a certain vibe to it that didn't really reflect Tom the man. It had a working-class sheen, with music played by and for the everyman American, greasy food that would make your stomach hurt if you ate too much of it, and the prerequisite pool table and dart board.

There were several big TVs mounted around the room—most tuned to game six of the World Series at the moment—but since Detroit wasn't playing, the gathered crowd was only peripherally interested. Memorabilia from Tom's time with the Tigers adorned the walls, along with keepsakes from other Michigan franchises like the Red Wings, the Pistons, and to a much smaller extent, the Lions.

We didn't like to talk about the Lions.

"What can I getcha, pretty lady?" Kitty pulled up in front of me, a rag draped over her shoulder and an apron tied around her waist. She wore the standard Tom's uniform of a black T-shirt with the neon-orange *Tom's* logo stitched onto her chest.

"You ever find it weird wearing your brother's name on your shirt?"

Kitty set a glass down in front of me, shrugging as if she got asked this a lot. "Nah. We had his jerseys when he played. Not much different."

"Except those said Cunningham, and you are also a Cunningham."

"You don't actually want to pester me about my uniform, do you?"

"No." I set the coaster I was holding down, and she poured me a beer. A light one, because I was getting older and frankly, every year I got further away from thirty and closer to forty, the less alcohol and I agreed with each other.

"So what brings you by? I thought I was going to see you after my shift."

"If I said nachos, would you believe me?"

"I would not." She smiled, jutting her hip out to one side and resting her fisted hand on it, a gesture that managed to scream *Spit it out already* without her having to utter a single word.

"If I told you I wanted to go spy on someone but didn't want to go alone, would you believe me?"

Her posture relaxed instantly, and she leaned across the bar, conspiratorially close. Some of her glittery eyeshadow had fallen onto her cheeks, making her look like a fairy princess, if fairy princesses smelled like deep-fried cheese and pilsner. "Who are we spying on?" she whispered, though it was more of a stage whisper, since there was no one beside me and the music was too loud.

I quickly gave her a rundown of what had happened this morning and how the appearance of Mayor on my doorstep had me turning my suspicions toward Mick. What I didn't mention was how my suspicions had previously fixated on Bruno. I didn't think Kitty would be rushing to be my partner in crime if she knew I thought her current crush might be a killer.

Kitty let out a low whistle, then leaned away from the bar, looking thoughtfully around the room. "I know the guy can be a real piece of work, but do we really think Mick could kill someone?"

I gave a half shrug, because that was the same conversation I'd been having with myself all day long, and the answer always came back unclear.

"We don't really *know* him all that well, you know? He's not exactly a community joiner, and whenever he does participate in things, it's usually just to stir the pot in some way or another. And look, I don't want it to be *anyone* we know, but if it has to be someone . . ."

Dislike wasn't reason alone to suspect Mick, but there were certainly plenty of pieces of circumstantial evidence pointing me in his direction. Nothing that a jury would convict him on, or even that Tom could arrest him on, but that was also why I wanted Kitty to come with me and scope things out. Tom couldn't ignore it if both of us saw something worth sharing.

Plus, there was safety in numbers, and I felt like I'd be less spooked if I did this stakeout with someone besides just me.

"All right, look, I think this is more than a little nuts, but also you know I'm up for any adventure, no matter how weird it might be. Things close up here at eight. I'll meet you at your place, and we can go do . . . whatever this is you want to do after that, okay?"

I nodded, but there was a knot in my stomach. I was happy my friend was willing to help me, but a small part of me had been hoping she'd tell me not to do this or talk me out of it somehow.

I should have known better.

If you wanted the voice of reason, you didn't go to Kitty Cunningham, that was for darned sure.

Chapter
Twenty-Three

Kitty showed up at my cottage door at 8:10, wearing a bright-red winter coat and a sparkly beanie with an enormous fur pom-pom on the top. Subtle stakeout attire it was not.

"What are you *wearing*?" I asked, exasperated.

"My clothes?"

"You're going to stick out like a sore thumb in that no matter where we go on the island. You might as well be wearing a billboard that says *Look at Me!*"

Kitty seemed nonplussed by the whole thing, pulling off her hat as she stepped over the threshold.

As she did, a tiny gray streak darted past her and made a beeline in the direction of my bedroom. Kitty shrieked. "What was *that*? Was that a *rat*?"

She should have known better than anyone we didn't have rats on the island and hadn't since Smokey started his multi-generational cat colony. "No, I think that was the kitten. She must have been waiting outside and saw her moment when I opened up the door."

The kitten had slept hard on the couch the night before but woken me well before dawn to be let out, part of the reason I'd been so early getting to work and had time to witness what was going on down at the docks. I should thank her for multiple reasons. First, she had asked to go out instead of inviting herself to use one of my potted plants—which were all fake, so they would have been pretty hard to clean—and second, she might have helped me get one step closer to whoever Jeff's killer really was.

Maybe she was the real detective here.

Which convinced me the name I'd come up with for her was perfectly suited, after all.

"She's just letting herself in now?" Kitty asked, peering around the corner to see if she could spot the small bundle of fluff. Good luck; the cat made herself known only when she wanted to. This also settled things once and for all: I was going to have to buy some cat supplies, because it looked as if the universal cat distribution system had finally fixed its eyes on me, and I'd been chosen.

She wasn't giving me much choice in the matter.

"In fairness," I said, "she was always letting herself in. I think we've just reached the point where she's stopped asking for permission. I guess she's decided she owns the house."

"Yeah, I've heard that'll happen. Are you going to tell her she's wrong?"

"Wait until you see her, and you tell me if you could ever kick something that cute and fluffy out of your house." I shook my head. "No, I think I've just been suckered into cat ownership."

"You seem really torn up about it."

"I'm not, but I'm sure some of my furniture will be." My attention turned back to Kitty's bright-red jacket, and I gave my head a shake. "I can't believe I told you we were going to spy on someone and you decided to wear quite possibly the loudest coat known to man."

"It was what I wore to work. I wasn't going to go home and change," she protested. "Besides, say someone sees us. We're out and about, doing whatever. What looks more suspicious— two ladies in head-to-toe black, or two ladies just out in their cozy winter apparel trying to look at some stars or go for a walk or whatever it is we can pretend to be doing? If we get spotted."

I had to admit she had a point. We'd look way less shady if we just pretended we were out for an evening stroll as opposed to hiding in Mick's bushes like we were burglars. Perhaps I should give Kitty a bit more credit for her foresight, but I was also pretty sure she had just made up that entire excuse on the spot to make up for having worn the jacket.

At least I knew she'd be able to think up a story on her toes if someone did ask us what we were up to.

I pulled on my own winter jacket, a puffy tortoiseshell number that went all the way down to my ankles. If you can't beat 'em, match 'em. It wasn't quite cold enough for me to need this jacket yet, but at the same time I didn't know how long we'd be out, and this would keep me warm for several hours if need be.

I hoped it wouldn't be that long, but I also didn't know precisely what I was hoping to see.

I had no idea how one even *did* a stakeout; everything I knew was something I'd seen in a movie, and that usually involved an exhausted cop or private investigator spending hour after hour in their car with bad fast food, cheap coffee, and too much time to think.

We didn't have cars, fast food, or days to sit around and keep an eye on Mick. I had to hope we spotted something fishy pretty quickly, because we couldn't just sit outside his house in our winter jackets until Thanksgiving.

Kitty and I donned our gloves, and I called into the house, "Okay, Nora, the big, scary humans are leaving. Try not to destroy anything while I'm out."

"Nora?" Kitty asked as I locked the cottage door behind us.

"Well, funny story about the name. Nora was a Dashiell Hammett character, from the Nick and Nora books. I actually got Nick and Nora confused with Tommy and Tuppence, these characters from books by Agatha Christie I really liked. Tuppence was this young upper-class wife who ran a detective agency with her husband, and they kept pretending to be great literary detectives as they tried to solve their cases. Christie got pretty meta with those ones, because she would reference Poirot as being a literary detective, meaning the characters in the Tommy and Tuppence books would have read Christie's other books."

"Sounds kind of full of herself, don't you think?"

"I mean, she was a best-selling author; I guess when you have money and fame, you can have a little fun with your own books. I don't know. Anyway, by the time I realized I'd mixed up the names, I'd already started calling her Nora, and it just kind of fit. I don't think I can call her Tuppence. I think if she was an older cat, I would have gone with Marple or something like that, but this seemed to suit her more."

"I'll take your word for it. Aside from that picture you sent me, all I've seen so far was her doing her best impression of the Flash."

Without our even realizing it, our conversation had taken us up the main hill of Split Pine, past Tom's place, and right up to the Gorley estate. Mick had paid handsomely to get this piece of property, because the Gorley family wasn't from Split Pine originally and every piece of land on the island was generally willed down through families. To buy in as an outsider, you either needed to develop new—which was rarely allowed—or you needed to find a property being sold off by the family. There were rules about owning property on Split Pine, all part of how the original founders had wanted to keep a close-knit community. If you didn't have family or an approved nonfamily party to will your property to after you passed away, then ownership of your property would revert back to the island on your death, and it would be up to the town council to decide on the appropriateness of allowing nonlocals to buy it.

There was less oversight in terms of who could buy property *from* locals, and that was how both Tom and Kitty had managed to buy places here with minimal fuss. Tom, first, because the person he'd bought his home from had been an enormous baseball fan. Kitty was already considered a local by most because she had been living with Seamus, so allowing her to buy her place from an elderly couple who decided to move to the mainland had been an easy decision all around.

But Mick hadn't charmed anyone; it had been his fortune that bought him onto the island, a rare occurrence. While the town council typically overlooked people looking to buy local real estate at a premium just so they could turn around and flip it or turn it into a short-term rental—which was not forbidden, just frowned on—they couldn't ignore Mick when he made an offer on the old hotel. His proposal to revamp and restore it to its old glory was simply more than the council could refuse because of how it would help support local tourism. When Judy Revere, who owned the largest estate in town with its prime location on top of the main hill on the island, passed away with no next of kin, the estate had returned to the island.

And oh boy had Mick wanted it.

Many members of the council wanted to turn it into a museum of local history—which it was frankly too big for—or make it another hotel. But ultimately Mick must have offered to pay about three times its value, because they agreed to sell it to him, and the rest was history. He got a mansion, one that he continued to retrofit and renovate until it basically looked like it had been dropped out of a Jane Austen adaptation onto a small Michigan island.

You could see it from the harbor, which I think was what Mick was most proud of, because that gave it a castle-like air of importance. People would go out of their way to walk by and photograph it as if someone important lived there, not just a really irritating man with a lot of money.

I didn't particularly care that Mick had bought the estate—no one else here could have afforded to keep her in such good repair—but I didn't love the message that Mick took away from the whole business. Because now he believed that everyone in town had a dollar value and that no matter what he wanted, if he put the right number of zeroes on a check, he could have it.

That was probably why my family had resisted all his attempts to buy our undeveloped piece of land.

Now, looking up at his huge home from the road, more than anything, I felt annoyance. I was annoyed at how he had bought his way into this town and then resisted any measures to actually become a *part* of it. Even his house being at the highest point on the island spoke volumes: Mick thought he was above us all.

If I knew anything about wealthy people from years and years of serving them my pies, it was that they often believed they were entitled to things merely *because* they were wealthy.

Perhaps that was just my bias showing, because I was far from rich, but on more than one occasion someone had offered to buy the "secret recipe" for our lucky pies, as if it were just an extra pinch of nutmeg or some fancy seasoning that caused the magic to work.

No matter how often it happened, whether to me, my parents, or my grandparents before them, we'd told them the same thing: you can't buy luck. I think the idea that there was anything money *couldn't* buy really bothered them. Someone had once offered to buy the whole diner if we wouldn't sell the recipe, and someone else had insisted they'd buy a nearby property and develop their own diner to put us out of business, but that was just an idle threat. The town was designed to eliminate the concept of competition between businesses. Another diner would never be approved unless its menu was markedly different from ours.

Needless to say, that particular threat never came to be.

But all of Mick's threats, veiled and otherwise, about the property Grampy had set aside for me were starting to feel less like words and more like the promise of something seedier and possibly more violent.

Was Jeff's death just the first step in a plan to get me and my family out of the way? It seemed like a logical stretch, and I kept coming back to that invoice clutched in Jeff's hand. Was that just a coincidence? It felt too pointed to mean nothing.

Not to mention Mick's name on the harbor sheet, and the fact that he'd been out of the hotel when it was likely Jeff was being murdered. It wasn't *just* dislike that made me wonder what Mick's involvement in this might be.

Thanks to the scant amount of available land in town, fences were required to add charm, not appear as a deterrent, so Mick's estate was surrounded by a pristinely painted post-and-rail fence instead of the big gothic iron one he'd wanted.

This meant it was not only easy to see onto Mick's property but also easy to *access* his property, which was probably the exact reason he'd wanted the big scary fence to start with. I doubted that anyone until right this moment had had too much interest in sneaking into Mick's yard before. The Gorleys didn't hand out candy on Halloween, which one might think would make them a target for irritated local children, but instead the place just got left alone, as if no one wanted to take the trouble.

Except for me and Kitty. But we weren't planning to throw toilet paper in his trees; we were trying to see if he was hiding the darkest secret possible.

If he was hiding evidence that he was the killer, where would he put it?

"Let's check his shed," whispered Kitty, even though there was no one around to hear us.

A few lights were on in the house, one in a front room facing the street and another in an upper room I assumed was a bedroom. There were no signs of movement inside, and as far as I could tell, none of the lights at the rear of the house were on, since the backyard was pitch black, with nothing from the interior shining out to illuminate it.

The shed was a good suggestion. No one in town had garages, but a few people had sheds or carports to store their golf carts and other summer paraphernalia in. Those who could afford it might have boat storage on their property, but most people used the boatyard on the far side of the island, as it was a much easier way to get boats out of the water in the winter without a car or truck to tow them. Based on the size of Mick's shed, it looked as if his boat was stored with everyone else's in the yard.

Meaning there was plenty of room to store other things he might not want people to see if they visited his house.

We went to the very far end of his fence, as far as we could get from the house, before getting to the end of the property, then easily climbed over the post-and-rail fence. I was hoping this was far enough from the main windows for us to escape being spotted by anyone inside as well as to avoid setting off any motion detection lights Mick might have had installed.

As we climbed over, it occurred to me that if we *were* busted, this was going to be really hard to write off as a nice evening stroll. I decided to hope for the best rather than try to come up with a good lie in advance. I wanted to be in and out of here as quickly as possible. My greatest hope was that Mick had been so overconfident in himself and in his intelligence that he had messed up somewhere along the way in a super-obvious way and that Kitty and I would luck into finding the evidence tonight.

Breaking and entering hadn't exactly been on my agenda when I'd asked Kitty for her help tonight, yet the moment we'd arrived at Mick's property, this had just seemed like the logical thing to do. I knew we weren't going to take anything, but if there *was* evidence to be found, we could at least put Tom on the right track to finding the true killer.

He'd told me to stay out of things, and instead I'd gone and roped his sister into helping me. I knew it was all a terrible decision, but I'd gotten myself so fixated on figuring out this mystery that I knew I wouldn't be able to focus on anything else until I got an answer one way or the other about what Mick's involvement was.

Kitty and I snuck across the side yard and along the far side of the shed, the side facing away from the house. To call the thing a shed really was an insult to the building, because even though it wasn't big enough to fit Mick's boat, it was certainly big enough to fit several pieces of large equipment. It was probably the same size as my little cottage, and based on its condition, I wouldn't be surprised to learn it had cost more as well.

I should ask Mick one day; I was sure he would love to tell me that his riding lawn mower lived in a nicer house than I did.

There were large windows on all four sides of the shed, giving us a clear view inside and all the way through to the house. As I'd predicted, there were no lights on in the back. I'd actually been in Mick's house a small number of times, as he occasionally liked to throw a party to lure investors to the hotel, and he would invite all the local business owners on the island. He did this every few years or so, and I was pretty sure one of the major reasons he did it was to show off whatever new and exciting renovation project he'd just completed. With those few exceptions, I didn't think he'd ever had anyone over.

The mansion's large kitchen was in the back corner closest to us, and Beth, Mick's full-time cook, would be off for the night. Unless someone had snuck downstairs for a late-night snack, the kitchen would remain dark. I just needed to hope no one decided to peep out at us from the upstairs windows, because they'd have no problem spotting us and we'd have no clue we were being watched.

I tried the latch on the side door of the shed and was genuinely surprised to find it unlocked.

Inside the shed was a pristine golf cart with the Gorley name on a vanity plate on the back and the hotel's logo on the front. The aforementioned riding mower was parked behind it. An array of garden instruments were neatly organized on one of the walls, while general tools and two sets of golf clubs were stored on the opposite wall.

There was quite a lot of sports equipment in here, which maybe shouldn't have been surprising. The hotel offered a robust variety of services, and it stood to reason that Mick and

Jersey would take advantage of those offerings. There were tennis rackets on the wall and tidily stacked cans of fresh yellow tennis balls. Several buckets were filled with golf balls—there was a driving range about a quarter mile out of town—and two kayaks were neatly strapped to the rafters.

Two bright-red bicycles that would match nicely with Kitty's coat were stationed behind the riding mower. It was absolutely remarkable how clean everything in here looked, as if it was all ready to be photographed for a catalog shoot.

Not even a musty rag or pile of garbage to be seen in the whole place, let alone anything that had a giant neon sign hanging over it screaming *Evidence!*

"What exactly are we looking for?" Kitty asked, keeping her voice hushed. Even though we were a good distance from the house, it was impossible to know if someone might step outside for a breath of fresh air, or in Jersey's case, a noxious puff on her vape pen.

"I don't know. If it was him on Jeff's boat this morning, then anything that might connect him to the boat or to Jeff. He would have had his own invoices, as they did business together, so that wouldn't help, but anything that looks like it shouldn't be here."

Kitty glanced around the space. "I hate to say it, but the only thing that looks out of place here right now is us. My *house* isn't even this clean. My shed looks like someone opened a gardening magazine and set off a bomb, then threw all the debris in together just to see what would happen."

I had seen Kitty's shed, and this was actually a very fair assessment of the chaos within.

I sighed. "I'm not really sure. There has to be *something*, though. I can feel it in my gut that it was him. We just need a reason to make Tom see that's the case."

"Este, I know maybe it's a weird time to say this, because I'm literally squatting in someone's garden shed with you, but do you think it's possible that Tom could come to these conclusions on his own?"

I sat down on the rear seat of the golf cart, pulling my jacket around me more tightly, which made me realize just how cold it had gotten while we were out here. I scrubbed my palms over my face, taking in my surroundings and Kitty's gentle smile.

Sure, she had followed me here, she had been gung ho to participate, but she had a point. What was I *doing* here? Even if I found something, I couldn't take it with me and hand it over to Tom. He'd need to find a different legal reason to come get it himself.

I was just so focused on finding out who had killed Jeff that I'd somehow decided I was the only one who could do it, which wasn't fair to Tom. Still, I just felt a *need* to get to the bottom of this. It wasn't even about proving myself innocent. I just needed to know.

"Oh, Kitty, I feel like an idiot. Of course Tom could figure this out on his own. He's smart."

"Well, we're already here; we might as well see if Mick actually is a killer and not just a grade-A jerk." She shrugged it off as if this were a perfectly normal way for us to be spending a girls' evening, rather than making valiant efforts to learn how to knit or sampling the newest brainchild I had for a pie special.

She was already starting to go through some drawers at one of the nearby counters when suddenly the back kitchen and porch lights on the house both turned on. The pair of us ducked in unison, me still next to the golf cart and her across the shed where the tools were stored.

Kitty, whose vantage point was closer to the house than mine, slowly inched her way upward until she was just beside one of the windows and able to peek out.

"*Kitty*," I hissed. "Get *down*." It was really hard to project a sense of urgency when you were loudly stage-whispering, but I did my best.

She waved a hand at me as if brushing me aside and continued to peer out the window. After a moment she dropped to the ground like she'd had her ankles taken out from under her and waved at me again, this time more urgently and in a *Come here* gesture.

In the most elegant manner possible while hunched down in a squat and wearing my bulkiest winter jacket, I shuffled across the room until I was beside her.

"It's Mick," she whispered. "And Jersey."

I wish I were a better person and that my immediate response to hearing Jersey's name weren't making a face.

We waited a moment, either to see if the lights went out again or if the Gorleys had spotted us and were on their way over to the shed right now to swing the doors open and tell us they had called the police.

Seconds ticked by, and nothing happened.

As my knees began to protest from staying crouched down, I finally decided to risk taking a peek. I followed the method Kitty had used earlier, staying to the side of one of the large windows so the top of my head wouldn't give me away as I stood up, and then when there was just enough room for me to see, I peered out the window across the lawn.

I wasn't sure what had called Mick and Jersey outside, but Mick was still standing on the back deck, and Jersey was pacing the grass a few yards away, furiously puffing on her vape pen. It was obvious she hadn't been planning to come outside for long, as she was wearing her pajamas underneath her jacket, and her hair was done up in satin rollers. It was hard to tell from this distance, but I was pretty sure she had gel patches under her eyes.

Between puffs on her vape, which billowed out into the air around her like exaggerated dragon's breath, I could hear her voice rising, even though I couldn't quite distinguish the words.

The window next to me had a crank to open it, and I decided to take the risk, in case I might actually be able to make out whatever Jersey was shouting about.

I reached over and gave the window crank a few turns, letting out a breath of relief when it didn't make a loud squealing sound and opened easily for me.

"—don't think it's very fair that you make all these promises and then nothing happens."

"Jersey, come inside. This display of histrionics is beneath your status, and certainly not what I would expect from someone your *age*." The withering emphasis Mick placed on the word was enough to make me recoil in resentment, and I wasn't even the one he had been insulting.

Jersey said nothing, or at least nothing I could hear, but I was disappointed not to be able to have seen her reaction better.

I darted a quick glance over at Kitty to make sure she was hearing this too, and based on her rapt expression and leaned-in posture, she was absorbing every word right along with me.

"No, Daddy. This is it. I've had enough. You say *Jersey, one more year and you'll be in charge. Jersey, five more years and you'll have your own hotel. Jersey, if you're just patient, then moving to this stupid island will be worth it.* But *when*, Daddy, when will it be worth it? Because I'm tired of waiting."

Whatever Mick said in reply to that, I couldn't hear much of it, but it made Jersey laugh in a way that had nothing to do with humor and sent a chill down my spine.

I knew full well how petty, vindictive, and downright cruel Jersey could be. I'd been on the receiving end of a fair share of those nasty laughs in my time, and I wondered if Mick realized just how much of a monster he had created in his spoiled daughter.

"Oh, is that the case?" she snarked. "Well, you keep that up and maybe I'll find my own way to get what I want."

"And what does *that* mean?" His own tone was icy. It was hard to imagine that this was a father and daughter who, at least sometimes, seemed to love each other. They more easily could have been labeled mortal enemies.

Though I supposed no one could get you where it hurts quite like family could.

"Let's just say that if I don't see some progress on this new hotel plan of yours, and *soon*, then I'm going to tell them everything I know about you and the fruit man."

One more cloud of smoke billowed out into the air, and Jersey stomped up the back stairs of the house. As she brushed past her father, he grabbed her by the arm, hard, and held her in place.

A breath caught in my throat. I squinted at them through the window, unable to hear if he was saying anything to her but wondering if a moment might come when Kitty and I needed to come out of hiding and do the unthinkable by saving Jersey.

Whatever was said between father and daughter wrapped up quickly, and she pulled her arm free of him and made her way back inside. Mick stood on the back deck a few moments longer, probably letting himself cool down, or letting her words sink in—it was hard to tell which. He stared out into the dark night, his eyes grazing over his property, and I realized almost too late he was about to look directly at us.

I dropped down, hoping I hadn't been too slow, and held my breath. The light coming from the house would probably have obscured his view inside the glass, and we were fairly well hidden, but nevertheless, things could always take a turn south in a moment.

Seconds ticked by. The lights at the back of the house went out, and finally I let out my breath, knowing we were in the clear.

I waited a few more seconds for good measure, just in case it was a plot to put us at ease so he could catch us out in a more dramatic fashion, and finally I pushed myself back up to my feet.

The plastic container I was using for balance tipped and rattled precariously, almost sending me sprawling back onto the ground or creating a new ruckus by falling over itself. I held it tight, steadying both of us.

Which was when I realized I was hugging an open recycling bin. Something inside glinted in the low moonlight, and in spite of telling myself I wasn't going to touch any potential evidence, I reached in and grabbed it, thankful I had worn gloves tonight, since my ability to resist temptation was basically zero.

It was a plastic container.

More specifically, it was the exact same kind of plastic container I'd found in the case behind my diner. An empty strawberry clamshell. But whereas the ones I'd discovered before had borne the Evergreen Produce label, this one was different. It depicted an illustration of an island and several bright strawberries surrounded by vines and sweet little white flowers.

The name on the package was *Summer Island Farm*, but what caught my attention was the notation under that name: *Split Pine, MI.*

This label was for a fruit farm on this island.

But we didn't have any produce distributors on the island. Unless you counted the farm, but they were only growing items for themselves and for the summertime farmers' markets; they weren't a major business. Split Pine wasn't an export economy. We were a tourist island.

One corner of the label was peeling, and my gut told me that, as if it were a hangnail, I should keep picking. So I pulled back the label as best I could with my gloves on, surprised by how easily the Summer Island sticker peeled away.

Revealing the old Evergreen Produce label underneath.

Chapter
Twenty-Four

When I'm nervous, I bake.

In fairness, baking is generally my first response to almost any heightened emotion. But baking was just a way for me to put my body on autopilot so my brain could shift into deep thinking mode.

Kitty and I were back at my cottage, and I'd grudgingly left the mysterious clamshell behind. I couldn't exactly walk it over to Tom's place and explain where it had come from, but I really wished I had it with me still. Partially because I didn't want it to vanish, and partially because I was worried I had imagined it. It had been so dark in the shed, after all, and part of me wondered if I'd made it up.

I had tried my best to snap a photo of it in the dark but hadn't dared use my camera's flash, so there was no telling how the quality would turn out, even if I was able to use it for anything down the road. I'd just needed something, some kind of proof to take with me that I'd seen what I'd seen, even if I didn't understand what it meant.

Kitty was perched on one of the barstools at my kitchen island, sipping a mug of homemade hot chocolate and watching me work. She knew when I got into moods like this it was often best to let me move around the kitchen like a flour-coated dervish until my brain finally calmed down enough for me to carry on a normal conversation.

Nora was still here when we'd returned and hadn't—to my knowledge—destroyed anything or marked her territory in any of my fake plants. She had warmed to Kitty enough that she was hanging out in the same room, but she wasn't about to sit on the stool next to her. In fact, it seemed from the kitten's serious expression that she was a little annoyed to have a human sitting on *her* regular chair.

Instead, Nora was in her loaf form on the back of my couch, struggling to keep her eyes open but jerking to alertness the second one of us spoke or moved too much. She seemed to want to go to sleep very badly but still wasn't totally sure she could trust us.

I hadn't pulled out any pie dough before we left on our adventure to Mick's, so instead of making a pie, I was mindlessly assembling a crumble. I still had some nice apples on the counter from our last produce delivery, some lovely Honeycrisps that would give off a nice, sweet flavor. Normally when baking, especially baking pies, I favored a Granny Smith, because the green apple had a tart bite to it that offset the more sugary aspects—especially in our signature caramel apple pie—and kept things from being too sickly sweet.

With a crumble, though, I found it was okay to rely on anything you had on hand.

I set about peeling the apples while the oven warmed up.

With the fruit in my hand, I circled back to my biggest question, the one that made no sense even now.

"Why *strawberries*?" I asked.

While the question was more rhetorical, Kitty decided she didn't want to be left out of my one-sided conversation with the universe.

"What do you think it means? The strawberries, that is."

I started to peel another apple. I wasn't going to make a huge dessert, as it was just the two of us, but I also didn't want to deny either of us the option of having seconds. Anyone who designed a meal and didn't allow for there to be seconds was a cruel person indeed. Always make too much food. Leftovers are welcome any day over leaving someone feeling like they didn't get enough.

That was always my Gran's motto, and I carried it with me still.

"I don't know what to think, honestly. But everything keeps coming back to strawberries. That was what Jeff shorted me on my order. It was what the containers I found behind the diner were for. And now this weird fake-labeled shell? And what does Mick have to do with all of it? Was the clamshell a mock-up, maybe for some kind of business he was planning to start? All I can think is that maybe he was trying to buy the business off Jeff but something went south, and when the deal fell apart, Mick killed him."

"Over strawberries."

Out loud, it sounded insane. Who would murder someone over fruit? But the idea that Mick might have been trying to buy Jeff's business certainly fit. It would give him a total monopoly on our produce here, and Bruno and I would be forced to turn to him for our orders, meaning he could charge us an arm and a leg for his goods.

The town council would back him, because the island's noncompete arrangements would bar Bruno and I from finding an outside vendor that we could go to more cheaply than going to Mick. In a way, it was genius. After years of the council using our age-old rules to deny Mick the things he had wanted to do in the past, he had finally found the perfect way to twist those rules into a weapon.

But there was one small hitch: Mick didn't own a farm. So unless he was planning to use Jeff as his grower, I wasn't sure how the rest of the plan came together.

It was, however, easy to see that the plan had fallen apart.

Was the first crack when Jeff had failed to show up with the berries this week? He'd brought a small number for the grocery store, but he hadn't had enough for my order, let alone for all the empty cartons I'd found in the case where Nora had gotten trapped. Did Mick's entire fruit empire plan hinge around being able to sell us on that first batch? Heaven knew I'd been looking forward to getting my hands on fresh berries all month; I probably would have paid twice what they were worth.

Did Jeff simply not have the fruit? It was November, after all, and strawberries were naturally a June-bearing fruit in Michigan, with some varieties giving off berries for months to follow. But the brightest and best of the bunch usually came in June. Typically, any other fruits we received through the season were shipped in from California or Mexico, meaning they were never quite as tasty as the locally grown stuff, but I was always more than happy to take what I could get for that little taste of summertime when the first snow hit.

I started to cut my apples into slices and then cubes, then dumped them into a big mixing bowl. To the bowl I added just the tiniest bit of flour, a healthy amount of sugar, some lemon juice to keep the apples from browning while I prepared the rest of the dish, some melted butter, and a few spices. Most recipes called for only cinnamon, but I couldn't leave things alone when it came to "basic" recipes and always erred on the more-is-more side, even with my seasonings. If I was already adding cinnamon, why not cardamom? And if I was adding cardamom, then why not just the tiniest little bit of freshly grated nutmeg?

I poured the apple mixture into a baking dish and quickly tossed together the crumbly part of the crumble, which was basically just sugar, oats, flour, butter, and sugar, mixed until it looked like . . . well . . . a crumble. At work I used a stand mixer to make things easier and faster, but at home I liked to revel in the simple pleasures of baking and did as much of it by hand as I could. With the glossy butter-coated apples waiting in their dish, I took the crumble ingredients and tossed them with my hands. I squeezed the room temperature butter between my fingers, feeling like a little kid playing in a sandbox. But this truly was the best way to make a crumble. With the ingredients combined into perfectly imperfect clumps, I dumped that on top of the apples and threw the whole thing into the oven, all while contemplating this new avenue we had discovered tonight.

"You enjoy that way too much," Kitty said. "An hour ago we were hiding in a shed trying to find a potential killer, and now you're covered in cinnamon looking as happy as a clam."

I couldn't help myself; I licked the buttery spice mix off my thumb before washing my hands.

"It helps me think. But I still can't wrap my head around anyone getting killed over fruit," I said.

"Me either, but you just need to open a newspaper on any average day to find two or three stupider reasons for someone getting killed. It doesn't take much, it seems, if someone is looking for an excuse."

"We'd just met him, though. No one had even heard of Jeff before he got to the island. So what could make someone go from meeting a stranger to murdering them?"

"Except I think what we're learning is that Jeff and Mick weren't strangers."

"If that's the case, do you think Mick was the only reason Jeff was here? And what about Denny? I still don't think his death could have possibly been a coincidence."

"That's where you lose me, hon, sorry. I know you want to have this all be some super-elaborate puzzle where every sneaky, terrible thing is connected, but I think there's a real chance that Denny just died—may he rest in peace—and Jeff and Mick saw an opportunity."

We mulled over the possibilities until the oven timer chimed. Unfortunately, Kitty needed to excuse herself from enjoying the crumble fresh with ice cream, as she needed to get back home. Piper was with Seamus for the night, but since he started work a lot earlier than Kitty, they had to meet in the morning so Kitty could take on school drop-off duty.

I sent her home with a Tupperware container that had enough for both her and Piper and then some, and once she was gone, I served myself some of the crumble.

I baked to settle my brain, but I didn't actually want to eat sweet treats constantly. Which was probably a saving grace for me at the diner, because if I *was* inclined to sample all my goods throughout the day, my waistline would be in real trouble.

The crumble was good, especially with a dollop of ice cream on top, and it didn't take long for a certain kitten to get a whiff of what I had in my bowl. She crept along the top of the couch until she was right behind me, then placed a tentative paw on my shoulder.

I froze.

Nora had been content to be in the same room as me, even on the same couch as me, and I had been happy with those baby steps, assuming it would be quite some time before she braved letting me pet her or considered getting cuddly. I also knew that even if she stayed, she had been outside at least several months, based on her size, and I shouldn't be surprised if she was *never* a cuddly cat. A few of my friends on the island had taken in reformed ferals, and while they became good house cats, they never lost the uneasy edge of having been out in the wild at the start of their lives.

Yet Nora now had two little paws on my shoulder, and I could hear her purring loudly.

Sure, it was because I had ice cream, but if I could buy a cat's affection with the tiniest bit of dairy, I wasn't too proud not to. She sniffed the side of my face aggressively, then stepped farther down my chest until she reached the bowl in my lap. I was already done, but there was still a bit of the melted ice cream pooling in the bottom of the bowl. I coated my spoon with it and lifted it up for her.

At first my movement made her tense, and I thought she might run, but the allure of food was simply too strong.

She sat on my lap and daintily licked ice cream off my spoon until it was totally clean, then she settled herself in and started to groom her paws and face, all while sitting with me.

And that was it.

She had officially manipulated me into keeping her.

Chapter
Twenty-Five

I arrived at work the next day early, but not so early that my curiosity would have an opportunity to get the best of me. After yesterday's encounter on the dock and my too-close-for-comfort experience in Mick's shed, I knew I had to take a few steps back.

Finding what I had in Mick's recycling bin had convinced me more than ever that he was the most likely killer. And even if he *wasn't* the killer, he knew more than he'd been sharing about his connection to Jeff.

A restless sleep hadn't offered me any further insights into the strawberry scheme, but when I'd woken, I'd decided to do a search online for the name on the new packaging label. A domain had been registered to Summer Island Farms, but no website existed, and my limited detective work in seeing who owned the page came to a very annoying conclusion.

Jeff Kelly.

While that did make the little hairs on the back of my neck stand up, it was also a useless revelation. I'd assumed he was involved, and it did nothing to tie this enterprise to Mick. All I had was a picture of a label for a farm that didn't exist.

I set about my morning routine of getting the coffee started, pulling out the premade doughs to allow them to come to room temperature, and getting the raw ingredients out to make fresh dough to replace those. I popped several pounds of butter into the freezer so it would be nice and cold when I needed it but not completely frozen.

With the morning chores done, I was feeling just about ready to take on the day. I had enough time to set up the Thanksgiving display outside before we opened. Normally, I'd have done it right after Halloween, but I'd only gotten as far as taking down the spooky-season decor and hadn't actually done anything more involved for the next big holiday, which was just around the corner.

We had a small storage locker right outside the diner's side door that was painted red to match the rest of the building, but the two units weren't connected, meaning I had to go outside if I wanted to get access to my decor items.

The sun was starting to come up and Seamus would be here any minute, so I wasn't feeling too uneasy about rummaging through the storage unit by myself. I really hoped Tom would figure out who had killed Jeff—if it was Mick or someone else—sooner rather than later so I could go back to living my life without jumping at every shadow.

I'd lived in this town my entire life, and this was the first time I could ever remember being anxious about being here.

I left the back door to the diner open a crack while I went into the locker, mostly so I could hear if Seamus or Rosie arrived through the front but also so I could more easily bring the boxes inside without needing to fuss about opening multiple doors.

The storage locker wasn't as professionally organized as Mick's shed had been, but there was a certain logic to its chaos.

Aside from a few outdoor lawn games we kept around to use in the summer and multiple sandwich boards that would guide people to our diner from the harbor, the whole unit was just for seasonal decor. My grandparents hadn't been too keen on holiday decorations, thinking the luck motif inside the diner was probably more than enough when it came to distinctive theming. My mom, on the other hand, was wild about holidays. Obsessed might have been the better word for it. She would start planning her holiday DIYs months in advance. Right after Christmas, she would be hand-stitching heart garlands for Valentine's. When the New Year rang in, she'd be crafting St. Patrick's Day–inspired pom-pom wreaths and blowing the yolks out of eggs so she could have enough real eggshells ready to dye before Easter.

The woman had never met a holiday she didn't love. If there was a holiday we could celebrate without being culturally insensitive, she was doing it.

The March family was a nice modern blend of Jewish and Catholic but practiced neither aspect with any kind of regularity. She figured if we could be a little of everything, so could the diner.

She'd also done a remarkable job of keeping the decor in logical order, and I'd done my best in the years after her death to keep her traditions—and most of her handmade decorations—alive in her stead.

The boxes in the locker were all color coded by event. The red ones on the bottom shelf—which were the most numerous—were all Christmas, Hanukkah, and winter-adjacent holidays. Green was for St. Patrick's Day, pink was for Valentine's Day, yellow was for Easter, and orange was for Halloween. Once one holiday ended, we pushed the next one up to the front of the shelves and moved the last one to the back. It meant things were always cycling their way forward.

Orange was now at the very back of the unit while one large brown bin awaited me, a slim barrier between me and the oncoming wall of Christmas decor.

I took the brown bin down from the shelf, not needing to read the custom *Thanksgiving* label pressed to the top, and set it aside while I locked the storage unit up again, then hauled the bin back inside and right through to the front of the diner.

The hay bales I'd set up for Halloween were still piled up out front and sprinkled with fake leaves and a few real pumpkins. By taking away the skeletons and witches, I'd been able to give myself a seasonally appropriate reprieve for a few days.

Opening up the tote, I was greeted by a collection of old friends. On the very top, to keep it from being damaged, was an elaborate plaster turkey statue my mother had discovered at a thrift shop on the mainland probably thirty years earlier.

I had to assume it had never cost a lot of money to begin with, and when she bought it, she said she'd paid two dollars, but she had also spent hours lovingly repainting it and drilling tiny holes into the plaster to add in meticulously arranged feathers, giving the whole thing kind of a hideous heirloom quality.

It wasn't fine art, but I loved it, and our patrons seemed to love it as well. It had gained the nickname Gordo at some point when my mother was still alive, and people were still calling him Gordo to this day.

Gordo was about the size of a beach ball, and I placed him on top of the highest bale of hay at a place of prominence, where everyone coming and going would be able to see him.

Seamus ambled down the path toward me as I was working. "Gordo season here already?" he asked.

"You know it."

"Might need to start thinking about something Gordo themed for the menu," he mused. "A Gordo-dito, perhaps. Like a turkey-themed quesadilla situation."

"I can't decide if that's one of the best ideas you've ever had or the most disgusting thing I've ever heard you say."

"You know what they say about genius, boss; it toes the line between madness and perfection."

"I don't think anyone has ever said that before today."

Seamus shrugged. "You need help with the display?"

"No, but thanks for offering. Thanksgiving might be the lightest box of them all. This won't take long."

Because the display would be up only about three weeks before giving way to Christmas, Mom hadn't been nearly so dedicated to turkey-day crafts, but the popularity of Gordo more than made up for the scant number of other decorations.

There was a bunting on twine that spelled out *Happy Thanksgiving Turkeys*, which I strung along the middle bale. We had an old green metal milk jug that we used for seasonal sprigs. I removed the blackened dead branches, which were covered in spider webs, but added in a few more festive cotton branches with stems of cheerfully colored autumnal leaves.

The rest of the box had decor for inside the restaurant, so I followed Seamus in and went from table to table, adding a stem of maple leaves tied with feathers into the small vase at each. When I was finished, the effect was subtle but charming, giving the restaurant a decidedly fall vibe.

I took a leaf garland from the bottom of the bin and put it inside the glass display case so that anyone stopping to buy treats to go would also get a cheerful reminder of the season. The last item was a little countertop-sized turkey holding a sign that read *Gobble Gobble*, which I set on the cash register.

Happy with my efforts—and successfully distracted long enough for someone to join me—I took the bin out the back door and to the storage locker.

After putting the empty tote back in its place and locking things up again, I turned to head back inside and stopped dead in my tracks, all the blood draining from my face and a gasp sticking in my throat.

There, pinned to the back door of the diner with a steak knife, was one of the Evergreen Produce invoices, identical to the one I'd seen Jeff clutching in his hand.

But this one didn't have my order details on it.

In bold black pen, it simply read *STOP LOOKING. OR ELSE.*

Chapter Twenty-Six

Tom stared at the invoice pinned to my door for a while before turning his attention back to me. The expression on his face said volumes. There was a tiny bit of *This is concerning* with a nice dash of *Why me?* and a more-than-healthy dose of *I told you so*.

For a moment, all he said was, "Mmm."

"Mmm? Mmm what?" I waved my hand at the door. "Come on, Tom, this is nuts. Someone on this island is a killer, and now *this*?"

"Mm-hmm," he elaborated. "Remind me again what I said to you the other day when you came by with bribery pie?"

"It wasn't bribery. It was buttermilk."

"What did I say?"

"You told me to stay out of it."

"And I'm going to hazard a guess here, because I'm such a good cop, that you probably decided not to listen to me and you *didn't* stay out of it. But I'm just guessing." His eyes cut meaningfully to the note and the knife.

I didn't answer.

"Mm-hmm," he said again. He pulled a pair of rubber gloves and a bag out of his jacket pocket but paused to snap a few photos on his phone, both close up and also a few steps back, to show the note as it was attached to the door. Once he was satisfied he had captured the whole scene, he removed the knife from the door and put both it and the note in his waiting evidence bag. "Tell me everything one more time."

I went over my activities that morning, knowing that whoever had done this must have been nearby, perhaps watching me from the woods, as I went through the storage locker and took out my things. They'd waited until I was out front before approaching the diner. Which meant they'd either come right before Seamus arrived, or they'd been bold enough to act while he was inside.

I'd had the stereo in the kitchen on, but I was still surprised that neither Seamus nor I had heard someone jamming a *knife* into the door.

My overly suspicious brain did briefly consider that it might have *been* Seamus, but I threw that notion away almost as quickly as my brain offered the suggestion. Not only did he not make sense to me as a killer—largely because he was my friend—but it would have been pretty risky for him to try to pull this off when I was expecting him, or while I was inside setting up the tables. There were too many chances I'd catch him in the act.

That same logic did tell me that whoever really had done this was bold, and bordering on reckless, because they'd done it when I was so close by.

Someone willing to take such a bold risk—especially with the sun rising and a chance they might be seen—was either sure they wouldn't be caught, or they didn't care.

And I had to admit that both of those options frightened me.

I thought I'd been careful enough on the dock yesterday morning to avoid being seen, but it was obvious that someone must have spotted me after all and waited until an ideal moment to issue their threat, rather than coming for me at the time.

They'd made their case pretty clearly: I was stepping over the line and getting too close to something big.

And while this did make me want to back off—in fact, it made me want to go hide in my cottage until all this blew over—it also told me that this person was getting concerned because I was close to the truth.

I had to tell Tom what I'd found, because at this point keeping it hidden was only going to get me into more trouble.

"Okay, so I may or may not have been doing my own poking around. You already know what I saw on the dock yesterday."

"Please tell me you weren't on the boat. I know you said you saw it from your deck, but you have to appreciate I'm not going to take your word for that, given everything else that's going on."

"I wasn't on the boat," I said indignantly, though it was probably fair of him to assume I *might* have done something that silly. I resented the implication nevertheless. "I was on the dock."

"Yeah, that's so much better." He heaved a sigh. "So when I told you to stay out of things, your best way of doing that was to go—the very next morning, I might add—and snoop around at a crime scene."

"*Near* a crime scene. I was trying to see if there were more of those cases on board, because the whole strawberry container thing was bothering me. And it *should* have bothered me, because I found something else yesterday." I pulled out my own phone and showed him the poorly lit photos I'd taken in Mick's shed.

"What am I looking at here, exactly?" He squinted, holding the phone up close to his face when zooming in failed to give him the clue he was looking for.

"That's a strawberry clamshell from Mick Gorley's recycling. It has a label for a fruit farm on Split Pine that doesn't exist, and under that was a label for Jeff's farm. They're connected." I kept gesturing to the phone screen.

"Este."

"Tom."

"Do you need me to ask you how you got a hold of Mick's recycling?"

I flushed, having known this was inevitable but also having hoped that my breakthrough might be enough to distract him from that particularly glaring issue.

"It was in his shed." I realized after saying this I should have just lied and said it had blown out of his recycle bin when it was on the curb, but that fib ran the risk of Mick being able to deny that it was his garbage.

"And did he let you into his shed?"

I bit my lip.

Tom handed my phone back to me. "Please keep the back door locked today, okay? When are you finished your shift?"

"Three." And then I would need to head to the pet store to get some items for Nora.

"I will be here at ten to three to walk you home. If you could avoid going anywhere by yourself for a while, that would be very much appreciated. I know your schedule is . . . difficult, but perhaps you could coordinate with your grandfather, or Seamus, to make sure someone is always with you."

"You think this person is serious, don't you?"

"I don't think people leave notes like this for fun. Which leads me to my next request. *Stop it*. Stop looking at this murder.

You're going to get yourself into trouble, Este, and I don't particularly feel like having to solve *your* murder too. Capisce?"

"Your concern for my well-being is touching," I said sarcastically.

"I like you alive, so please let me do my job, okay?"

"Okay." The truth was, even though I was digging my feet in like a stubborn mule, that was just my gut reaction to being told what to do. I was plenty scared by the warning and had no interest whatsoever in finding out what *or else* meant to this person.

"I'll see you at three. And try to avoid touching the outside of this door, if you don't mind. I'm going to see if I can lift any prints off it when I come back. Not that it'll help much; I'm sure your staff have theirs all over the place, and it might be hard to find anything unique. I'm hoping the note gives me more to go on." With that, he wandered off, staring into the contents of the evidence bag and shaking his head like he couldn't believe his dumb luck.

I felt for him. You move to an island where the regular population is only around five hundred people and there's a decades-long record of it being one of the safest towns in America, and suddenly you're stuck unraveling a murder. So much for a nice, peaceful career.

I returned to the kitchen, locking the back door behind me, and found Seamus and Rosie both standing in the diner doorway staring at me. They'd both seen the note, because I'd been outside for so long gawking at it that Seamus had come looking for me, and Rosie had seen it because she wanted to know why both of us were hanging out outside instead of opening the restaurant.

"Does he know who did it?" she asked. Today she had swapped her normal uniform of Taylor Swift–themed shirts for a pink-and-black tee with a Barbie logo on it.

I shook my head. "He's going to see if there are any prints, but I'm not holding my breath. If someone wanted us to know who they were, they would have signed it. I'm sure they wore gloves."

"Gosh, that's scary," Rosie breathed. "Maybe we should get a security camera?"

The same thought had occurred to me since Tom arrived. If we'd had a camera positioned outside the back door, we could have seen who'd done this, and even before that might have been able to spot whoever had left the container in the woods. I had never really thought about having a camera installed before, because there'd never been a reason, but right now it was seeming like a pretty good idea.

"I'll order something, but you know how it is getting stuff here from the mainland in winter. It'll be ages before it gets here." We didn't have an electronics shop on the island; there was nowhere I could just pop in and get an outdoor-friendly camera. Meaning that for the next week or so, we would be totally blind to anything happening behind the diner.

Rosie rubbed her arms and wrapped her cardigan around her, even though the kitchen was toasty warm, with multiple ovens heating and Seamus's grill primed for the breakfast rush.

"Hey, hey," I told her. "It's okay. Nothing is going to happen. Someone just wanted to spook me, and they did a great job of it, but that's it. We'll be fine. Tom says as long as I stop sticking my nose into things, I shouldn't have anything to worry about."

Seamus let out a snort. "If your life depends on you minding your own business, you might be in real trouble."

I swatted him. "Uncalled for."

"But true." He dodged another slap.

"Go back to making breakfasts before I fire you," I said.

This normal banter seemed to bring Rosie back to a grounded state, but before she went back into the restaurant area, she crossed the gap between us and wrapped me in a big hug. Rosie was a petite girl, and her hug radiated a protective ferocity I wasn't expecting from her. The gesture was so lovely I let it linger until she finally released me, nodding like it was a job well done. "Don't you dare let something happen to you, understood?"

I had to keep a sudden emotional wave at bay to keep tears from springing to my eyes. These people were as much family to me as my own flesh and blood were, and I sometimes almost took their presence in my life for granted. It felt good to be reminded of how much I mattered to them. It told me that I should be careful, not just for my own benefit but for those around me as well.

Resolved, I returned to my baking station, ready to let the entire mystery go and leave it to Tom to solve. No more late-night sneaking around; no poking around website data or scoping out crime scenes. I had told Tom my theory about Mick, and now it was up to the island's actual cop to figure the rest of this out.

But in spite of my best intentions, there was a nagging feeling in the back of my mind that I shouldn't take a cowardly threat like the one on the door lying down.

I was so close.

I shook off that terrible instinct and unwrapped a premade pie dough. If I couldn't be trusted to mind my own business, then I would just have to keep myself busy until Tom came back.

Chapter
Twenty-Seven

The result of my working myself to distraction was a particularly delicious pie of the day that I had never made before. I had an abundance of carrots in the fridge that were on the older side—still good, but not fresh enough to be enjoyed raw anymore. I decided to do a spin on a pumpkin pie and make a carrot pie instead.

The unusual but seasonally fitting pie was a runaway hit, and when Tom showed up just before three, as promised, I had barely been able to snag a leftover piece for Grampy.

"What the heck is that?" Tom asked, lingering near the back entry as I put the remaining slice of orange pie into a takeout container.

"I'm pretty sure we've established that the thing I'm most well known for is pie. It's pie."

He rolled his eyes. "Don't be cheeky with me because you're annoyed I told you to stop acting like Nancy Drew."

"I'm not annoyed. It *is* pie."

"You know I meant what *kind* of pie."

"Carrot."

"Okay, now you're just making fun of me." He came a few steps closer and stared at the piece of pie sitting on the container. "Carrot? That looks like pumpkin pie."

"And yet. Carrot." His unwillingness to believe that the pie was made of a root vegetable was so endearing to me that I knew Grampy wasn't getting near this last piece. I handed it to Tom. "Here, try it. I promise it's not bribery pie. It's really good."

He looked as if he might reject the pie on principle, but I could tell his curiosity was getting the best of him. "If you insist."

"For science," I said. "Or luck."

"Is it lucky?" He gave it another long look, as if there might be some visual sign telling him.

"Could be." It wasn't.

I grabbed my jacket and waved to Rosie and Marcel before heading out the back door.

"Be honest with me about something, Este."

"As long as it isn't legally binding, sure."

"I'm not sure I want to know what that means, but I have to ask you about the pie. Whenever I bring up the whole luck thing, you're evasive about it. Is that all just a town rumor that your family embraced, or what's the deal? You can tell me the truth."

I had to laugh. Of all the things he could have brought up in this moment, with everything going on and all his annoyance about me snooping, he still wanted to know about the stupid *pie*.

"Let me put it in a way I think you might be able to appreciate. In baseball, pitchers want to throw strikes, right? That's pretty much their whole goal, to get out there and strike out three batters in a row. And your job as a batter was to go out and make that *not* happen."

"I'm not sure where you're going with this, but yes, you're right so far."

"Think of life as the strikeouts. That might be a little grim perspective-wise, but you go through the days and things just kind of go according to plan. Right? Okay, well, in baseball, sometimes a pitch gets thrown and something happens. The pitch was dead perfect leaving the pitcher's hand, but for some reason, something that can't be explained by science, that pitch *rises*, it doesn't fall into the glove, it goes right to the perfect spot, and it just *finds* your bat. Bam. Home run. Those moments feel like magic sometimes, right? You couldn't tell someone later how it worked, but it was just meant to be."

Tom was quiet, but I could tell he was with me.

"That's sort of how the pies work. They aren't all lucky, but some of them are. And when you get one of those slices? Bam. Home run." I spread my hands out, miming fireworks, which was mixing my metaphors a little, but I assumed he would understand what I was trying to say.

Tom nodded, though he still looked a bit uncertain. "I think that still counts as being evasive, you know?"

"You find a better way to explain magic to someone who doesn't believe in magic, and I'll give you a new way to explain my pies."

"So they *are* lucky."

"Sometimes. You're really getting stuck on this lucky-ver-sus-not-lucky thing, and that's not how it works. The pies *are* lucky, yes."

"And you make the pies."

"Sure, but that's doesn't mean I'm, like, a good-luck token or something." We were approaching the pet store, and I realized Tom had just followed me here, knowing it wasn't on my way home, without asking me where we were going.

"I don't know; that still just sounds like it could be a coincidence. Like someone eats your pie and something good happens to them, you say the pie chose them; someone else eats the pie and nothing happens, too bad for them."

I stopped in the doorway of the store and looked back at him. "Well, the pie doesn't *choose*; it's not sentient. It's pie. But if it makes you feel better to think it's a coincidence, I'm okay with that."

"You know, it's really frustrating to me that you won't just tell me how it works."

At that I had to smile, because there really was no easy way to explain it, and I thought it would frustrate him more to know that I had no answer to give that would appease him. But it wasn't just coincidence, and maybe one day he would get to try the right piece of pie on the right day, and he would understand. Until then, I was used to skeptics, but I wasn't accustomed to one who was so willing to be convinced, if only I could show him the right graph, or a formula, something that might allow his brain to accept what everyone in town had already told him to be true.

If there were a formula for magic, though, it wouldn't be magic anymore.

He seemed to realize for the first time where I'd taken him as he glanced up at the Four Paws UP sign, which was a cute nod to both the clientele and also the shop's location in Michigan's Upper Peninsula, known to pretty much every native Michigander as the UP, as in U-P, not the word *up*, but the double meaning worked well here.

The shop was owned by Dr. McKnight, the veterinarian, and there was a small clinic in the back. Dr. McKnight was due for her *real* retirement soon, so she liked to stick with vaccinations and checkups and standard spays and neuters, but she would never say no to someone in an emergency or a pet who needed advanced care over the winter. Otherwise, if it wasn't immediately life threatening, she would refer them to a mainland vet.

I was glad to be visiting her on a more fun errand than anything emergency related.

Dr. McKnight was sitting on a stool behind the cash counter, a book laid flat on the countertop in front of her and a pair of reading glasses so low on her nose I wondered how they hadn't fallen off.

"Why, Este, what a surprise. How are you doing today?" She flipped her book over and set her glasses down beside it. Dr. McKnight—Abigail, if you wanted to be casual—was in her late sixties, though she looked much younger. She kept her hair in a short silver pixie cut, and as always, she wore scrubs in a lively pattern. These had a teddy bear print on the top.

I'd known her my whole life and still had a vivid memory of the top she was wearing the day we had to have our dog Misfit put down. It had been covered in balloons. As sad as that day had been, I remembered not being scared of her, so maybe the scrubs had helped after all.

"I'm well, Dr. McKnight. You good? Haven't seen you in the diner for a few weeks."

She patted her perfectly flat tummy. "Gotta watch my sugar, the doc says. And you know no one can resist your pie if they come in there. I'm sure my resolve will only last so long; you know how much I love your lemon meringue."

"I'll keep a slice waiting for you," I said with a wink.

"Temptress." She looked behind me to where Tom was lingering in the doorway. "Well, hello there, Sheriff. I can't say I was expecting to see the two of you in here today. Not that I was expecting to see much of anyone. Was thinking I might even shut it down early, but now you're here, so how can I help?" She was looking specifically at Tom, who even after years of living here still sometimes got the tourist treatment, but I decided to save him from her scrutiny.

"I seem to have been chosen by one of Smokey's clones," I said.

"Oh, one of them finally got to you, hmm? Was bound to happen one day or another. Not sure I had you pegged as a cat person, though."

"Me either, but I guess she knew better."

"They always do. Do you have anything for her? What's her name? Can't be Smokey; you know the rules."

There was indeed a pet bylaw on the island prohibiting owners from naming any newly licensed cat Smokey. As far as island rules went, it was weird, but not our weirdest.

"Nora."

Dr. McKnight gave me a thoughtful look, and I wondered if she would ask me the meaning, but she just gave a quick nod of approval, which told me it wasn't a stupid name, at least. She must have heard her fair share of real doozies in her time.

"We'll get you set up with the basics, then." She got out from behind the counter and moved around the room with surprising speed. Soon there was a stack on the counter: a litter box, litter, food, dishes, toys, snacks, and a *Cats for Dummies* book that I didn't think I needed but also didn't dare put back.

Once she was done collecting all the essentials and I'd paid my eye-watering bill, she turned her attention to Tom. "And you, Sheriff, what can we do for you?"

"Oh." He seemed bewildered to have been spotted, as if he'd believed himself to be invisible this entire time. "Um, no. No pets." His gaze drifted toward a wall display where Dr. McKnight had a small number of pets on view—a few hamsters, a rabbit, a gecko, a snake, and some basic starter fish—and it seemed like Tom was briefly trying to determine what he would pick if she forced him to take something. Instead, she just nodded.

"Just here to help with the carrying. I see how it is." She gave me a quick wink that turned my cheeks, ears, and neck all red, and Tom swallowed wrong and started to sputter. If he was planning to correct her, though, he didn't, and instead just let her thrust several plastic bags into his hands.

We were back out on the street before either of us had gathered up the wherewithal to correct her assumptions.

Tom glanced down at the bags in his hands, then back at me. It seemed that for the first time since we'd arrived at the shop, he finally realized what I'd been buying.

"You got a cat?"

Chapter Twenty-Eight

It was weird having Tom in my cottage.

Being at his place the other day had been surreal, because it was odd that I'd never seen it before. But my cottage was my refuge; it was a place for me to have some peace and quiet in a space that was all my own.

It was okay to have Kitty here, because she was my best friend, and everyone knows that best friends don't care if your dishes are done or if you accidentally leave your bra on the back of the couch. But having Tom here was an entirely different story, because even though he was Kitty's brother, he was *not* Kitty.

My eyes scoured the small main room, terrified of what horrible embarrassment I might find that would convince him I was some kind of hoarder goblin and not a functional adult human, but aside from an unwashed cereal bowl and mug in the sink and a T-shirt I'd discarded on the couch when I'd changed my mind about what to wear at the last minute, the space was clean enough that I didn't feel the need to apologize for it.

Nora had been waiting for us at the door, and while she had momentarily run away when she spotted Tom, I'd left the door open, and it took her less than a minute to sneak her way inside, darting past him in a flash and going to hide in the safety of my bedroom.

"So that was the new cat, was it?" He peered past me in the direction of my bedroom, but the cottage was shaped in a way that meant my bedroom and bathroom were hidden down opposite ends of the same hallway. So Tom couldn't see my room, where I couldn't remember if I'd made my bed this morning or not.

Small favors.

"That's Nora."

"Are you going to keep her indoor only or let her out during the day?" At first I tried to gauge this question to see if it was a trick and he was trying to get me to admit to breaking some kind of bylaw. I didn't think anyone would care if Nora spent time outdoors, since there was no traffic for me to worry about her getting into, but I honestly hadn't decided that yet. We had a lot of outdoor cats in town, some feral, some not.

"First thing is to get her spayed. Then I guess I'll see how she feels about it."

He set the bags he'd been carrying on the island, and I riffled through them, taking the litter box and litter into my bathroom, which felt like too small a space to put them in, but there wasn't really anywhere better suited, so it would have to do. Then I unpacked the ceramic cat bowls I'd bought and filled one with water, setting it down at the side of the island where I walked less often, and the other bowl with dry food.

Dr. McKnight had suggested a mix of dry and wet food, especially since I believed Nora was a kitten and kittens needed quite a lot of calories to keep them running. I half expected her to emerge from my bedroom at the sound of the food dish filling, but she had made her choice between food and hiding from Tom.

Tom watched me do all of this and helped by passing me whatever it was he thought I might need next. He had good instincts, and with his assistance I was able to get the house cat friendly in short order.

"Do you mind if I ask you something?" he asked.

"You've been doing it all day; I don't see why you'd stop now."

"Why did you get so focused on solving this case? I know you're going to try to tell me it's because I questioned you, but I don't think this is about proving your innocence. You know I had to question you as a formality."

I leaned against the island and crossed my arms in front of me, itching to bake something so I could distract myself from this slightly too real line of questioning.

"I wish I could tell you it was something really noble, like wanting to find justice for Jeff. That would probably make me seem like a better person."

"I guess that really depends on what the real reason is."

I picked up an apple from the fruit basket by my elbow and rolled it back and forth between my hands. "I wanted to sleep better at night. I mean, it really did start as me wanting to point you to someone other than me. But I just hated the idea that anyone I knew could be capable of doing something like this, and I got it into my head that the sooner I could find the person who had done it, the sooner Split Pine would go back to being the place I love. Somewhere you feel safe with your doors unlocked."

"I used to live in Detroit. I'm not sure I'll ever get used to the idea of anyone leaving their doors unlocked." He glanced around the cottage, and I wondered if he was trying to find pieces of me in its decoration. But my house wasn't like his. This wasn't ever meant to be my permanent residence; it was just where I'd moved when I came home from school to give me a bit of adult freedom. That had been years ago, but I'd never gotten around to making it mine. I think I was still waiting to build my own house, figuring I would let myself come through then.

As it was, the place with the most Este-like personality to it was the kitchen, where beat-up flour-coated cookbooks lined the countertop and vintage dish towels hung from the oven door. The fridge was covered in magnets I'd collected on various trips. If he was trying to find a part of the cottage that was *me*, it was the kitchen.

Instead, he stopped looking around and refocused on me with such direct intensity that I had to drop my own gaze down to the countertop to keep from blushing at him.

"So you did it just for the good of public safety, then?" He didn't sound like he believed me.

"I hope that's not so impossible to believe."

"I guess I just thought there would be more to it than that. But I'm also aware that you and I don't really know each other that well."

I looked up at him again, taking in those rugged Steve McQueen, all-American good looks, and I wished his expressions weren't so darned inscrutable, because I couldn't tell if he was trying to imply he *wanted* to know me better or just reminding me how much we were still like strangers even after living so close after all these years.

"If I'm being totally honest, maybe I thought I would be able to see something you didn't. Because I've been here longer, and I've known most of these people my whole life."

He observed me quietly for a moment, then nodded. "I could see that. But I think what you might have forgotten is that knowing people well also lets you turn a blind eye to the obvious. Sometimes we like people so much we don't want to believe they could be something else . . . something darker. And I think you have to consider that if this killer *is* from our community, it could be someone you like."

"So you don't think it was Mick?" I was suddenly standing straight up, my fingers clutching the edge of the counter.

"I-I didn't say that at all." He must have been taken aback by my sudden change of demeanor.

"Well, you said it might be someone I like, so that immediately rules out the Gorleys."

That made Tom laugh for the first time since he'd been here. It was a rich, masculine sound, and it eased a pit that had been building in my stomach. "That's the other thing about playing detective when you know all the players involved, Este. Sometimes you might *want* someone to be guilty just because you already dislike them. To answer your question, it wasn't Mick this morning at the diner. I did listen to what you told me, and I went to visit him. Before you ask, no, I didn't bring up the berries. I can't exactly confront him about evidence that you found illegally." He gave me a pointed look. "But I did ask where he was all morning, and he got to the hotel early and was doing rounds of the property when someone left that note on your door."

"But he—"

"He showed me camera footage. There was no way he could have made it all the way to the Lucky Pie Diner and back in time to be on the clips he showed me. I also spoke to a few employees who confirmed he was there."

I wanted to ask if those employees also vouched for Jersey, but I bit my tongue. Based on what I'd heard last night, Jersey wasn't part of the murder scheme, but she *did* know something and was on the cusp of being ready to spill everything about her father.

I wasn't going to stick my nose into the investigation any further, but if I happened to bump into Jersey, it would be rude of me not to have a friendly conversation with her.

Chapter
Twenty-Nine

We were busy at the diner the next morning. Incredibly busy by November standards. There were also a surprising number of customers who just wanted coffee or other hot beverages to go. At first, I thought perhaps news about my sinister note had spread and business was booming because people now knew I wasn't the killer.

It wasn't until Safia Hamdi, one of the co-owners of Elevated Grounds, showed up around seven thirty that I gained some insight into our boosted morning numbers.

"Power is out for half the island," she grumbled.

"Oh *no*."

"Yeah, seems to have only been an issue for the east side, so basically everything west of Main is fine. They're working on it right now, but I'm really hoping things get up and running before nightfall, because I can't deal with frozen water lines on top of no power."

That part hadn't even occurred to me. The daytime temperatures were still pretty mild at the moment, but temperatures were definitely getting below freezing some evenings. If the power didn't come back or we didn't find enough generators, things could get bad very quickly for the businesses and homes on the east side of Main.

Which included both Grampy's house and my cottage.

I gave Safia our largest-sized coffee on the house. "If you need to hang out here and use the phone to call anyone, go ahead, okay? I know you said they're working on it, but let me know if you need anything. Whatever it is, I'm here to help."

"Thanks, Este, I appreciate it. This was really just the last thing we needed, you know? Business is already so slow in the offseason; every day we can't work feels like we're burning money we don't have."

I was very keenly aware of the offseason plight that she and all our local businesses faced. I knew we would never let a local business go under, especially not one as beloved by islanders as Elevated Ground was, but it was only natural for a business owner to be keeping an eye on their bottom line during the leanest times of the year. If she got a frozen pipe or other unexpected repair, it could spell disaster for whatever winter savings she'd built up during the busier summer months.

Again, a problem I was all too familiar with.

"Here." I grabbed a to-go container and pulled out a piece of Blueberry Billions pie, which was just a massively overstuffed blueberry pie, made from local berries that I'd frozen over the summer. "I think you need this today."

Safia took the pie from me, giving me a long, knowing look, then squeezed my free hand with hers. "Thank you. Thank you so much."

I nodded at her, knowing that in some small way it would make her life incrementally better.

Safia wouldn't need to worry about her pipes, at least. For some people that was as much luck as they could ever want or need.

I spotted a few people in the familiar brown clothes worn by the folks in the farm collective. A couple of them had pulled some tables together, while two others waited in line to place their orders. I would never get used to seeing everyone wearing identically colored clothing, like some sort of unofficial uniform. I'd been told time and time again they weren't a cult, but those clothes always made me do a double take.

I knew I shouldn't place so much judgment on them; every time I'd met a member of the group, they'd been kind to me, and their produce in the summertime was so good I often didn't need to place orders from the mainland for weeks.

One of the members arrived at the counter, and Rosie took their order while I poured coffees and got pies ready. We needed all hands on deck at the front with this unexpected rush of customers, though I now knew this was mostly just folks from the east side of town trying to find somewhere to stay warm until the power came back on.

About twenty minutes later Tom arrived, waltzing through the front doors like he was prepared to make a speech. It was obvious from the way he was carrying himself that he was in full sheriff mode, projecting an air of austere professionalism.

"Folks, folks, hello, if I could get everyone's attention." The buzz that had filled the room only moments earlier fell silent in an instant, and all eyes turned toward the sheriff. In a town where our mayor was a literal dog, we did need to look to someone as our primary authority figure, and Tom seemed to have decided that role fell to him.

We weren't close enough friends for me to call him Town Dad after this, but I was going to keep that nickname in my back pocket in case we arrived at a time in the near future where he'd decided to put up with me long enough that I could tease him.

He stood in the doorway until he was sure he had everyone's complete attention before he began. "Look, I know most of you are here waiting for word on when we're going to get the power back up and running, and I wish I had a better answer for you, but right now I'm afraid that we still don't know. We've got a lot of folks working on it, and since things on the lake are still smooth sailing with there not being any ice to speak of, we do have a call in to an emergency repair crew on the mainland if we're not able to get things going again in the next hour. I promise you we're doing our best, and we should have some backup power running before dark, so everyone should be nice and warm at home tonight, okay?"

"And if not?" someone asked from the back of the room. "What are we supposed to do if the backup generators aren't working? I thought they were supposed to kick in automatically when something like this happened."

"Well, the way Reynold explained it to me is that it's just been so long since we've needed the generators that they weren't as primed and ready to go as they should have been. Now, that's an oversight, and I know it's not what you wanted to hear, but they are working on it; we've got a lot of people much smarter and handier than me out there getting things going, and worst-case scenario we bring in outside help, okay? I promise you this isn't going to last long, and better it happen now than in January, right?"

A few people in the crowd muttered their grudging agreement, and there was some discussion among people at individual tables, but then someone from the collective table piped up.

"What about the hotel?"

This created a buzz, and Tom had to lift his hands to get everyone to calm down.

"Sorry, what did you say?"

"I said, what about the hotel?"

"Well, the Pine Hollow Hotel is on the east side," Tom said. "It'll be out of power too."

"Except it won't be, because Mick installed his own generator, independent of the main grid," one of the other members said. "So, if for some reason we can't all go home tonight, he should let us stay there."

Now the crowd was *really* buzzing. They'd gone from being irritated by the idea of not having any power to being completely thrilled by the notion of getting to spend a night at the fanciest hotel on the island. Except, of course, Mick hadn't promised any such thing, and I couldn't imagine him wanting to.

"Okay, folks, let's calm down for a minute, please. I will talk to Mick about his power situation and see what he thinks about the idea. But you're right; at the very least, one of the conference rooms would be a good place for people to stay warm if this carries on into the evening. Now, good news is I looked at the forecast, and we aren't at a freezing risk tonight. I know some of you were worried about your plumbing, but we should all be okay."

I realized then that Tom's place was also on the east side of Main, so he had just as much to lose. The police station was on the west side, so he probably had a place to stay and keep warm if need be, but that wasn't true of the rest of us.

"Good luck getting that tightwad to help anyone," someone in the room said, though I couldn't catch who it was. The chorus of chuckles and agreeing nods meant it could have been anyone.

Tom left, giving me a nod before he headed out the door, but I knew he was heading directly into an uphill battle. If only Mayor were really in charge, the old dog would let anyone stay at the hotel for the cost of one generous belly rub. His owner, unfortunately, was more likely to charge everyone a double rate to stay in his warm hotel rather than letting everyone in for free.

The crowd started to thin out a little an hour later, though people came and went in batches and it didn't really slow down for the whole day. Around eleven o'clock Grampy showed up, looking like he had every single day he'd worked a shift here, with his button-down plaid flannel and favorite Levi's jeans. There was a hardcover book tucked under his arm, but he graced me with a greeting before stealing away to one of the booths.

He came into the kitchen and wrapped me in a one-armed hug so he wouldn't lose his book, then pressed a kiss on the top of my head. Taking a step back, he gave me a once-over. "I don't get to see you work that often, angel. My goodness but you do look like your grandmother, you know that?"

This wasn't the first time he'd told me this, but it made my heart sing every time he did. My grandmother Ruthie had been a beautiful woman, not just in her youth but throughout her entire life. Her beauty hadn't been the kind that came from delicate features, but she was incredibly striking. You took notice of her. She was also the one I'd inherited my red hair from, so it was a true compliment to hear him compare us to each other.

"You go get settled in, and I'll bring you some lunch. Sound good?" I shooed him out of the kitchen. As much as this had once been his restaurant and I was more than happy to have him come by, it was *my* restaurant now, and I sometimes got a little edgy if Grampy or my dad lingered too long in the kitchen, because I felt absolutely certain they wanted to intervene and tell me how to do things differently.

Grampy let me kick him out, not putting up any kind of fight, and headed toward an empty booth at the far side of the diner. It had a great view overlooking both the harbor and the lake, but that was lost to my grandfather as he opened the book and began to read.

I brought him the sandwich of the day—the previously promised Gordo-dito—which had been a surprising hit with the lunch crowd so far. I could tell he was holding back commentary on the Thanksgiving/Taco Bell mutant combination, but I'd tried a bite of the first one Seamus made and had to admit it was delicious.

"Try it before you judge it," I told him. "Or you don't get any dessert."

"I would never pass judgment without a taste test, I promise."

I knew this was entirely untrue, coming from the man who always did a scouting mission at potlucks before putting a single thing on his plate.

The rest of the afternoon went by in a blur, with people coming and going from the east side, giving us gossip as the day progressed, and completely selling us out of pie before my shift ended at three.

Under normal circumstances I would just close early in a situation like this, but these weren't exactly normal circumstances, and I didn't want to take away one of the only warm places people had easy access to.

Seamus was still working away in the kitchen and Grampy hadn't moved from his booth, though his book was now much thinner on the back end than it had been when he first arrived. Quite a few people were lingering, and I knew no one was in a real rush to leave. Rosie's place was on the west side, but she was also the kind of person who hated to feel like she had been left out of anything, so I could tell she would avoid going home at all costs in case something interesting happened the moment she was gone.

I *wanted* to go home. The cottage had a fireplace, meaning it didn't matter much to me if I had power. But then I reminded myself of the note on the diner door and Tom's warning that I shouldn't be alone. It wasn't like I couldn't lock my door with the power out, but there was something kind of spooky about the idea of being home alone in the dark when a killer was keeping a watchful eye on me.

So I decided I'd stay, at least until we knew what was happening. If I was around others, I was safe, and since almost everyone I cared about most was already in the room, I didn't need to worry about anyone else. Tom's Bar would be closed from the outage, so I anticipated Kitty would probably come by after Piper got out of school. Might as well stick around here, in that case.

"Well, if I'm going to pull an accidental double, I might as well make more pie." I slipped my apron back on and pulled a few rounds of dough from the fridge. They'd need some time to warm up, so I could start with making the fillings.

Given the situation we were in, I thought people might want something hearty going into the evening. Comfort food that would distract them from the unusual circumstances we found ourselves in.

"Seamus, why don't you start up a big pot of chili? I think we might get a second rush around supper time if things keep going like this."

He didn't argue, though on another day he might have reminded me that his shift was almost over. I got the feeling he also wasn't in a hurry to leave. There was tension in the air, though not necessarily a bad kind. People were looking around at each other, talking in short, distracted bursts. Knees were bouncing, and there were so many people drumming their fingers on our tables that I was about to ask them to at least pick a single beat they could all stick with. It was as if everyone in the room was waiting for something important to happen, and no one wanted to miss it.

Seamus headed to the pantry first, collecting onions and garlic for aromatics as well as our home-canned diced tomatoes and a few containers of store-bought kidney beans. After that he went into the walk-in to get ground beef and ground pork, then set to work putting together a tasty chili con carne for the evening crowd. Chili was one of those great crowd pleasers, because you could smell it the moment you walked into a room and it somehow managed to be just as delicious to eat as you imagined it would be when you first caught the scent.

For the pie, I wanted something that would be equally satisfying, and decided that a good sugar pie would be just the thing. There was something to be said for turning the most basic ingredients into a truly delicious pie, like yesterday's carrot pie or the buttermilk pie I'd made for Tom. And like the tourtière I'd made earlier in the week, sugar pie was a Canadian staple I'd discovered during several trips to Quebec and had brought back to the UP with me. Canadians had a tremendously popular dessert treat called a butter tart that they served mostly around holidays but was available year-round. The sugar pie was basically a pie-sized version of that infamous butter tart.

Sugar pie also couldn't have been easier to make; this was where the phrase *easy as pie* had come from. I set a couple of sweet crusts to blind-bake and got the rest of my ingredients together. I melted my butter, and as I poured it into a waiting bowl, I already knew I was making a lucky pie. My fingertips tingled, and with each new ingredient I added to the stand mixer—brown sugar, vanilla, flour, milk—I envisioned each part of the pie bringing something good to the person or people who would eat it. The mixture blended together beautifully.

It always did when the pie was magic. The lucky pies never had burnt bottoms or filling that didn't set.

I whisked the eggs, smiling as they filled with frothy bubbles, then added that to the mixer as well.

While a standard sugar pie called only for brown sugar, I cheated a bit with my recipe. I loved the dense, rich taste brown sugar brought to the pie, but it wasn't quite enough for me. The last step before adding my filling to the shell was mixing in the secret ingredient. I drizzled the tiniest bit of molasses into the mixer. It would add just the right final flavoring to the pie to make it unforgettable.

I wanted enough pie to treat the evening crowd if we did have a rush, so I made three pies. If we had more people than that, well, we'd just need to start going through the frozen take-home pies.

I contemplated the three shells briefly, questioning my own magic in a way I never had before. Maybe it was because Tom had been asking me so much about it and I'd told so many half-truths over the years. Maybe it was because I didn't totally understand the gift myself, but I had to wonder.

I had baked three identical pies with the same ingredients at the same time, and yet I knew with every fiber of my being only one of them was lucky.

Not for the first time, and certainly not for the last, I missed my mother and grandmother with a deep ache in my soul. I wasn't sure if they would have the answers I wanted, or if this gift had been a mystery to them as well, but I wished very badly that they were both still here to ask.

I wondered if they'd ever shared any of those secrets with the men in their lives. I'd never really talked about my gift with Dad or Grampy—since making lucky pies was something only the women in my family could do—but maybe they knew something that their wives had shared with them over the years.

Resolving to ask them about it when my *current* mystery was solved, I shook the sadness off, not wanting it to dampen my motivation.

The pies would take about an hour to bake completely, so I set aside the dough to warm slightly, prepped my three pie pans, and let the oven preheat. Once I got the dough rolled out and blind-baked, it would just be a matter of waiting for the pies to bake. They were single-crust pies, so I didn't need to work on any elaborate lattice or even double the crust amounts.

It meant I had time to make homemade whipped cream, which would help balance out how sugary the pie itself was. Since that involved just literally whipping cream, I set my mom's mixer on medium and let it run. I'd add a little sugar, but I wanted to keep it almost plain so it would work well with the pie.

With dessert prepping done, I started doing some extra work for the dinner service. Chili was good, but chili with fresh cheddar jalapeño biscuits was probably better, and since I had a jar of homemade pickled jalapeños—which Grampy had made with the peppers from his garden—in the fridge and some time to kill, I figured I might as well. The process of baking, as always, was a welcome distraction for me. Mixing the crumbly biscuit dough first in the stand mixer and then by hand meant that I got all the ingredients incorporated—a little bite of jalapeño for everyone—but that the biscuits would still have a nice rustic quality in the end. With my hands coated in flour and flecks of cheddar cheese, I hand-shaped each biscuit and put them on a tray, ready to pop in the oven once it was free. Before I knew it, the pies were cooking, the biscuits were done, and the predicted evening crowd had started to roll in.

Kitty and Piper had joined Grampy at his table, and a few of the faces from the morning rush had come back again, this time settling into tables and scouring menus instead of just taking their coffees to go. Safia was back, as were a handful of the brown-clad farm members, though I recognized only two of them from the morning.

Rosie and Marcel were kept busy taking orders, and the chili was just as popular as I'd predicted it would be. Likewise, the dense, comforting sugar pie was snapped up in no time, and the next time I looked at the clock, we were at closing time and I was scraping the last piece onto someone's plate, doling it out with a big double serving of whipped cream to finish off the batch I'd made.

People were lingering in spite of the OPEN sign being flipped, and I didn't have the heart to kick anyone out, because there was a nice sense of community bonding in the room. We'd found a few old board games tucked under one of the benches by the door where we kept toys to occupy children, and a rowdy game of Monopoly was taking place at one of the group tables, while another crowd shrieked with delight and horror when someone declared, "Uno Reverse."

Grampy was still reading, which didn't seem to bother Kitty; Piper watched a video on her tablet and Kitty flipped through a magazine she'd brought with her. It was nice to see my blood family and my chosen family getting along in such an unusual but fitting way.

Tom opened the front door, and this time he didn't need to say anything at all to get our attention. The room fell silent, and Seamus even emerged from the kitchen as if he had sensed the sheriff's arrival.

"Evening, everyone," Tom said to his captive audience. "Just letting you know that the backup generator is still having some issues. The technician will be out in the morning."

Groans filled the room. This was not what anyone here had been hoping to hear, and now the once-jovial community gathering had turned into something more uncertain. Where would everyone go? I could certainly offer to let people sleep in the booths, but this wasn't really an ideal setting to act as emergency shelter. I waited to see if Tom would make a better suggestion.

"Now, I hear you, I know. It wasn't the news I wanted to be delivering either. But I'm also here to tell you that we've spoken to Mick Gorley, and he has graciously offered to open up the hotel to residents tonight. So why doesn't every get whatever they need and then go head over there? Now, keep in mind, that's a lot of people and only one hotel, so if you have a generator at home or other means to stay warm tonight, please take those options instead, okay?"

This last warning fell entirely on deaf ears. Everyone had heard they were getting a free night at a fancy hotel and had simply stopped listening. The rush for the door would have offended me in any other scenario, but I was also eager to head out.

Despite the fact that I had a perfectly functional fireplace at home, I found that I preferred the idea of heading to the hotel as well. For one thing, I wanted to stay with the crowd rather than being the only person on the east side of the island silly enough to go home by myself.

The other factor making me want to follow the crowd to the hotel was probably one I should have ignored, but I simply couldn't resist: being at the hotel meant I might bump into Jersey, which would give me a perfect opportunity to goad her into telling me something about her father.

That was a chance I just couldn't say no to.

Chapter Thirty

We closed up the diner, and as a way of making myself at least somewhat welcome at the Pine Hollow Hotel, I grabbed a banana cream pie out of the freezer. There were other options I could have selected, but in my personal opinion, banana cream was the best pie to have while it was still frozen.

Rosie also packaged up the last remaining slices of my daily pies that had been left over so I could share those around with anyone who ended up at the hotel.

Which, as I walked up to the Pine Hollow entrance, I realized wasn't going to be a small number of people.

It was remarkable to see how many had shown up to the hotel, given that only half the town was out of power. I had to imagine that at least some of these people had power still but were a little curious to see inside the hotel, or possibly just had some FOMO and didn't want to stay home when half of Split Pine was having a glorified slumber party.

Most people had come from their homes and not work, so I saw a good number of overnight bags and duffels thrown over people's shoulders, and I immediately regretted not stopping at home for a toothbrush.

I followed a group of about a dozen people through the lobby, and some of the stragglers who had spent the evening at the diner trailed behind me. All said, there were probably about two hundred people here already, which felt enormous by town standards.

I noticed that even though there had been farm collective members hanging out at the diner in larger-than-usual numbers throughout the day, there were no telltale brown outfits in the crowd at the hotel. Since they were an off-grid community, I knew they had their own sources of power—or at least alternative means to stay comfortable overnight—but it did make me wonder what had brought them into town that morning.

I supposed curiosity about town drama didn't disappear just because you decided to live in an unusual self-sustaining community. They *were* still residents of the island, after all, and there were at least a hundred of them out there. It stood to reason that they would want to know what was going on in town when something like this happened.

But that must not have extended to them wanting to spend the night with us.

Who could blame them, though? Quite a few of the people here would rather be sleeping in their own beds tonight. I was one of them, but the urge to have a moment to talk to Jersey, and also my desire not to be alone when there was a killer prowling the island, meant I had little choice but to say good-bye to my bed for the evening.

I followed the flow of people into the hotel's main ballroom, where all the banquet tables had been opened and people were pulling up chairs, looking both confused and expectant. I stood near the doorway, out of everyone's way, and clutched my pie boxes close to me.

A few moments later, Kitty came in and immediately homed in on me. Piper wasn't with her anymore; Seamus lived on the west side of town, so no doubt he had taken her home with him. I was sure he would have offered a place for Kitty as well, but she seemed to be enjoying the drama.

"I'm not sure I've ever seen this many Pineys in one group indoors before," Kitty said, using her nickname for townsfolk.

She had a point. While we did love to gather in large groups for festivals and events, we were also a very outdoor community. With the exception of perhaps Christmas Eve mass, there weren't a lot of things that happened in town that might cause more than a hundred people to be in one place together at the same time.

"I think this might be the only room on the island that can *fit* this many people," I reminded her.

Since the ballroom had been designed to host weddings and other large-scale events that would bring in crowds from the mainland, it had no problem holding almost half of the town's population without seeming overcrowded.

I spotted Mick and Jersey near the stage. Jersey had a look of general disgust on her face as she scanned the crowd, and Mick just looked annoyed at having to be here. So basically they were acting completely normally.

I stared until Mick's gaze swung my way and we locked eyes. I wanted desperately for him to give a sign of acknowledgment, something to let me know he had been the one to leave that note on my door. I knew Tom had said he had an alibi, but I wasn't convinced.

But instead of looking either nervous or smug about my presence here, he just nodded once, then continued to scour the room like he was looking for someone specific.

For some reason that ambivalent acknowledgment made me nearly incandescent with rage. How dare that man threaten to hurt me and then look at me as if I were nothing more than another fixture on his wall? I could strangle him with my bare hands.

My greatest hope in the world was that Tom would find whatever final piece of evidence he needed while we were all here tonight and haul Mick off in handcuffs in front of the entire town. Now *that* would be a sweet way to end the evening.

The crowd coming through the door seemed to taper off, with Bruno being one of the last to arrive. He spotted Kitty and me, and it didn't escape my notice that when his gaze landed on Kitty, a pink flush covered his cheeks. I felt incredibly bad for making assumptions about Bruno's guilt. Yes, there had been some decent reasons I'd believed he might want Jeff dead, but those were the same reasons someone could point a finger at me.

Bruno was just a businessman trying to keep himself afloat in a very unusual and sometimes volatile retail environment. Who could blame him for getting mad?

But now, seeing the way he was looking at Kitty, as if he were suddenly a teenager again and had eyes only for her, I almost wanted to apologize to him. I was grateful I'd never come right out and accused him to his face. That would have made for a very awkward time of going grocery shopping for the rest of my life.

"Hey, Bruno." I waved him over to us, and he joined without hesitation. "Is the General Store okay?"

His shop, like so many others, was east of Main.

He nodded vigorously. "We had a generator installed some years back after that lightning storm took out power and I lost all my frozen food right at the height of summer. No ice cream in tourist season? *Que saco*! So I said never again, bought a generator the very next day. I haven't needed it since, but today . . . today I am glad for it."

This would easily have been the worst time of year for Bruno to lose his frozen and refrigerated food supply, with restocks being so few and far between. I was happy for him that he wouldn't need to worry. Perhaps it was time to start thinking about a generator for the diner as well, because heaven knew we had thousands of dollars' worth of food and frozen product in our coolers. Losing that would be a nightmare, especially in summer, like he had mentioned.

I'd have to ask him later where he'd ordered his and how much it had cost. The diner wouldn't need as much power as the General Store, but it would be a good place to start my research.

Kitty was gazing up at Bruno adoringly, as if this story were the most interesting thing anyone had ever talked about. I glanced across the ballroom and noticed that Jersey was all by herself on the opposite wall, looking bored and a little angry.

"If you guys will excuse me for a minute," I said, lifting the pie box so they could see my built-in excuse. "I'm going to go deliver a hostess gift. Why don't you enjoy these together, though." I handed them a few slices of leftover pie, then headed across the ballroom before either of them could protest my obvious attempt to leave them alone together.

A matchmaker I am not, but if I see an opportunity to force a little proximity, I figure there's no harm in making the effort. I got the feeling that Bruno especially would need a push to ask Kitty out, so perhaps if they could enjoy some pie together in this unusual circumstance, it would give them a funny story to tell their grandchildren about how they realized they were meant to be.

A gal could hope, right?

Bruno seemed a much more logical fit for Kitty than Seamus. Seamus was too dour, too serious. As much as I loved him, he was very much the opposite of the outgoing, bubbly Kitty. Perhaps that had been what drew them together initially, because it was almost impossible to meet Kitty and not immediately fall in love with her, but over time I had to imagine it was hard for Kitty to always be the positive one in their relationship.

Bruno was calm, he was level-headed, and from what little I knew of him personally, he seemed like a generally happy person—unless his *fútbol* team was losing; then misery would trail after him like a gray cloud. But that could be said of just about anyone on the island who took their sports more seriously than they should.

Mick was up on the stage, joined by Tom, and I suspected we were about to get a speech on what to expect for the evening ahead—probably a lot of rules—so I seized my limited opportunity to sidle up next to Jersey.

She started, as if genuinely shocked that anyone would come stand beside her, and gave me the longest once-over I'd ever experienced from someone who wasn't checking me out.

"What do *you* want?" she said, sneering openly.

I said a silent prayer that some supernatural power above would give me the necessary patience to get through this entire conversation without saying something mean.

Honestly, it was kind of impressive how Jersey had managed to maintain her mean-girl persona so long after high school. Most people as they grew up and got older learned that cruelty and unkindness didn't get you too far in the world, but Jersey had somehow learned the opposite lesson. This likely had a lot to do with her upbringing, and for the first time in a long time I actually felt sad for her. She hadn't really been given an opportunity to *be* a good person, because the man who had raised her had taught her that the most surefire way to the top was by stepping over anyone who got in your way.

I wondered if his lessons extended to killing anyone who crossed you.

I held the pie out to her, and for one moment her expression shifted. It was a microscopic change, one that I wouldn't have noticed if I hadn't been looking right at her face when it happened, but she visibly softened. There was a flash of excitement and pleasure in her eyes, something that lasted only as long as a breath before it was replaced by her usual steely mask of indifference.

"A pie? How groundbreaking."

"Well, my grandmother always told me you never go anywhere empty-handed, so consider it a hostess gift."

She took the pie from me, hesitant at first, then lifting the lid to look inside. She darted a quick glance in my direction. "Is it . . ."

I paused. I shouldn't lie. I *never* lied about my pies. People would ask me if their slice or their whole pie was lucky, and I'd always hedge. I would rarely tell them it was, even if I knew. Moments like this afternoon with Safia were few and far between, but sometimes I felt like someone *needed* to know it was lucky, like they just had to have that extra nudge to keep them going. But I'd never tell someone their pie was lucky if it wasn't; that was just setting a bad precedence for my reputation.

I'd tell them that it was never a sure thing and that the luck chose the person, which was and wasn't true. This particular pie was just delicious, not lucky, and Jersey was never going to be the benefactor of one of my truly lucky pieces. But tonight, just this once, I thought a white lie might be okay.

"Yes." I nodded slowly, the single syllable burning on its way out. It felt *wrong* to tell her this, so much so that I almost immediately took it back, but I needed her on my side for a few minutes if I had any hope of getting something useful about Mick from her.

Her eyes widened, and she got a greedy look on her face that made me wonder if she was about to run off and grab a fork to start tucking into the banana cream immediately.

"It was really nice of you and your father to put everyone up tonight," I said, stealing her attention back, however briefly.

"Yeah, well." She made a scoffing sound. "Sheriff Hot but Annoying didn't give us much of a choice."

I almost choked when she mentioned Tom like this, not having expected such a snide but almost perfect nickname to come out. I'd give Jersey this: she could boil someone down to a single vicious yet accurate sentiment within minutes of meeting them. She'd called me Little Miss Grease Trap for the entirety of our high school experience. Lovely. Though I did work in a diner and sometimes worked mornings before school, so no doubt I'd periodically gone through the halls smelling of pie dough or fryer oil.

Most people didn't notice or care, but Jersey sure had.

"Still, Tom's insistence aside, you're doing something really lovely for people. Thank you."

She grunted but didn't actively deflect the compliment this time. Minor success.

I decided not to idle around the conversation too long. She was going to get bored of me quickly, and more than anything, she probably didn't want to be seen having a long chat with someone who had my paltry bank account balance.

"I bet it was your idea too," I continued, even though this flew in the face of what she'd just said about Tom. I figured she'd probably already forgotten saying it. "Not at all what your dad implied you were like. He should know you better."

That got her attention. She turned toward me, hugging the pie box to her chest, wearing a fierce and immediately angry expression. "What's that about my father? Did he say something to you?"

"Oh, gosh, I shouldn't have said anything. I'm so sorry. Just pretend I didn't say that, okay?"

She would do no such thing, and I knew it. "No. Come on, Este, please. Tell me what he said." Her tone was pleading, but her eyes were so filled with rage I almost felt bad for doing this to Mick. Or I would if he weren't most likely a killer.

"It was just something I overheard him saying to someone in the street the other day. Someone was asking about you, and I . . ." I paused for dramatic effect, and she leaned in close. "Well, he said he wished he had someone he trusted to leave his company to someday. He said that you were flaky and didn't care about anyone but yourself."

This last little bit was the best way I knew to goad her. While it was more what I personally thought of her rather than something her father had said, I knew Jersey was enormously worried about other people's perceptions of her, especially her own father's. This little meanness would do the trick perfectly to set her off on a tangent about him, and if I knew her, she'd immediately go to whatever it was that would hurt Mick most.

It probably wasn't very nice of me to play on Jersey's insecurities like that, but if Mick had secrets, this was the most foolproof way of finding them out.

"Oh, he said that, did he?" Her voice was quiet, but her tone was so ice cold it made the hairs on the back of my neck stand on end.

Hell hath no fury like a Jersey scorned.

"You know, it's funny he would say that, when *he's* the one who spends all his time thinking about himself and how to make a quick buck from the idiots who live on this stupid island." She let out a long breath, puffing up her blonde bangs. "If you only knew some of the things he'd done to keep himself on top out here."

Here we go, I thought.

"Like what?" I tried to keep my tone from sounding too eager, which wasn't easy. But I didn't want to spook her, so I hoped the way I'd asked sounded only casually curious, like it didn't matter to me whether she told me anything or not.

"Well, just between you and me, he's been really in the town council's ear about that piece of property your grand-father owns. And I think he's just about convinced them that it really isn't doing the town any good to have a vacant lot on such prime real estate."

This was *not* what I had expected her to say. I'd thought she might tell me something about Jeff or imply her father's participation in his murder. I had *really* hoped she would tell me something about Summer Island Farms. But of all the ways I had imagined this little discussion going, I hadn't anticipated her juicy gossip to be about my own family.

But now that her words were out in the open, those nasty little jabs she'd made to me at the diner earlier in the week sud-denly bubbled back to the surface under a new light.

"What are you talking about?"

She must have loved the way I sputtered out the question, because she knew I hadn't seen this coming. Even though days earlier Mick had been on my case about the property, I hadn't really believed he had the power to do anything about it. We'd had that land for generations; it was *ours*. More importantly, it was *mine*, and I had legitimate plans to build my dream house on it. Everyone knew that. Just because it was taking longer than I'd hoped didn't mean the plan was dead; it just meant I had needed to delay it a few times.

"Daddy made a pretty compelling argument that if the town bylaws dictate we need to use all available property to the betterment of the town itself, then your grandfather is actually in violation of the bylaws by doing nothing with it. The council is going to issue an ultimatum that if your family doesn't start to do something with that land in the next six months, then the city will buy it back at the original sale cost and sell it to someone who *will* develop it." She looked weirdly triumphant about this, and I knew it was because of the promise her father had made her about the new hotel he planned to build on that land.

I was flabbergasted. I'd come into this conversation thinking I would be able to manipulate Jersey into ratting out her own father for murder, and instead she had just shared a family secret I hadn't known I had.

Did Grampy know this was a possibility? If so, why hadn't he said anything to me? I had never been in a rush to develop the property because I'd thought I'd have time.

And six months? What an impossible deadline to issue. That was basically the entirety of winter, a period when we wouldn't be able to get contractors or equipment out to the island and it would be too cold and snowy most of the time to get anything done. Mick had managed to back us into a corner where we could either sell to him and make some real money now, or he could just bide his time and wait for us to have to sell it back to the island.

For the original sale price; wasn't that what Jersey had said? We'd owned that land for over a hundred years. The original sale price was probably less than ten thousand dollars. Land like that would sell for hundreds of thousands now. It was prime real estate in a market where things almost never went up for sale.

I felt like Jersey had just punched me in the stomach.

Why had I been left in the dark like this? That was supposed to be my land, and now I was finding out the horrible news from the last person on the island I wanted to know this information.

Maybe this was the universe's way of telling me I shouldn't have been digging into this murder investigation, because if I'd just minded my own business, I wouldn't have found out. At least not like this.

I scanned the room, looking for Grampy, but he must have decided to head home and set up in the living room by his own big fireplace. He wasn't one for crowds, so I wasn't surprised, but I was still frustrated to not be able to talk this out with him.

I was brimming with anger, not at Grampy but at Mick for his unrelenting greed and how it had driven him to finally use the town's bylaws to his advantage. There truly was no limit to the depths he would sink to.

I took one look at Jersey, who was hugging her pie box and glaring up at the stage, and I knew she was furious, not at what her father had said about her but that he'd said it to some unnamed stranger and I'd been there to hear it. She was lashing out at me simply because she believed I'd overheard her father sharing his very real thoughts about her.

That family really was a mess.

It took all my self-control not to knock the pie box from her hands or tell her that I'd lied about the luck. At this point none of that mattered. I needed to get out of here and go talk to my grandfather. I was already mentally checking my very sad bank balance and wondering what work we could possibly get done over the winter that would allow us to keep the property in our family name.

Surely there were some basic measures we could take that would qualify as activity. The council wouldn't be cruel enough to punish us for the limitations brought on by the offseason, would they? That didn't seem fair.

I walked away from Jersey without saying goodbye and headed back toward the entrance just as Tom took the microphone to greet everyone. I didn't want to stop; I was tired of being here and needed to go home. I'd pictured this night going very differently in my head, and rather than uncovering a criminal, I'd only managed to make myself feel sad and hurt that Grampy hadn't said anything to me.

As I reached the door, Bruno and Kitty were still huddled together in conversation. When they saw me, Bruno straightened to attention and gestured toward me before I could leave. I thought about pretending I hadn't seen him, but that would just be rude. I moved in their direction.

"I forgot to talk to you earlier about our very lucky news," he said, a huge smile crossing his face. I could see why Kitty found him so handsome.

"Our?" Was he talking about him and Kitty?

"Yes, I was very sad to hear about what happened to Denny, and this upsetting business with Jeff I think means we will not get any more produce from Evergreen Produce, yes? A shame. For both of us." He shook his head.

"I'm sorry, where is the good news?" I was so miserable right now I didn't want to be reminded of all the other things going wrong. At the moment I didn't even care about Jeff's murder. Tom could solve it on his own, as far as I was concerned. I was done.

"It is good timing because of the new vendor on the island. Just think! Fruit from ten minutes away, not a thousand miles." He beamed as if he couldn't imagine anything better.

"I don't know what you're talking about."

"Well, the farm, of course." He seemed confused, as if he expected me to know all about this. When he could see that I wasn't making the connection, he reached into his jacket pocket and withdrew a slightly dented business card. "I thought they had talked to you."

He handed the card to me and looked back over at Kitty. "I never imagined we would have something like this right on the island. Fresh produce all winter long. What a joy."

I glanced down at the business card he'd handed me.

Summer Island Farm.

Split Pine, MI.

The same design and information I'd seen on the clamshell package in Mick's shed.

"Bruno, who gave you this?" I held the card up, as if he might have forgotten giving it to me only seconds earlier. "Was it Mick?"

His brows knit together in a quizzical expression. "Mick? No, no, Este. It was . . ." He looked thoughtful for a moment, snapping his fingers as he tried to remember. "Calvin. Calvin from the Sunrise Acres farm. They've built a four-season greenhouse. Produce all year round, right in our backyard."

I glanced down at the card.

Strawberries.

Strawberries to die for.

Chapter
Thirty-One

Any notions I had of going home to have a heart-to-heart conversation with Grampy vanished completely.

I stared at the card Bruno had handed me, completely dumbfounded as to how one tiny piece of paper could change everything I thought I knew about Jeff's murder.

At first, I'd believed this was just about bitterness over bad business, someone pushed too far by Jeff's ridiculous prices. It would have been a horrible reason to kill someone, but it was believable. The little time I'd spent with Jeff certainly indicated he was capable of inspiring that kind of rage.

Then I'd been so certain Mick had been the one to kill him, because Mick didn't like to be scammed out of his money. If he had believed Jeff was unfairly overpricing his goods, I could absolutely picture Mick going to the last resort.

I'd been thrown off by the seemingly random-appearing strawberry clamshells. This murder was about something more, not just bad prices and bad business.

Now I was holding a card in my hand that pointed me right to the people who might have all the answers I needed.

I looked back toward the stage, where Tom was busy explaining to everyone how things were going to go this evening, reminding people that the hotel was to be treated respectfully, to which Mick interjected that if anyone even *thought* about loading their bags with stolen hotel soaps and shampoos, he would know.

This was the kind of situation I shouldn't go into alone, but I also knew if I told Tom what I was planning, he wouldn't let me go at all. And I was desperate to know how organic berries had been the cause of a man's murder. I had so many questions and only one place to go for answers.

I ducked out the side door, promising myself I would text Tom on the way to let him know what I'd discovered and where I was going. He couldn't exactly send me home if I was already *at* the farm, right?

Plus, I had to imagine that even if Calvin and a handful of others from the farm knew the truth about what had happened to Jeff, they wouldn't be stupid enough to do something to me if others knew I was going there. They would need to play nice.

Nice like leaving threatening notes?

I was already halfway up Main when I remembered the note that had been stuck to my door. The ominous and not-so-subtle threat telling me not to do exactly what I was doing now.

But it was too late.

The walk from town out to the farm wasn't long; getting anywhere on the island didn't take much. However, it felt a lot different walking there in the dead of night with the chill of winter clinging to the air, turning my breath into white clouds. The moon glimmered through the pines, giving me enough light to see by, but I wasn't used to taking long night walks in the woods. Every few minutes a branch snapping or the creaky groan of trees rubbing together would give me pause.

The closer I got, the more I regretted my impulsive choice to come out here. Was I just going to burst into their compound and demand to speak to Calvin, then grill him about his involvement in the murder? No. No one would tell me anything, and worse still, it could potentially derail Tom's investigation.

I remembered, then, my promise to text him. I pulled out my phone and quickly sent a message saying where I was and just the words *Secret strawberries*. I hoped it was enough for him to figure out where my thinking was. A few minutes of total silence had me wondering if maybe I shouldn't turn around and reconsider this whole thing.

The woods were downright spooky with most of the lights on the island out, and even though the path to the farm was well worn, it still felt like I might be getting myself lost somehow. Wouldn't that be the ultimate kick in the teeth for overstepping my bounds on this investigation—getting lost in the woods and freezing overnight?

Just as I was about to give up and turn around, I noticed light glinting through the trees. I followed the glow until I reached an arched sign over a packed-dirt entry path that read Sunrise Acres in large hand-painted letters. Underneath that sign was a new one that had clearly just been painted and hung recently.

Summer Island Farm.

I swallowed a lump in my throat.

The self-preservation voice in the back of my head was screaming at me to just turn around and go home, but I couldn't. I didn't know why, but what had started as just a nosy attempt to learn the truth about Jeff's murder had become an insatiable need to uncover a much deeper mystery. I needed to know what was happening on my island, what *had* been happening right under my nose while I'd believed I was living in an idyllic northern paradise.

"Are you lost?" a voice asked from behind me, making me jump half a foot in the air and let out a surprised yelp.

The voice chuckled, and a hand clamped down on my shoulder. "Oh, good heavens, I'm sorry. I didn't mean to startle you. My partner is always telling me I'm too quiet out here and I need to put a bell on." He laughed again, and I turned to see who was talking to me.

It was one of the farm collective members, wearing head-to-toe brown, and I recognized his face. He'd been in the diner earlier that morning and a few other times in the past week. I was embarrassed to realize I had no idea what his name was.

"Sorry, I didn't mean to scream like that," I said. "I just wasn't expecting anyone behind me."

With one hand, the man gestured to his other arm, where he cradled bunches of dry pine branches and sticks. "We're having a community fire tonight; I was just getting extra kindling. Why don't you come join us?" He nodded toward the arch over the entryway. "All are welcome at Sunrise Acres."

"I . . ." Well, if he was just going to invite me in, that seemed like fair game. "I was just coming out to make sure you guys were okay with power and everything. Mick Gorley is offering to let anyone who needs it to stay at his hotel. You know Mick?" I narrowed my eyes at him, trying to gauge his response with only the overhead light of the moon to show me his expression.

"Sure, I know Mr. Gorley. That's a nice gesture of him. And of you too, to come all the way out here. But we're comfortable. We've got all we need for power in our solar banks. Nice to make the sun work for us a little sometimes." He smiled and gave a friendly wink.

If this was who they sent out to find new members for the farm community, it was no wonder they had over a hundred people living here. He was charming and friendly and had an approachably handsome face that was nice to look at without being so attractive as to make him too memorable.

"I'm Este," I said, offering to shake his free hand. "I own the Lucky Pie Diner in town."

"Oh yeah, I knew your face, just not your name. You make great pies. We usually take care of all our own food needs out here just living off what we can grow and make, but we do certainly love any good opportunity to come in and have some pie. And wouldn't you know it, we haven't figured out how to grow our own coffee beans just yet, so we do like to get a nice cup of joe every now and again." He started walking into the farm's main yard and turned back to me. "Este, my name is Calvin, and I'm glad you came out here tonight. I know you're trying to be neighborly, but I think I might have a bit of a business opportunity for you."

Chapter
Thirty-Two

Having never seen the farm in person, I hadn't really been sure what to expect. I knew it was a four-season community, and yet for some reason, whenever anyone talked about people living out here, I imagined them living in tents with makeshift, temporary quarters. Knowing that the people living at the farm liked to be left alone, those who lived in town kept their distance out of respect. There were hiking trails nearby, but I'd never been to the compound itself.

My imagined version of the camp was the exact opposite of what I found as Calvin walked me through the farm grounds. There were dozens of beautifully made bunkhouse cabins, all with lights aglow inside and smoke billowing out from the stone chimneys. He pointed out the farm's main building, even though it was hard to miss, a two-story cabin with a large wraparound porch.

"That's where the kitchen is, and also where we have the day care center and our main offices." He pointed to another long building connected to the main cabin on one side. "That's the community center, where everyone comes together to eat."

People were just filing out of the community center as we arrived, everyone wearing their same mismatched brown

ensembles, even the children. Calvin either noticed me looking or was used to people being curious, because he spoke the
answer to a question I never would have dared to ask him.
"We wear brown because we want to avoid a life where we fall
under the spell of consumerism and capitalist greed. When
everyone dresses the same, we no longer see status in clothing.
It's just something to cover ourselves in, not a statement of our
value."

I felt weird about my jeans and jacket, wondering what the
brands I'd selected said to him about me. Then I reminded
myself of why I was here and told myself I should stop worrying so much about what this man thought of me.

But I found that difficult. He was warm and inviting, and
it didn't take me a long time in his presence to find that I
wanted him to like me as well. Certainly I'd been mistaken
about the connection between the farm and Jeff's death. There
was no way Calvin could have been the killer.

He guided me through the compound, and while I saw
many people milling around, none of them approached us.
Most just watched us pass with thinly disguised curiosity.

In the distance, past where people were gathering for the
fire and outside the circle of cabins, something was glowing
pale white-blue in the trees.

"What's that?" I asked, gesturing toward the glow.

"Well, that's what I wanted to talk to you about. Why
don't you come with me?" He dumped the kindling he'd been
carrying in a pile by the fire, touching a few people by shaking hands or squeezing shoulders as he passed by. If I'd been
unsure of Calvin's role here when I first arrived, I wasn't any
longer. It was obvious from the deference people were paying
him and the way everyone we passed looked at him that he was
the leader.

We continued to walk through until we passed by the last of the cabins and down a short path away from the warm light of the little village. For the first time since arriving here I caught myself thinking that this wasn't necessarily the best idea, to be walking alone into the woods with a man I didn't know.

Breaking through the tree line, I let out an audible gasp.

"What *is* this?" I said, unable to hide the gobsmacked tone of my voice.

"*This* is Summer Island Farm. Or the first part of it."

We were standing together in front of an enormous greenhouse. It was several interconnected domes stretching hundreds of feet back into the woods to a point so distant that I couldn't actually tell where the glow ended.

"Come on in." He opened the door of the dome in front of me and ushered me inside. Immediately I was hit by a blast of summer-hot air that was so humid my face began to sweat when we were only a few feet inside. While the exterior had been impressive, the inside was even more so.

Everywhere I looked were rows upon rows of verdant vegetation. One dome seemed to be entirely filled with trees, with lush, vibrant fruit hanging low on branches—lemons, oranges, all huge and ready for the picking. Calvin walked slowly through the domes, where trees gave way to raised cedar beds. Labels in the soil told me I was looking at carrots, beets, and kale. Potted plants lined the entire outside of each dome, with staked cucumber and cherry tomatoes practically spilling over the edges.

Anything I could imagine in the way of fruit, vegetable, or herb, it was all here.

"We've adapted a six-acre spread here to being a veritable cornucopia of fresh produce. No more denying yourself what you want in the winter or settling for subpar food flown in

273

from other countries. Whatever you want, we're growing it."
He stopped in front of a huge raised bed and pushed back some
of the ruffled leaves.

Strawberries. Dozens and dozens of huge, bright-red
strawberries. He plucked one off the stem and handed it to
me. "We've engineered the zones throughout every dome for
optimal hydration and warmth. We've basically created a space
where it's permanently summer. Now you don't need to wait
for a farmers' market to have what you want. It's right here.
Este, we want you to be a part of this. We know how much
you were spending on bringing produce in. It's not easy to get
everything you need to make those pies of yours from scratch.
But what if I could cut your grocery bill in half and you didn't
need to wait for any of it? If you ran out of peaches in February,
we could have them at your doorstop that day."

As sales pitches went, it was incredible. I could certainly see
how he had gotten Bruno so excited so quickly.

My mind was reeling, because obviously I wanted this. I
was so in love with this that I wanted to move in and never
leave the strawberry room. When I bit into the berry he'd given
me, tears unexpectedly sprang to my eyes. Store-bought berries
were fine, but this, *this* berry was incredible, so sweet and juicy
that I was immediately planning strawberry tarts and rustic
strawberry galettes.

If only that voice at the back of my head would shut up and
stop reminding me that something about this was *wrong*. I was
no detective, but everything I'd uncovered about Jeff's case, every
little thread I'd followed, all seemed to point here, to this farm.

"How did you get this set up so quickly? I don't remember
any of this being here when I did some hiking last year, and I
feel like this would be an enormous undertaking." A lot of the
fruit plants, especially the trees, looked well established, so the

farm had to have been in development for some time. But since the farm hadn't been operating as a business—at least not at any of the summer farmers' markets—and was only putting out feelers now, where had they gotten the money to do something like this?

"We had an independent investor." Calvin glanced around the space, looking as proud as if it were a beloved child. "A partner, if you will, who wanted to see us succeed."

I paused a beat, thinking of the container in Mick's shed. "Mick Gorley."

Calvin paused, surprised to hear me say it. For a moment it looked as if he might deny everything, but I think he must have realized that my mention of Mick wasn't a question.

"Yes. Though that isn't public knowledge, and both Mr. Gorley and I want to keep it that way."

So that explained Mick's connection to Summer Island Farm. He had a financial stake in the company. And like any good investor, he must have known that the best way to corner the market would be to eliminate all the competition.

"I hope you don't mind me asking you this, Calvin, but don't you feel like it's an unusual time to start telling local businesses like me and Bruno about your product?"

"Why would you think that? *No time like the present* is always my motto. You never know what could happen to you tomorrow, so why wait?"

I was sure Jeff would have liked a few more tomorrows. He certainly wouldn't have wanted to be bumped off for the sake of organic strawberries. All the warmth I'd initially felt toward Calvin began to slip away as I heard him speak so calmly about this.

"Well, sharing your card around less than a week after our last produce vendor died might come across as a little cold-hearted, no?"

I watched him carefully, trying to gauge what his response to this might be. We'd kept things light and casual up until now, so I hoped my mentioning this wouldn't make him realize what had actually brought me out here tonight.

I was also starting to wonder where the heck Tom was. I'd sent him a text probably fifteen minutes ago, and it didn't take all that long to get out here from the hotel.

Unless he was so busy with everything happening that he hadn't bothered to look at his phone.

Or if the phone tower is running off east-side power, I realized.

I hadn't even considered that possibility. When I'd sent the text, I hadn't been looking at my bars of service or even checked to see if I got a send confirmation; I'd just put the phone right back in my pocket. And now that I was alone out here with Calvin, I was seriously beginning to wonder if the message had gone through at all.

Tom might not be coming.

Which meant I needed to tread very carefully, lest I get myself into some seriously hot water.

"You know, it's really amazing what people will believe when someone comes around with a logo and a business card and starts asking for money."

There were a lot of things Calvin could have said in that moment that I would have been able to reply to. I was prepared for just about any response. But this was not what I'd been expecting at all. I'd figured he'd keep playing it cool and aloof, I'd tell him to give me a formal quote, and I'd get the heck out of here before anything had a chance to go sideways, kicking myself the whole way home for coming out here to begin with.

Instead, Calvin had taken us to the top of the tracks on a roller coaster and decided we were going down *fast*.

"I'm sorry, what?"

"Jeff. Jeff the supposed produce man? The guy you all let into your businesses and made payments to? All he had to do was tell you he was replacing someone else, and none of you asked a single question. Don't you think that's a little bit odd?" While the words themselves weren't menacing, his tone had taken on an icy-cold tone that made my skin crawl.

I glanced around the room, trying to gauge where my nearest exits were while also trying to figure out if there was anyone else in here except for us. A big part of why I'd felt secure coming out here was my belief—however unfounded—that Calvin wouldn't hurt me in front of witnesses.

But there weren't any witnesses in here.

Now he was talking in the vaguest terms about Jeff and I felt like he was on the cusp of admitting something, and while I was desperate to know what he was about to say, I was way more interested in getting out of here alive. There was no point in solving a mystery if you wound up dead at the end.

"Jeff took over from Denny."

"Oh, Este, don't be stupid; I know you looked him up. I know you couldn't find a single thing about him being connected to that company. You know how I know that? Because you looked at *our* website, and you found it was registered to him."

I'd almost forgotten about that search. But how had Calvin known what I'd been looking into?

"I have an alert set up for anytime someone does a search on our domain registration."

"If you're that paranoid about it, why did you leave his name attached to the site?" If he was going to admit following my internet search, I might as well get some answers. I started moving slowly, just shuffling really, in the direction of a nearby exit, hoping he wouldn't notice and I could get enough distance between us to make a break for it.

"As it turns out, the host site requires a formal request. We were in the process of changing it when you had to go digging your nose into things. No one else even knew the site existed, but there you went, poking around. So that's when I decided you needed a warning to mind your own business. I even came by today to make sure you were being a good little girl, and I thought you might have listened, but then I saw you out front and I knew you were never going to stop being trouble."

"Funny, that's what my sixth-grade teacher told my parents about me too. Guess I never grew out of it."

"Este, don't you see? This is going to be a beautiful, symbiotic relationship. We can do great things for this island. Why can't you just let it be?"

"Sorry, but it's just not in my nature to overlook a murder."

"That's a real shame. Because I don't think there's been a year since this island was founded where *two* people have died by homicide in the same week."

I darted a quick glance toward the door. "Yeah, and don't you think that people are going to think that's a little suspicious? I texted Tom Cunningham on my way here, by the way."

"What a pity that he won't get to see that text until the power comes back on, then."

And there it was, my lifeline cut, and my one hope of keeping myself alive now foiled. The cell tower must be on the east side. I swallowed hard.

"Look, you don't have to do anything to me. I can sign whatever agreement you want with the produce. I'll be your best customer, and we can pretend none of this happened. You haven't actually told me anything." I took another small step toward the door.

"Told you what? That I killed Jeff? Yes, I can see how it would make a difference to hear it said out loud. But I think you want to know why, don't you? And I so want *someone* to understand how it came to this, even if you won't be around to tell anyone else."

"No offense, Calvin, but if it's between knowing the truth and getting out of here alive, I'm okay not knowing the truth."

He shook his head. "This isn't going to be the kind of situation where you have options. I already gave you an option when I left you that note. You should have listened to me."

Well, that was at least one point he and I agreed on.

"Fine, if you're desperate to tell me, just do it. Jeff wasn't who he said he was? Doesn't seem to matter now, does it?"

"Jeff was a member of our community here."

Now *that* was something I hadn't expected him to say. "No, that's not possible. I'd never seen him before in my life. I might not know all of your names, but I know your people to see them. There's no way."

"Do you, though? Do you know us to see us, or do you see our clothes and just look away?" He gave me a long look, and I realized he was right. The faces of the farm collective members seemed to blend together in my mind; all I could see was their matching brown ensembles. Nothing else about them stuck out in my memory. "You see, it's a pretty smart way to make sure you're memorable without anyone actually remembering anything about you."

"Why would someone from your farm pretend to be an outsider? And how did he take over Denny's business?"

"He didn't. You see, this little farm of ours has been something we've been planning for a long time, and we were just waiting for the right moment to introduce our setup to the island. We wanted to make sure everything was ready, but the main issue we had was how damned devoted you people can be to outsiders. You've been using that same blasted fruit company for generations, so we knew it might not be easy for you to switch."

"Did you kill Denny McAvoy?" I gawked at him. I *knew* that boat accident had sounded fishy.

"What? No." He looked genuinely offended by the suggestion, which was rich, considering he'd just admitted to killing Jeff. "But his death *was* the open invitation we needed. You see, Mick was the first person to find out about Denny's death. The widow called to explain that the last delivery of the season wasn't coming, and she wanted to apologize to everyone personally. Mick told her not to worry and he would let the rest of the accounts in town know."

"Except he didn't."

"No. He *did* get her to tell him exactly what you, Bruno, and the others were expecting, though, saying he would help find a replacement solution, because he's such a nice guy."

"So where does Jeff come in?" I inched closer to the door again, and while Calvin hadn't seemed to notice, I was sure he'd see what I was up to soon. But I wasn't close enough to escape before he got to me. I just needed to keep him talking a little longer.

"We needed to break your loyalty to the brand. If you knew Denny was dead, you would stick with his family. If we sent someone else, someone who was nasty and unlikable and said they were the new owner, then it would be a lot easier to come in and be the new best thing on the market, wouldn't it?"

"I still don't get it, though. You got what you wanted. Bruno and I hated Jeff. He overcharged us, shorted our orders; we would have switched companies in a heartbeat. So *why* did you need to kill Jeff?"

"Greed."

"Greed?" What I was thinking but didn't say out loud was that Calvin's entire scheme seemed rooted in greed, so why did it matter if Jeff was feeling a little demanding?

"Jeff was a longtime member of our collective here. He and I were very close." In saying this, Calvin almost looked sad. "I trusted him to do his part of the plan so we could do what was best for us. For our community. This would have gone a long way to our ultimate dream of one day having a space that we didn't have to share with outsiders at all."

"You wanted your own island."

"This one can only let us grow so much. I thought Jeff shared a vision with me. He was so devoted to this farm that he hadn't wanted to take the outside investment from Mick. He'd been against it from the beginning. He *hated* me involving Mick further by telling him not to share the news of Denny's passing with anyone."

Now he was losing me. Right up to this point I'd believed Calvin and Mick had been in on the entire thing together, including the con and Jeff's murder, but now the way he was talking implied that Mick might not have known what Calvin was actually up to.

"Mick didn't like it. He knew that Denny's passing would open up the market here, and he was excited about that possibility. But I asked him to just be patient for a few days. And that's where Jeff decided to get greedy. He told me that if I didn't give him a hundred thousand dollars, he was going to tell everyone in town what I was trying to do."

"You were starting a business," I said. "People in town haven't cared a lick about bad business practices for decades; how do you think Mick still makes so much money? Why do you think they'd care about this? People would *love* to know we had this option for locally grown food."

"Well, you see, we're not just growing food, are we?"

"If you're not growing food, what *are* you growing?"

Calvin looked at me in a way that said *You're not that stupid, are you?*

My mouth fell open.

Of course.

Of course this wasn't about strawberries; it wasn't about organic farming. Indeed, how could I have been so stupid?

This was a good old-fashioned drug operation.

"He was going to tell everyone you were growing and selling drugs."

"I just wanted enough money to get out from under Gorley's oversight. We needed his money to start all this." He waved his hand around, looking at the beautiful bounty of delicious food, and in his distraction, I took another step closer to the exit. I was pretty sure I was close enough to beat him to the door now, especially with the raised bed between us.

"So Mick didn't know about the drugs?"

Calvin scoffed. "That man only asks questions if he starts losing money. He saw an investment opportunity and didn't care how it was run as long as it was going to make him money. But if Jeff had told him how we were planning to pay back our loan, I don't think he would have appreciated us tying him financially to that kind of business."

And there it was.

Drugs and blackmail were at the bottom of it, and the sinister strawberries had all just been a front.

"So Jeff brought *your* produce, packaged to look like it belonged to Evergreen Produce, but he was obviously planning to take a different kind of product with him when he left the island; that's why he had so many empty containers, isn't it? I found those by my diner. Is that why you went back to the boat? Because you were trying to see if he'd left anything else behind that might point back to you and the farm?"

"Ah, you saw that little visit, did you? I knew I was cutting my timing close."

I wasn't sure what disappointed me more: knowing that Jeff had just wanted to get his hands on the farm's drug money or that Mick *wasn't* responsible for his murder.

"You can't think that killing me is going to help you get away with this?"

"Well, that's where you're very mistaken, Este, because your death is going to clear me of all suspicion entirely. When you decide, tragically, to walk into the frozen lake and end it all, you'll leave behind a note admitting to what you've done, how you killed Jeff and simply couldn't live with the guilt anymore. Then I'm free of both of you."

I actually laughed out loud at this. "No one will believe that."

"People will believe just about anything if the evidence is looking right at them." At this, he decided he was finished talking and moved around the end of the raised bed, now holding a spade in one hand that must have been leaning against the other side. "Don't make this any harder than it has to be, okay?"

I planned to make it as hard as humanly possible.

I made a break for it, dashing in the direction of the exit door with a speed he must not have seen coming. The door was a direct exit back into the woods, and coming outside from the humidity and warmth inside the greenhouse felt like being slapped in the face with a bucket of ice-cold water. The sudden shift in temperature was so jarring it stole my breath, leaving me disoriented and gasping for air.

Run.

I had to get back, had to find people. If Tom wasn't coming, I had to save myself, and that meant finding a place with as many witnesses as possible.

I bolted in the direction of the farm village. While I knew those people would be at least partially devoted to Calvin, I had to hope they wouldn't look the other way while he killed me.

Crashing noises and a loud grunt told me he was right on my tracks, so I ran, oblivious to the sticks and branches clawing at my cheeks and hair, just running in a desperate attempt to get back to that bonfire before he caught up to me.

I tripped over an exposed root, sending me sprawling to the ground, pine needles digging sharply into my palms and the knee of my jeans tearing open roughly against the rough bark of a tree. Based on the stinging I felt on my skin, I was probably bleeding.

Still, the sound of Calvin behind me was all the motivation I needed. Adrenaline coursed through my veins, pulling me up off the ground like I had hands under my arms, lifting me.

It was only when I tried to run again that I realized I *did* have hands lifting me up. I screamed, thrashing away, assuming Calvin had caught up to me, and this was my last-ditch effort to save myself.

Instead, a warm, familiar voice said, "Whoa there, Este. Why are you running like the hounds of hell are after you?"

I looked up, my hair tangled and hanging in my eyes, but there was no mistaking Tom Cunningham's beautiful, perfect face. A moment later Calvin burst onto the path, a bellow caught in his throat and the spade lifted in the air. All three of us froze at once, Tom taking only a half second to realize what he'd interrupted. Calvin seemed to understand a moment too late what he'd just exposed.

Calvin dropped the spade and held his hands up even as Tom skillfully withdrew the gun clipped to his hip.

The adrenaline I'd felt disappeared the moment I realized I was safe, and I sank to the ground at Tom's feet, fighting to catch my breath.

I had certainly taken one lesson from all of this.

If a note tells you *or else*, you don't want to find out what they mean by that.

Chapter Thirty-Three

Three months later

Wind churned down the street, sending sharp blasts of ice pellets sailing through the air, attacking every bit of exposed skin I hadn't managed to cover. It was February, a time when you most wanted winter to be over but winter most seemed like it would never end.

The sky overhead was a deep steely gray, letting me know that Mother Nature had no intention of easing up on us anytime soon and it would be in my best interest to get back inside before the next storm hit us, which was slated to be any moment.

I hugged my jacket more tightly around me and pulled my beanie down around my ears until I basically like looked like a tube of down jacket with a furry pom-pom on top instead of a cherry.

Grampy stood next to me, wearing only a thick flannel jacket in a buffalo plaid print and a hat my grandmother had knit for him at least forty years ago, which was so threadbare in places I could see his gray hair underneath.

We were staring at what had once been a lot that held nothing but trees and a promise of *one day* but now had a sign mounted in front of it announcing imminent construction of a residential dwelling.

Jersey hadn't been lying when she told me that Mick had convinced the town to force our hand about the property. But as luck would have it—and luck was something my family was very keenly attuned to—the council seemed to put a lot more weight on keeping our family on the island than on helping Mick open a new hotel.

We were able to skirt the six-month rule by having several trees cut down and the roots dug out before the ground became too frozen to work, and as far as the council was concerned, that was enough to show good intention. We presented them with a blueprint proposal for my house, which passed the aesthetic overview and was given a go-ahead, and with signed documents from a local contractor saying he'd break ground in spring when it thawed, we were allowed to keep the property.

Funny, I had been so angry with Mick for making such an underhanded ploy to steal what was ours, but now I was almost grateful to him. I'd been putting off building the house for years, because it never felt like the right time to make such a big move or spend so much money on myself. But when I was forced into it—and with help from Grampy's formerly secret savings account—it turned out that building a place of my own was a luxury I actually could afford.

The wind plucked at our jackets, hunting for a way in, and I looped my arm around Grampy's elbow as we headed away from the lot and back toward his place. The cottage was perfectly suitable for me for now, but as I was no longer living alone, I wouldn't mind having a little extra space.

I gave Grampy a kiss on the cheek and headed back to my place, where the moment I stepped through the door, a small gray streak zipped out of the bedroom.

Nora jumped up first on the back of the couch, where she had come to realize I was perfectly able to give her head rubs as I came in from outside. She would then wait to see if I sat down on the couch with her, or head into the kitchen to decide her own path.

Today I was feeling like a nice soup for dinner, so I made my way into the kitchen, and she jumped off the couch and onto one of the stools at the island. From the fridge I gathered some fresh herbs and bacon, and from my bowl on the counter I collected a butternut squash and an apple. Seamus's fall soup had become a new staple in my rotation.

The herbs, in their custom packaging, bore the label of Summer Island Farm, something I was still having a hard time adjusting to, even months after Calvin was arrested.

He didn't fight the charges. Since Tom had busted him red-handed trying to murder me, Calvin must have realized there wasn't much sense in pretending he was innocent, and he'd opened up almost immediately about the plan and how Jeff had gotten himself killed.

I was grateful for a lot of things, but extra grateful I'd actually sent Tom a text when I'd left the hotel and that our power being out hadn't taken our already questionable cell service with it.

The case of clamshells I'd found had been a part of the ruse to convince us that Jeff was the real deal, but the Summer Island strawberries hadn't ripened on time and that part of the plan had been abandoned, which was how the order ended up shorted, and the case of clamshells—meant not for the strawberries but for much more illegal cargo—had evidently gone overboard during Jeff's struggle with Calvin.

The farm had planned on selling real strawberries as well—they obviously needed a decent number of *actual* strawberries in the crate to cover up what they were doing—and that was how one of the Summer Island containers had found its way into Mick's recycle bin. He'd had nothing to do with Calvin's drug operation. Mick, being one of the primary investors in the farm, had been given some of the first ripe berries. But Calvin had evidently not bothered to remove the Evergreen sticker and instead just covered it up with a Summer Island one, a lazy mistake on his part.

Of course Mick hadn't noticed, because why would he look that closely at produce? He had a chef; he likely hadn't even seen the container.

I was still a little miffed that Mick was completely cleared of any wrongdoing. I had been so convinced of his guilt that it was hard to change my mind now, even after I'd heard everything Calvin told me.

The farm had briefly been shut down because of the whole situation, but after an investigation, the farm was cleared of any accessory charges and allowed to keep the new business going. Mick, still owed for his loan, was smart enough to have had his investment protected with paperwork, and thanks to Calvin's accidental failure to meet the morality clause, Mick now owned the primary share of the farm.

I guess that boon had helped soften the blow of losing out on our property, because he hadn't stopped by the diner to make any snippy comments in the past few months. Jersey *had* stopped in to complain that the pie I'd given her was a dud, but that was the closest I'd come to a negative interaction with the Gorleys.

As weird as it was to have produce in my fridge that came from the farm where I'd almost been killed, I was coming around to the idea that it *was* really nice to have access to delicious fresh food in the dead of winter.

It would be a while before I bought any strawberries, though.

I'd started to fry up the bacon in a Dutch oven while peeling and cubing the butternut squash when a knock sounded at my door. Nora, who had no interest in strangers, zipped silently back to my bedroom. Sometimes I was half convinced she was a tiny gray ghost, but I didn't think ghosts ate as much as she did.

I hadn't outgrown the habit of locking my door, even if Calvin was now on the mainland awaiting trial, so I peeked through the curtain on my door to see Tom standing on my front step.

This was a bit of a surprise. He'd been stopping in at the diner a bit more since everything had happened, but he seemed to be avoiding any one-on-one interactions with me. I wasn't sure if it was because he wanted to distance himself from the investigation or because being around me made him nervous, but I had to admit I was sad we hadn't been talking as much since Calvin's arrest.

I unlocked the door and let him in. "Hey there. Make yourself at home. If you're hungry, I'm making a butternut squash soup with apple and bacon."

"Well, that sounds both weird and delicious, so I think I have to say yes." He sat at the island, taking his jacket off and draping it over the back of the second barstool.

I didn't want to tell him his ex-brother-in-law had given me the recipe. "What brings you by, Sheriff?" I tried to keep my tone light, but the curiosity must have snuck out in spite of my best efforts.

"Just figured it was about time I come by. Make sure you're doing okay. I know it's been a bit since things went down, but that was a pretty scary situation and I realize I never did ask you how you were handling things since."

I dumped the cubed squash into the bacon grease after removing all the bacon pieces and let it soften. "That's . . . unexpected. Thank you."

"So, you're okay?"

I set my cutting board back on the island, contemplating the plastic container of thyme, with its cheery, rustic label, and the fruit I'd purchased from Bruno, and I looked back to Tom with a smile. A real one.

"I will be."

Recipes

Lucky Pie Diner's Basic Pie Dough

Author's note: While this recipe comes straight from a handwritten stenographer's pad my grandmother kept recipes on, there's a real chance that—like Phoebe Buffay—my gran might have cribbed it from a women's magazine or pack of butter, so be gentle. I have merely adapted it to be made in a food processor, because I am very lazy.

2½ cups all-purpose flour, plus more to dust
½ tablespoon white sugar (omit if making a savory pie)
½ teaspoon salt
1 cup butter (2 sticks), cold, cold, cold and diced into cubes
1 cup ice water (you will need about 6–8 tablespoons; just
    have a measuring cup filled with ice water at the ready)

While you may feel motivated to mix this by hand (and all power to you if you are that person), this is significantly easier to make if you use a food processor.

In a food processor, combine dry ingredients and pulse to blend. Add cold butter (I cannot express enough how the butter needs to be as cold as possible). Pulse to combine the butter with the dry ingredients. It should begin to resemble sand at this point but still be dry.

Begin adding ice-cold water 1 tablespoon at a time until the sandy mixture begins to combine. Don't overdo it or overwater it; check the consistency frequently. If you pinch the dough and it sticks together, it's done.

Lightly dust your countertop with flour and roll the dough out. Form into a smooth ball, but do not overwork or knead. Divide the ball into two even portions and wrap each ball in plastic wrap. Each ball is good for one 9-inch pie shell. Keep in fridge until ready to make one of the tasty pies that follows.

Note: While Este does offer vegan pie options at Lucky Pie Diner, you cannot substitute the butter for shortening here with the same result. Stay tuned for future books to get the signature vegan-friendly crust option.

Additional note: Every single pie here can be made with a store-bought pie shell if making one from scratch is too intimidating or time-consuming.

Lucky Pie Spice Blend

1 tablespoon cinnamon
2 teaspoons cardamom
½ teaspoon nutmeg
¼ teaspoon allspice
¼ teaspoon orange zest

This is it, powdered perfection.

Combine all ingredients in a small bowl and whisk well. Store in a glass spice jar or any glass container with an airtight lid. It will last about six months, but you will probably need to make more before then.

Cranberry Apple Cider Pie

4 cups apple cider
4 cups fresh cranberries (frozen will work if fresh are out of
    stock); you can also opt to substitute in 1 cup of sweet
    apple in place of 1 cup of the cranberries
4 tablespoons cornstarch
½ cup white sugar, plus extra to sprinkle
1 teaspoon vanilla extract
3 teaspoons Lucky Pie Spice Blend
1 pinch salt
1 tablespoon butter
Zest of two oranges
2 batches Lucky Pie Diner's Basic Pie Dough *or* 2 9-inch
    store-bought crusts
1 egg
1 cup water

First you will need to reduce your apple cider considerably by
placing it on high heat and boiling until it reduces by half. It
should start to resemble a syrup.

Preheat oven to 400 degrees.

Coat cranberries in cornstarch, white sugar, vanilla, spice
blend, and salt. Once your apple cider has reduced by half, add
your cranberry mix and butter to the pot; stir until cranberries
have softened and begin to pop. Remove from heat and stir in
orange zest.

Pour mixture into prepared bottom pie shell.

Mix egg and water to make an egg wash; smooth a small amount over the exterior edge of the pie. Add a second pie disk over top, crimping the edges together with your fingers. Cut excess dough away from the edges, and cut several small vents in the top of the pie shell. Coat the top shell with remaining egg wash mix. Sprinkle with sugar.

If you're feeling super motivated, this is a great pie for trying your hand at a lattice top instead of a plain flat top. Look at some tutorials online for making a simple lattice and impress all your friends.

Bake pie for 50–60 minutes or until shell is a deep golden brown.

Buttermilk Pie with Berry Compote

For Buttermilk Pie

3 eggs, room temperature
1½ cups white sugar
½ cup butter, softened
3 tablespoons all-purpose flour
1 cup buttermilk
1 tablespoon lemon juice
1 teaspoon vanilla extract
⅛ teaspoon nutmeg, freshly grated if possible
1 batch Lucky Pie Diner's Basic Pie Dough *or* 1 9-inch
    store-bought crust

For Berry Compote

3 cups fresh or frozen fruit (try strawberry, raspberry,
    blueberry, cherry, etc.)
2 tablespoons orange juice
¼ teaspoon cinnamon
¼ teaspoon ground ginger
1 teaspoon white sugar

Preheat oven to 350 degrees.

Beat eggs in medium-sized bowl until they appear frothy. Add
sugar, butter, and flour and continue to mix at low speed until
smooth.

Add buttermilk, lemon juice, vanilla, and nutmeg; blend until combined. Pour into pie shell. Bake for about 50 minutes or until mixture appears set. Allow to cool, and while cooling, prepare berry compote.

To make berry compote, combine fruit and orange juice in a saucepan over medium heat. As mixture starts to bubble, reduce heat, and mash fruit with a potato masher or spoon.

Raise temperature to medium high and continue to stir occasionally, breaking apart any large pieces. As the liquid begins to reduce, the compote will thicken. Stir for about 10 minutes.

Remove from heat and stir in spices and sugar. Serve immediately with the pie or store in fridge for about a week in a glass jar.

Carrot Pie

2 cups chopped carrots
¾ cup white sugar
2 eggs, room temperature
2 teaspoons Lucky Pie Spice Blend
¾ cup 2% milk
1 batch Lucky Pie Diner's Basic Pie Dough *or* 1 9-inch store-
    bought crust

This is a quirky little spin on a more traditional veggie pie like
pumpkin or sweet potato. Because it can toe the line between
sweet and savory, feel free to serve with dinner rather than dessert as a little something different.

Preheat oven to 325 degrees. Blind-bake pie crust for about
10 minutes; once it's removed, raise oven temperature to
350 degrees.

Boil chopped carrots in a saucepan into fork tender. Drain the
carrots, then add to food processor and mix until smooth.

In a medium-sized bowl combine carrot, sugar, eggs, and spice
blend. Add milk gradually. Pour mixture into pie shell and
bake for about 50 minutes. Mixture should be firm when fully
baked, but don't worry it there's a little bit of a jiggle when it
comes out; that should firm as it cools.

Serve plain with dinner or with whipped cream or ice cream
as a dessert.

Sugar Pie With Homemade Whipped Cream

For Sugar Pie
2 tablespoons butter, room temperature
3 tablespoons all-purpose flour
½ cup 3% milk
1½ cups brown sugar, packed
½ teaspoon vanilla extract
2 large eggs, room temperature
1 teaspoon molasses (this can be increased to personal taste)
1 batch Lucky Pie Diner's Basic Pie Dough *or* 1 9-inch store-bought crust

For Homemade Whipped Cream
2 cups heavy whipping cream, cold
½ cup icing sugar
1 teaspoon vanilla extract

This sweet treat is a decadent delight, especially in cooler months. Bring it along to Thanksgiving or Christmas dinners where someone has already volunteered to bring a pumpkin pie.

Preheat oven to 325 degrees and blind-bake your crust for about 10 minutes. Turn oven up to 350 degrees once pie shell has been removed.

In a medium-sized bowl, melt butter, then add flour, milk, brown sugar, and vanilla. In a small bowl, whisk eggs. Once eggs are thoroughly mixed, combine with the butter-and-sugar mixture. Pour wet ingredients into waiting pie shell.

Bake for about 50 minutes. The filling may still be a little wobbly when you pull it out, but it shouldn't be liquid; if the filling is still liquid, put back in for 5 more minutes.

Allow pie to cool while making the whipped cream.

For whipped cream, your cream must be cold, so keep it in the fridge until you plan to use it. You may also want to put your bowl and beater attachments into the fridge or freezer until you're ready to use them. When you're ready, use a hand mixer with a whisk attachment, or the whisk attachment on your stand mixer, to combine all your ingredients in the bowl.

It's best to start slow here, unless you want to end up with whipped cream splatters all over your kitchen. Slowly increase speed as your mixture thickens. You will know it's done when stiff peaks begin to form. Resist eating too much right from the bowl, and serve with your cooled pie.

*Quick tip: You can freeze leftover whipped cream! Line a baking sheet with parchment paper and place dollops of cream on the paper. Toss in the freezer for a few hours, then remove the dollops and place in a freezer bag. Voilà—whipped cream anytime you want it.

Shepherd's Pie Este-Style

For Topping
4–6 large potatoes (depending how mashy you like your topping)

6 tablespoons butter

¼ cup 2% milk (or any milk substitute; I like to use Greek yogurt)

1 tablespoon creamy horseradish (can be omitted if you want to play it safe)

Salt and pepper to taste

For Filling
1 tablespoon olive oil

1 small onion, diced

4 cloves garlic, minced

1 pound lean ground beef

1 packet onion soup mix

2 tablespoons tomato paste

¼ cup water

2 cups mixed frozen vegetables

1 can condensed vegetable beef soup (the one with alphabet letters)

2 tablespoons balsamic vinegar

2 tablespoons Worcestershire sauce

2 teaspoons dried thyme

2 teaspoons dried mushroom powder (can be omitted if hard
    to find)
2 bay leaves

Peel and cube potatoes; add to salted boiling water, cook until
fork tender, then drain. Add butter, milk, horseradish, and salt
and pepper; mash to combine. Set aside.

Preheat oven to 350 degrees.

In a large skillet, heat olive oil over medium-high heat. Add
diced onion and minced garlic and cook until onion is translucent. Add ground beef and cook until done. Add onion soup
mix, tomato paste, and water, and stir until beef is coated.

Reduce heat to medium and add mixed frozen vegetables and
can of condensed soup. Add remaining ingredients and mix
well.

In a 10 × 14–inch casserole dish, spoon meat layer onto bottom
of dish. Top with mashed potatoes and evenly spread potato
over meat layer. Bake for 20–25 minutes until potato begins to
turn golden brown. Serve immediately.

Tourtière

For Spice Blend
2 teaspoons salt
1 teaspoon fresh-ground pepper
1 teaspoon dried thyme
½ teaspoon dried sage
½ teaspoon cinnamon
½ teaspoon ginger
¼ teaspoon nutmeg
¼ teaspoon allspice
¼ teaspoon mustard powder
⅛ teaspoon ground cloves
⅛ teaspoon cayenne (omit if you don't like spicy food)

For Meat Filling
1 large potato, peeled and cubed
1 teaspoon salt, plus more to taste
1 tablespoon butter
1 yellow onion, chopped
½ cup diced celery
4 cloves garlic, minced
1 pound ground beef
1 pound ground pork (can do 2 pounds ground beef if pork is hard to find)
1 cup retained cooking water from potatoes
1 egg

1 cup of water
2 batches Lucky Pie Diner's Basic Pie Dough *or* 2 9-inch
  store-bought crusts

Combine all spice blend ingredients in a small bowl and whisk to mix.

Boil potato with 1 teaspoon salt in water until potato is fork tender. Reserve 1 cup of potato water. Place potato in a small bowl and mash until smooth.

In a skillet over medium-high heat, melt butter. Add onion and a pinch of salt and cook until onion pieces become translucent. Add celery and garlic, then add the seasoning blend. Stir until onions and celery are coated.

Add ground beef and pork as well as the reserved potato water. Stir until meat is fully cooked and the liquid is almost evaporated; this could take up to 45 minutes, so be patient. Once meat is cooked, stir in mashed potato and remove from heat.

Preheat oven to 375 degrees and take chilled pie dough out of fridge. Put one rolled-out dough disk in a deep-dish pie pan, then fill with meat-and-potato mixture.

Mix egg and water to make an egg wash; smooth a small amount over the exterior edge of the pie. Add second pie disk over top, crimping edges together with your fingers. Cut excess dough away from the edges, and cut several small vents in the top of the pie shell. Coat the top shell with remaining egg wash.

Bake for 1 hour; cool before serving.

Acknowledgments

First and foremost, I don't think it's possible to write a book about a fictional island town in Northern Michigan and not give a nod of acknowledgment to the real-life Mackinac Island. Split Pine is *not* Mackinac, but the real island was certainly a source of inspiration. Specific thanks to TikToker @baileyyjanette, whose videos piqued my interest and made me think, *Man, what if someone got murdered there?"*

To my incredible editor, Melissa Rechter, who heard "magical pies" and said, "Say less." Thank you a million times over for your belief in me and these books. To the entire crew at Crooked Lane Books who make this possible.

To Dean Winchester. Because pie.

And last but never least, to the staff at Whodunit Mystery Bookstore. Michael, Laura, Aaron, and Wendy, you made my dream of being "a regular" somewhere a reality and were the first people I told when I finished writing my first cozy. You humor all my weird two AM book orders. Your unending support and kindness mean the world. Support indie bookstores, now and forever.